Bridle Path
Press

Also by Melissa Westemeier

Bassville Stories:
Across the River

Whipped, Not Beaten
Kicks Like a Girl

On the River

a novel

Melissa Westemeier

On the River is a work of fiction. Names, characters, places, and incidents are the products of the author's imagination or are used fictitiously. Any resemblance to actual events, locales, or persons, living or dead, is entirely coincidental.

Copyright © 2018 by Melissa Westemeier

For information or permission contact:

Bridle Path Press, LLC
8419 Stevenson Road
Baltimore, MD 21208

www.bridlepathpress.com

Direct orders to the above address.

Printed in the United States of America.
First Edition.
ISBN: 978-1-7321630-0-3

Library of Congress Control Number: 2018903922

Book Design by Elizabeth Ryan Cole
Cover Design by Mitch Miskoviak

Bridle Path
Press

For Doug, who is Loyal

On the River

ONE

THE WINTER HAD BECOME a test of endurance and patience, especially for those living in northern Wisconsin. Three friends, June Butterfield, Dottie Trayson and Arlyce Shanski, sat at the end of the bar near the Bassville Pub's kitchen and pored over knitting patterns, ignoring the grumbling men gathered to watch basketball on the wall-mounted TV set. A cold and snowy February had left behind three feet of snow, and now it was March 3, 1985, with no sign of a spring thaw. Even though the Shanskis had turned on every light, the bar still seemed dim. The huge windows overlooking the Wissipaw River let in little light on an overcast day and the view in both directions looked the same: a solid mass of unmoving snow and ice, except for the occasional vehicle crossing the bridge that connected both sides of Bassville.

"I'm sick of ice fishing," Gene Trayson declared, and thumbed a card free from the deck. He flipped it up with a grunt. He was a stout old farmer with a grizzled and balding head. "I'm worried it'll be a wet spring and keep us out of the fields." He looked across the bar to the bartender who'd agreed to play the fourth hand in their cribbage game. Gene glanced down the bar at his wife, Dottie, deep in conversation with her two knitting pals.

"My crib," Steve Shanski said gleefully, while he moved his peg two spots along the cribbage board between them. He reached into a cooler and replaced Gene's empty can of Old Style with a full one. Then he lifted each customers' can on the bar in turn, weighing them to determine who needed a refill before settling back on his barstool. Steve was a tall man, gone soft in the middle. He was easy-natured and quick with a joke, the opposite of his wife, Arlyce, whose face was creased from scowling and smoking.

"Lucky son of a bitch," Gene said, and laid down the eight of hearts.

"I'm sick of ice fishing, too." Maw Cooper topped Gene's card with the seven of spades and called out his score. "Fifteen. And ice fishermen. Cheap bastards. After the sturgeon spearing ends, I feel hermetic until the walleye run starts. The ennui about kills me." The bait shop owner tugged at his dark brown beard and waited for his friends to ask what "ennui" meant—it was yesterday's Word of the Day on his calendar and he hadn't yet used it in front of anyone.

"On-wee? What's that? Some kind of gout?" Dob Dohill asked Maw. Dob folded his cards with a quick flick of his calloused hands. Dob had a grin as broad as his barrel-sized chest and a voice that sounded like a mellow shot of whiskey. It seemed like his huge head rose out of his shoulders because his neck was so thick. Dob and his younger brother Dale owned a thriving construction business and enjoyed the winter months. It meant they could work indoors at a slower pace than they did the rest of the year.

"It means boredom. Boredom about kills me. And so does ice fishing. I hardly sell any bait." Maw had quickly gotten used to the

2

fame and insanity that followed last spring's unexpected promotion on a Chicago radio station. He'd done a brisk business selling bait through the fall, and continued to promote "Maw's Minnows" (*Belligerent, Cantankerous and Passive-Aggressive*) branded T-shirts and baseball caps.

"How's that mail-order business coming along, Maw?" Spade was crouched over the pool table, lining up his next shot.

Maw spun his barstool around to look at Spade, a scrawny, bearded man who wore coke-bottle glasses and a faded short-sleeved T-shirt. A swing shift worker at a mill, Spade spent most of his paycheck compulsively gambling. "It's going to be more of a spring and summer thing. I've got about fifteen shops in the southern part of the state ready to sell as soon as their traffic picks up. They like the logo Peg designed."

"I saw that—the minnow with the big teeth going after the bass," Spade nodded. He drew back his cue stick and sent the nine ball whirling into the corner pocket. "You just print up the stickers and slap 'em on the containers then?"

"Yep," Maw told him. "Shiny orange fish shape for Passive Aggressive, yellow for Cantankerous and red for Belligerent. I don't know what sells more, though, the names or the story behind them."

Maw Cooper had invented a story about the ferocity of his minnow stock almost a year ago when a Chicago disc jockey called his shop for a fishing report. His tale of strategically bred and genetically mastered minnows that *go after the fish for you* was such a hit that he now enjoyed a bit of celebrity status. Between his marketing genius (involving a Bikini Fishing Team and slapping the logo for Maw's Bait and Tackle on every possible item he could sell) and his propensity to dazzle with his homespun wit, Maw had become a raging success by anyone's standards, but especially by Bassville's.

Gene gathered the cards off the bar and was about to shuffle them when a movement on the street outside caught his attention. His eyes fell on Joanne and the guys at the bar followed his gaze.

A slim woman with long dark hair trudged through the slushy intersection outside. The front of her fringed leather jacket was unbuttoned to reveal her arm held fast against her midsection in a sling.

The bar fell silent as everyone watched her walk by until she was out of sight.

Straddling both sides of the Wissipaw River, Bassville looked like any other Wisconsin fishing town. It had a Catholic church and a Lutheran church, a few resorts up the river, Bud's Supermarket—which was noteworthy for the extensive collection of taxidermy decorating its walls—and several taverns. Farming and fishing kept the town's economy alive, but new possibilities lay on the horizon since Gene Trayson sold a hundred acres of his family's dairy farm to pay for his daughter's bone marrow transplant. That hundred acres would transform from cropland to a subdivision with a strip mall anchoring the eastern edge as soon as the developer started selling lots. Some optimists even predicted that the sprawling growth of Northfield, a city forty minutes east, would reach its borders, but the only thing to happen so far involved a surveyor setting up flags to mark the property. Paved roads and utilities, the foundation of any development, wouldn't go in until next summer. None of this mattered to Gene, though. For him it was business as usual on the remaining acres of his dairy farm, especially since his daughter, Angie, had celebrated her twelfth birthday in remission.

Like most river towns, Bassville suffered through off-season drought. Any delay of springtime meant one less weekend of rooms, drinks, meals, gas and bait purchased from the local shops. Each weekend of springtime fishing traffic helped the locals survive winter. Last week's blizzard and cold snap made everyone edgy. For at least another week, the ice would be thick enough for ice fishing, but then conditions would become dangerous until the lake and river fully opened up. The spring thaw could take anywhere from a couple of weeks to over a month, depending on Mother Nature.

Everyone suffered except for Maw, because he'd sell more bait and sundry with his expanded retail outlets, and Mona Butterfield, because she was in love and on the cusp of expanding last summer's vegetable business.

Mona's love life and business venture were the topic of conversation at the kitchen end of the bar. Her mother, June, and her employer, Arlyce, both considered themselves experts on Mona as they hashed out predictions of her next move while choosing their next knitting projects.

"I like this cable-knit," June said, holding up a Vogue pattern for a cardigan, "but the sleeves look bulky." Her own hand knit sweater, a mauve pullover, fit snug through the arms and loose over her hips.

Arlyce leaned forward for a closer look. Her thin lips moved while she read the stitch counts and her dangly earrings swung back and forth when she nodded. "I think we can adjust that. It's the armpit. If we take it up then the torso won't bag so much where the sleeve joins it."

"Will that be a pain?" June asked. She wasn't the expert knitter her best friend had become.

"Not at all. We'll just taper the sleeves in a bit more than the pattern calls for. It'll be a cinch." Arlyce reached across to retrieve her cigarette from the ashtray. "How's Sean doing?"

"Really well. He loves his professor at Ohio State and he says it's a kick teaching freshmen."

"Any girlfriend on the horizon?" Dottie asked. Her oldest was an eligible bachelor, but Scotty showed no interest in anything but working, hunting and fishing.

"Not a serious one. Not that he's told me about. He likes his roommates. One's a chemistry major, they work together in the lab. He's busy all the time. I don't think he's ready to settle in a serious relationship just yet."

Arlyce took a drag off her Salem Light and blew it out of the side of her mouth to avoid giving June a face full of smoke. "Sure are different from us. Kids these days go off to school, they don't get married until they're almost thirty. Heck, by his age you and Loyal were already married a few years and had your babies."

June looked out the huge picture windows lining the south side of the Pub. Drifts of snow had piled on the deck and the dock's pilings were snugged in tight beneath the ice. The weather would change the scenery, but it would still look the same in that way she'd come to resent. She and Loyal had been married twenty-five years. She'd spent more than half her life with him. More than half her life. And what was ever going to change? Eighteen years living with her parents, three at college, twenty-five living with Loyal. She hoped she'd live to be about eighty, which meant her life was more than half over and there was every reason to expect the next half of her life would look the same as the first.

She forced a smile at her friends and picked up the knitting pattern again. "Kids are different these days. Probably a good thing, if you think about it."

"But Mona's older and wiser than you were, right?" Arlyce prodded. "She's not straight out of high school, she's twenty-three. Do you think they'll get engaged soon? Jake's a great catch and it has been almost a year since they started dating."

"Ten months, and yes, she's older and mature enough to marry, but I don't think they've talked too much about their future. The construction business requires people moving around for work, and Mona's pretty rooted here between being on the town council and taking up vegetable farming. Those aren't exactly activities that travel."

"There are enough building projects in the area. Jake wouldn't have to move to get work," Arlyce said.

"No, and he does seem pretty committed to staying around Bassville. I think he expected things to move faster with the new development."

Dottie nodded. "We did, too. I don't mind things looking the same, but I really expected the lots to start selling by now. It seems there's more interest in building by the river than on our old cornfield." She wound a loose strand of yarn around her chubby pinky finger. "I heard there's been interest in the property next to the Swenson mansion."

"Mansion indeed. And to think that place is only a summer home. But it was built almost thirty years ago. Hard to believe anyone would want to squeeze another big house next to that one—there's not much buildable land off Dead Run Bayou." Arlyce began casting a buttery-yellow summer weight cotton onto size 4 needles. "I know this is the most impractical color for a toddler, but isn't it beautiful?"

June reached over and gave the ball of yarn a squeeze with her fingers. "It's as soft as her cheeks. Victoria will look cute as a button wearing this over her Easter dress."

"She will," Dottie agreed. "Gene was telling me the other night that a couple of buyers are interested in buying land back in that bayou. Guess they want to either knock down those little cottages and build over them, or somehow squeeze big houses in between." A crease deepened between her eyebrows and she shrugged her rounded shoulders.

"That would look awful—imagine a brick mansion like the Swensons' looming over one of those two-room shacks," Arlyce said. "But I question how much of a house you could build back there anyway, it's pretty swampy. Floods every spring. Seems like a lot of hassle to live on the river when there are perfectly good lots for sale by Dottie."

"Think Mona will sell her place if they marry?" Dottie suddenly asked.

"I don't think so. They each own their houses, one of them would have to sell or rent out. I imagine if they got married they'd buy a new place, bigger than either the cottage or Mona's little place in town." June removed her own knitting project—a skullcap for Loyal made of navy wool—from her bag and started purling across a row. "Anyway, there's no rush. She's got her new business and talked about taking more classes at the community college. Nothing wrong with a girl living a little before she gets tied down for the rest of her life." June heard the bitter edge in her voice. She sounded like a shrew.

Arlyce studied her friend with keen eyes. She gave her a brief nod and bent her head over the yarn and needles on her lap. After a moment she spoke. "I saw Joanne at the store yesterday. Her arm was in a sling."

"What story did she tell you?" June asked, glad the focus had shifted.

"The usual. *You know what a klutz I am. I fell down the stairs.*" Arlyce rolled her eyes.

"Was it a proper sling from a doctor's office or home-made?" Dottie asked, her brow wrinkled with concern above her bifocals.

"What do you think? It's terrible, but she keeps going back. How can anyone really help a person who keeps going back to the same bad habit over and over again?" Arlyce reached for her ashtray.

June thought about all the times she'd gently offered a hand, the times their husbands and other men in town had intervened on her behalf, just to watch Joanne return to sitting next to her boyfriend at the Riverside Tavern, like it was no big thing she boasted a bright purple shiner or a broken limb. "It's almost like she's addicted to him somehow. A bad habit is a good way to say it."

"They say love is a drug, but that's not love." Dottie sipped her coffee.

"I'm thankful Mona's never been in that kind of situation," June added. "T.C. always treated her well, and Jake is a gentleman."

Their needles clicked in harmony while they reflected on their good luck in marriage and love. Outside the clouds prevented spring for another day because snow and ice won't melt without sunshine and warmth.

TWO

Mona was misting a pallet of microgreens when the greenhouse door slammed open. She winced at the sound and turned to watch her best friend since grade school, Jenny Bender, stomp snow from her leather boots, the pointy heels driving tiny divots into the rubber mat beneath her feet. "Girlfriend, you will *not* believe what I just heard."

Mona redirected the thin spray of water on a pallet of green peppers that were proving difficult to grow indoors this winter. She'd done all she could think of—boosted the soil with nitrogen-rich compost, repositioned a grow light, watered them from the roots, misted the leaves—but they looked straggly and sparse. Distracted by the question of how to get peppers to thrive off-season, she vaguely grunted towards Jenny, who always brought drama. Even a broken fingernail could reach epic proportions in Jenny's world. "What did you just hear?"

"Guess."

Mona sighed. "Beau was spotted at a jewelry store looking at rings."

Jenny scrunched up her face and Mona caught a flicker of disappointment before the disgust. "As if," Jenny drawled. Her on-again-off-again relationship with Beau Longwell had been off for two weeks.

"Bassville's getting a Famous Footwear."

"Get real. You know ninety percent of this town buys their shit-kickers and tennis shoes at Fleet Farm."

"Well, if you can't find it at Fleet Farm, you don't need it." Mona curled her toes inside her scuffed sneakers and thought about how she'd actually bought this pair of Tretorns at the Northport mall's sidewalk sale last summer. "A Fleet Farm! Bassville's getting a Fleet Farm!"

"No, dummy. Give up?"

Mona knew Jenny was dying to share whatever piece of gossip she'd acquired, so she slowly walked the length of the greenhouse to shut off the faucet before nodding. "Spill it."

"Maw's lining up another calendar shoot for the bait shop—and he wants local girls to pose for it!"

Mona laughed. "That's not exactly news, Jenny. Even *I* heard about that already." She coiled the hose beneath a pallet of tomato seedlings and poked her index finger into the peat moss to test the moisture. The warm humidity of the greenhouse was a wonderful escape from the biting cold outside. She had spent most of her free time here this winter, had even dragged in a couple of lawn chairs so she could study between the cucumber vines and frilly carrot tops poking past the edges of the cattle troughs she'd repurposed as planters.

"Well, I thought you'd be excited for me," Jenny pouted as she flopped herself into one of the lawn chairs. She unbuttoned her wool coat and fanned her face with her hand. "It's like a sauna in here."

"Isn't it great?" Mona had talked her dad into building the greenhouse along the east side of the milking barn after showing him the sales figures from last summer's vegetable sales. What had started as a lark, growing the garden seeds she'd discovered in her grandmother's old dresser drawers, was becoming a full-fledged business venture. Loyal had given Mona five acres of the family's farmland to grow instead of the usual corn, alfalfa and hay for the cows. Appropriating the dairy farm's resources, including a tractor, cow manure and some scrap building material, she'd brought a weekly haul last summer to the Northport farmers market. But, she'd successfully argued to her father, the demand for year-round vegetables was where they could make real money. He and Jake had helped her construct the greenhouse from a kit, and she successfully cultivated a steady winter harvest of microgreens and root vegetables to sell. She was still working out the kinks in growing peppers and tomatoes, however, the two most desired vegetables people wanted to buy year-round.

Jake. The thought of him still made her stomach flutter. Who'd ever guess she'd call Bassville's hometown hero her boyfriend?

"You working tonight?"

Jenny's voice interrupted Mona's thoughts and she shook her head. "Steve is. I'm working tomorrow."

"Let's go out then. You don't have plans, do you?"

"No, Jake's still at the job by Milwaukee. What do you want to do?"

"Let's grab Judi and head to Northport. I heard a new club opened up downtown."

"That's not really Judi's scene."

"I don't really care."

"Not really my scene, either."

"Ugh!" Jenny whined. "No one's any fun anymore. I *hate* this. You're turning into a boring old farmer like your dad."

"Sorry, Jenny." Mona grinned. *That actually sounds like a compliment to me*, she thought.

Loyal hated sitting still. He stood at the kitchen window staring out at the clumpy, muddy field stretching into the distance and contemplated his options. Another month before he could get on his tractor, the cows were milked until evening now, and he'd changed the oil and spark plugs in every engine on the farm. He swallowed the rest of his midday cup of coffee and scratched the back of his neck.

"Looking for something to do?" June came around the corner carrying a stack of newspapers. "You can put these in the recycle bin."

"Sure." Loyal grabbed the papers and set down his mug in one motion. "I'm going to the barn."

"Again?"

"Yep."

June opened her mouth and then shut it. Late winter was a difficult time to be a farmer's wife. Nothing to do, yet nowhere to go, as long as cows required milking. They'd gone on a day trip to Northport last week and the whole time, instead of enjoying himself, Loyal had checked and rechecked his watch, anxious to get back. He suggested she take a trip alone somewhere, maybe Branson or even Florida, but June didn't want to go anywhere alone. She wanted to be with her husband. And her husband wanted to be with his farm. It was as simple as that.

Rinsing out his coffee mug at the sink, June half listened to *The Price Is Right* promote a Carnival Cruise on TV. Loyal's tall form disappeared into the barn across the yard and June wondered how a woman could feel lucky and disappointed at the same time. Loyal worked hard, he didn't carouse, get drunk or screw around. Her husband was a wonderful father to their children, provided for his family and had a reputation as a man people could count on. Many women would trade their partners for hers in a heartbeat. He was even still attractive at forty-eight, in a beat-up Clint Eastwood sort of way. She envied how his crow's feet and grey temples added a dignity to his appearance; while the same signs of age did nothing to improve on her looks. She'd begun to sag beneath her chin and her midsection had thickened, even her complexion was becoming spotted with moles.

June had been in high school when she started dating Loyal. He'd asked her to be his date for homecoming, that tall and broad-shouldered boy, dashing in his bright red Bobcats football jersey, number 17. She'd felt so proud wearing that huge jersey, her blonde hair swept back into a matching ribbon. He gazed up at her in the bleachers, standing a head above many of his teammates that October afternoon. His shy smile, his dimple and his bright blue eyes suddenly had her full attention.

She'd never dated anyone before Loyal, and never dated anyone since. When she left for college, he stayed on his parents' farm and worked. He drove up to see her once a month. They talked on the phone long distance once a week, and she sent him funny postcards from school telling him about the classes she took, the other girls living on her floor, the politics and craziness of campus life. Loyal never wrote back, but asked her questions when they talked on the phone and he listened, interested in every conversation. Once, during final exam week, he'd arranged to have a dozen red roses sent to her dormitory and the entire floor swooned at his romantic gesture.

Then she graduated, they got married and moved into the farmhouse his parents left him. She began her new life with vigor, painting bright colors on the walls, scrubbing and scouring every floorboard of the house and outbuildings, cooking huge meals for Loyal and whoever happened to be helping him at the time, even trying her hand with milking and plowing. Her college textbooks were moved from a bookcase in the living room to a cardboard box in the attic when their daughter was born. The last remnants of the woman she was silently receded to make room for children, PTA, Sunday dinners for the entire family. She stopped reading the newspaper cover to cover, let her library card expire, cut her blonde hair short and forgot to wear lipstick. Her degree in history never collected anything but dust.

Sean was gone now, off at college in another state. But June's discontent couldn't be written off as empty-nest syndrome. It had started five years ago at a girls' basketball game. The Bassville Bobcats had beaten the Liberty Polar Bears 57-46 and she was flushed after two hours of cheering for Mona's team. She stood with the crowd of parents, all people she knew well after years of church potluck dinners and school events. She tucked her arm inside of Loyal's and smiled and chattered her way out of the gymnasium, into the school's lobby where she glimpsed her reflection in the glass of a trophy case. Short and stocky, her dull hair streaked with grey no longer shone golden blonde. The sweatshirt did nothing to conceal the bulge at her waist and her white socks flashed between her too-short jeans and brown loafers. June looked like every unfashionable middle-aged woman she'd always despised. She only lacked polyester pants with a crease sewn down the center of each leg. This ugly woman reflected in the trophy case, oblivious to her ruddy cheeks, bad hair and ill-fitting clothes, clung possessively to the arm of a tall and attractive man in a flannel jacket.

The next morning June had called Weight Watchers and bought three fashion magazines at Bud's Supermarket. She looked over the bright photographs and studied the cut and color of the clothes. She tore out five particularly appealing pictures of women and laid them in her underwear drawer where she saw them every day to inspire her to eat more carrots and less cake.

That was five years and thirty pounds ago. Now her hair swung in a flattering golden bob that required regular appointments at the Best Little Hair House. She wore clothes purchased from Pranges instead of Kmart. Loyal never noticed or said much.

June got a new library card and borrowed books on politics, history and philosophy. She read the newspaper cover to cover every day, even looking over the classifieds for job opportunities. At supper, now just the two of them during the week, she would bring up subjects to discuss over new experiments in cooking. Over Indian curried chicken one night, she asked, "Do you think all this investing in the stock market is a good idea? Nothing can grow forever, even an economy. Are we headed for another crash?"

Loyal shrugged and scowled at the chicken. "Don't know. What *is* this? I like your fried chicken better."

June concluded that after updating herself, essentially *reinventing* herself, Loyal remained the same and didn't care one way or the other. Passion, adventure, drama—all the things she'd craved when younger and then squelched in the course of creating a family—once more filled her imagination. Meanwhile, Loyal's idea of romance was bringing home another dozen roses every Valentine's day, and later rolling over from his side of their bed to kiss her, expecting sex in return. Life had become limited and unsatisfying.

She loved her family. She wanted to stay married—leaving Loyal never crossed her mind. But she wanted to see the world! She wanted to be like the couples in advertisements, holding hands on a beach, laughing and gazing at each other affectionately over candlelit dinners. She wanted to feel useful—beyond doing laundry and dishes. June wanted something *more*.

In the barn, Loyal grabbed his toolbox and headed to the back door. Might as well fix that loose hinge and patch that fencing on the south side of the barn, too, while he was at it. He could hardly wait until next month when he could be busy again, instead of all this damned standing around. Maybe he'd build a few planting boxes for Mona to set out her seedlings when the weather got nicer. And a potting bench. Maybe two, one for June as well. She'd like that.

After bouncing Jenny from the greenhouse, Mona made sure everything was in order before shutting the door tight behind her. The weatherman said it would get down to 18 degrees tonight. She had too much at stake beneath those glass frames, and her bartending job at the Bassville Pub would not cover any losses.

Hugging her arms across her chest, Mona jogged down the frozen path towards her parents' house. Through the window she could see her mother at the kitchen table, her blonde head bowed over a book maybe, or a knitting project. She'd stop in for a quick visit before heading to her house in town.

Mona rapped on the door before letting herself inside.

"Mona!" Her mother pushed away from the table and dabbed at her eyes.

"Everything okay?" Mona asked. "Were you crying?"

"No," June sniffed. "I caught a little cold." She wadded up the tissue in her hand and gestured at the empty chair across from where she sat. "Sit. Want tea or anything?"

"I'm good." Mona slid the chair over and draped her winter jacket across the back. "What's new?"

"Nothing much. How's it going with the peppers?"

"Badly," Mona cracked her knuckles. "Sorry, I know you hate that."

"It's okay. But your seedlings for the spring planting are doing well. I sat out there last night for a while. The smell and the heat—it's like a shot of summer in that greenhouse. Not quite a beach vacation, but on a budget it'll do."

Mona smiled at her mother. "Can't talk Dad into leaving town yet?" She knew the winters were long for her mom. But her dad would not be budged from the farm for any length of time.

June shrugged. "I knew it when I married him. Dairy farmers don't take vacations."

"Baloney. The Traysons hired somebody to run their farm while Angie was getting her treatments. I bet Dad could get someone for a week."

"The only change your father enjoys involves a remote control for the television."

"Then you should go," Mona suggested. "With a friend." She thought of Arlyce and Dottie. The thought of plump, sturdy Dottie Butterfield in a bathing suit on a beach—or Arlyce for that matter! Her mouth twisted into a smile.

"Speaking of friends, I saw Jenny came out here earlier. What's new with her?"

"She's excited about some calendar Maw's putting together for the bait shop. I think she's still holding out hope she'll be discovered and become a famous model."

"You never know. Who'd have guessed Maw would make it big selling minnows?"

"Who'd guess *anyone* would make it big out of Bassville," Mona agreed. "It surprises me that she sticks around town, though. You'd think she'd want to live in a big city as much as she loves to shop and all that."

"Do you think Beau keeps her here?"

Mona considered this for a second. Beau Longwell was attractive, but sleazy and a terrible flirt. "No," she decided. "He's the most attractive option here for Jenny, but she knows there's no future there."

"Too comfy living at home?"

"No. Her parents would set her up anywhere she wanted to go.

That's not it."

"Maybe your friendship keeps her here."

Mona laughed. "I think it boils down to Jenny not having any better plan, at least not right now. Anyway, the only plan I know she has involves going to Northport tonight."

"What's she doing there?"

"She wants to check out some new club. Probably some skeevey meat market under strobe lights. Ick." Mona stuck out her tongue. "I think I'm getting old or something because that sounds like torture to me."

"Not going then, huh? When's Jake back from Milwaukee?"

"Only for the weekend."

June reached across the table and clasped Mona's forearm. "You're so independent and confident, I'm proud of you."

Mona raised her eyebrows. "Thanks. You sure everything's all right, Mom?"

"Yes. Everything's fine." June patted Mona's arm before pushing back from the table. "You sure you don't want a cup of tea?"

"I'll take a cup of hot chocolate if you have any." Mona grinned. "Look at me. Wasn't so long ago I'd be chomping at the bit to go out on the town with Jenny and get out of your kitchen. Things have sure changed."

June pushed her chair back and walked towards the pantry where she kept the cocoa powder and powdered milk. "Things are different for your generation. Hopefully you'll never find yourself discontented."

"Oh, Mom. That's a crazy thing to say." She ticked off the good things in her life on her fingertips. "I've got a sweet little house, my own business started, a great boyfriend and a town council seat. Plus friends, good health and great parents." She stood up and gave her mom a hug. "You don't need to worry about me at all!" But it was strange, Mona thought, that her mom would say such a thing to her.

THREE

Maw hung up after placing an order for can coolers with the bait store's new minnow logo and crossed that particular item off of his to-do list. The rest of the list made him cranky; none of the things he had to take care of were fun. He didn't want to change the furnace filter, figure out why Peg's car was making a weird clicking noise or finish taking inventory. Across the house he could hear his kids messing around, and contemplated hiring them to assist him. Minimally, he might be able to train them to handle the inventory and stock shelves. "Kids!" he yelled. "Get in here!"

A scrambling thumping on the stairs commenced, and Maw's offspring shoved their way past one another into the kitchen where he sat at the table. He studied them. The oldest actually had a job, he remembered. She washed dishes at the Pub when the season got busy. The middle one was almost twelve, tall for his age and skinny, but not very bright. The youngest was seven, chubby like Maw, and had a quick mind. "Okay, you two," he pointed his finger at the younger two, "I have a job for you." He waved the oldest away by flapping his hand. "You're dismissed."

"Aw, Dad!" they whined in perfect chorus.

"Come on." Maw stuffed his arms into his winter coat and held the door open for his children, who sulked past him into the muddy parking lot that separated the house from the bait shop. "This'll be fun."

"Fun for grownups is never fun for kids," the youngest one mumbled.

Maw flung open the door to his bait shop and ushered the boys inside. He crouched down with his hands on his knees to look them in the eye. "As you two have figured out by now, your mom and I provide you with all the things you need—food, clothing, shelter. We also provide you with all the things you *don't* need—baseball cards, money when we go to the county fair, TV."

"I could live without TV," the middle one offered.

"Great. But meanwhile, you two are going to contribute."

"This sounds bad," the youngest one said to his brother, who nodded in agreement.

"Not bad. I'll even pay you." Maw watched their expressions morph from wary to interested. "I'll give you each five dollars for the job." He knew better than to pay them by the hour—they were his kids, after all. They'd milk that deal for all it was worth. "I need you to stock all the shelves in the store and then fill in this inventory list so we know what we need to order."

Maw spent the next forty minutes explaining his system of taking inventory, which involved several different order forms, lists and folders. Then he showed them the stock room, an eight-by-ten room overflowing with boxes of every size stacked in precarious towers.

"Jesus," the younger one breathed when Maw showed them the

stock room. "What a mess."

"Yeah." Maw looked around. There was hardly any space to move through, yet somehow the boxes had crept into the middle of the room, blocked the window, probably multiplied when he wasn't paying attention. He scratched at his chin through his beard, considering the situation. In less than a month the walleye run would start and they'd be bang into the middle of fishing madness, if last year's success continued to breed. Maw watched his sons start pulling assorted reels, spinners, packets of hooks and sinkers out of one of the boxes. Maybe he shouldn't've placed such a big order with the Berkley rep.

"Okay, fifteen bucks each if you can clean up this mess, too."

"Cool!" the middle one said, high-fiving his brother.

The boys stood around for a minute assessing the mess before diving in. "Let's put all the lures over here," the younger one suggested.

Maw retreated back to into the shop, satisfied he'd successfully tackled the biggest challenge on his list. He grabbed a pencil out of the cup by the register and started to chew on it. It was raining out, a sleety drizzle. He didn't want to monkey around with Peg's car in this weather. A stack of catalogs and other mail lay strewn across the counter and he started to doodle a fish getting caught by a hook on the back of an envelope. He'd drawn his way to the edge of his next grand marketing scheme when the phone rang.

"Maw's Bait and Tackle," he answered, "Home of Maw's minnows."

"Hey, hey, hey," a low silky voice curled into his ear. "Can you give me a fishing report?"

"Dave LaMay!" Maw yelled to the Chicago DJ on the other line. "Holy shit, what's it been—almost five months!"

"All of that. How's it going, man?"

"Great. Getting geared up for the season here, of course. Been working on the next strain of minnow. It's a top-secret project, but I can tell you it involves shark DNA."

Dave laughed. "Excellent. I'm glad you brought that up, because I met a guy who does documentaries and he'd like to make you his next subject."

Excitement surged through Maw's veins—fame and money gave him the biggest rush, and starring in a movie about himself was bound to produce both. "What are we talking here? A behind-the-scenes look at the glamorous life of a bait shop salesman?"

"Bit more than that, Maw," Dave drawled. "He's really curious about the science stuff. I don't know all the details. I only told him I'd put him in touch with you."

"Okay, how's this gonna work?" Maw flipped over the picture he'd sketched of a fish and got ready to take notes.

"His name's Boyd Douglas."

"Uh-huh." Maw scribbled down the name.

Dave relayed the rest of the contact information before telling Maw he'd call again soon to set up his spring fishing trip. "There better be booze, babes and white bass, buddy. In that order!"

"You got it, buddy!"

Maw hung up feeling more inspired than he had in months. He dialed Boyd Douglas to hear his pitch.

"What I'm looking to do, Maw, is create a series of science videos about the ecology of different sports for a new cable TV channel called *Discovery*. For example, I just finished shooting *Turf's Up*, which tells the story of grass on golf courses—how it's developed, how it grows, what it takes to make the different landscapes from driving range to putting green. It featured a botanist, a chemist from Monsanto and a physics instructor from MIT who talked about the effect of different textures on how a golf ball moves."

Boyd Douglas went on to describe his last project in greater detail while Maw stifled a yawn. He couldn't see how this opportunity would lead to anything worthwhile, but he did subscribe to the old adage that no publicity was bad publicity.

"So, what I'd really like to do is come to Bassville and film your operation. Really dig into the science behind your minnows, how you raise them, how you've tapped into the DNA protocols to create world-famous bait."

The nagging voice of reason said Maw should tell the truth to this man, explain that all he did was take an ordinary golden shiner and slap a name on it. He should confess that his minnows were only world-famous because of his marketing ploy, they weren't any better than any other minnow out there. However, if he told the truth, he wouldn't be in a movie, and if he wasn't in a movie, he wouldn't get more attention. Attention led to money, which always led to happiness.

Through the bug-smeared window overlooking the muddy parking lot, Maw saw Peg's Buick. "Sure thing, Boyd," he said. "You come on over and I'll show you how we genetically engineer the minnows at Maw's."

All he had to do, he reasoned when he hung up, was turn the stock room into a science lab and set up some kind of process that looked legitimate enough to pass inspection. He'd research some jargon and rig up some equipment. "Kids," he called down the hall, "we've got to get all of that stuff outta that back room and out on the shelves here. Your dad's about to become a mad scientist."

FOUR

In winter, entire days could pass without a single customer walking into the Bassville Pub. Brutal wind chills and icy roads kept the locals hunkered down at home around their fireplaces. Aside from the occasional groups of snowmobilers racing down the river and the ice fishermen coming inside for a quick pizza and pitcher of beer, no outsiders came through town.

Steve and Arlyce Shanski had tried various promotions over the years to persuade people to visit the Pub, but the locals stubbornly refused to budge from in front of their television sets when the temperatures plummeted. The weekly pool league hardly paid the electric bill, but an experiment in shutting down until spring pissed off the few people venturing out for a fish basket and beer to break up the monotony of staying home. To strike a balance, Steve ran the bar alone, giving Mona the extra hours while Arlyce stayed home with their kids. It was hell on their marriage; they liked spending their day together running the kitchen and bar. But, they reasoned if only one of them could afford to be working, it should be Steve shooting the breeze with thirsty farmers and fishermen.

A seven-inch layer of ice covered the river and snow seeped into mud along the street. Arlyce bundled up her four children and bustled them out the front door of her house and down the street to Bud's Supermarket. She wistfully glanced across the street at the Pub—by the end of summer she hated working there but when she was trapped at home all winter she missed it. At least at the Pub she made money and got to talk to people. Staying home with the kids meant doing the same chores over and over again: laundry, making snacks and stepping across the plastic strips of racecar tracks her kids set up through the house.

Waddling like overstuffed chickens, the three oldest followed their mother while she dragged the baby through the slushy parking lot beside Bud's. Steve used the truck to get from spot to spot along the river and public hunting lands he frequented after he left the Pub, so Arlyce walked through her errands—pulling her groceries and children behind her in a huge red wagon. She herded the children down the sidewalk to her mother's or to school during the day and then she walked to the bank, the post office, the church. Once a month, when she and Steve headed to Northport to shop at the big stores, Arlyce would kick her feet up on the dashboard and enjoy the novelty of riding to her destination.

The string of jingle bells clanged against the glass door when she swung it open.

"Hey, Arlyce!" Joanne called to her from behind one of the two checkout lanes where she sat reading a tabloid and sipping a diet cola.

"Hi, Joanne." Arlyce's foot braced the door for the three boys following her into the store. Four short aisles displayed canned and boxed goods. The produce cooler consisted of two refrigerators along one side of the store and dairy products chilled along the back wall. A separate room was used for meat. Bud butchered anything anyone brought in, and the last, largest aisle of the store held beer, liquor, soda and potato chips. Bait and sundry items were located in front, next to the glass doors.

"Hey, Arlyce!" June called from aisle three. Arlyce waved to her friend while steering her way down aisle one, canned goods.

As Arlyce selected her cans and boxes and lined them up beside the baby, the boys raced silently up and down the aisles. Thump, thump, thump, their rubber boots echoed through the store, squeaking when they cornered the ends of each aisle. Victoria sat in the wagon and stared up at the walls above the shelves where Bud displayed an impressive taxidermy collection. Mottled foxes with their sharp noses and beady eyes stood still in mid-stride. Huge muskies, silvery scales dulled by dust and time, arched away from their mounts, forever fighting a current of central air instead of water.

Joanne followed them over to aisle four where Arlyce stood studying the display of canned corn on special this week—two for ninety-seven cents. "How's this little cutie doing?" Joanne leaned forward and chucked Victoria heartily beneath her chin. Victoria stared back at Joanne and kicked her chunky legs twice, breaking a strand of drool that attached her chin to the front of her bunting.

"Oh, real good. She's a keeper." Arlyce took two large cans of store brand creamed corn and set them in the wagon behind her. Then she took a closer look at Joanne's face. "What happened *now?*"

"Nothing." Joanne moved her hand up to her face and lightly touched her right eye.

"Nothing doesn't look like a bruise, Joanne."

"It's nothing." Joanne smiled down at the baby, who solemnly examined her hands.

Arlyce studied the puffy purple bruise around Joanne's right eye, barely camouflaged by a thick, clumsy layer of beige foundation, a shade too dark for her pale complexion. Joanne also wore a sling around her left arm, and the fingers of her left hand had a blue tint. Arlyce moved forward to pick out beans, pulling the wagon behind her with her free hand.

"He doesn't mean to do it," Joanne said quietly.

"When are you going to get a spine and leave that bastard?" Arlyce spun around to face her. "Your face got punched, your—what—arm or shoulder or wrist bound up. What'd he do?"

"It's complicated."

"Yeah, it's complicated. He gets drunk, he comes home, he uses you as a punching bag. You stand there and take it. The cycle repeats itself. Hard to figure where it gets 'complicated.'"

"He loves me." Joanne's voice rose slightly.

"He loves whisky. Beer. Hunting. Fishing—"

Joanne turned and walked back to the cash registers at the front of the store.

Arlyce felt awful. They'd had this conversation before, but she wouldn't quit on Joanne. She knew she was hurting Joanne's feelings, but that was nothing compared to other kinds of damage. She called after Joanne's retreating figure, "You deserve better."

Mona walked in then, clutching a shopping list. "Hey, Joanne. I'm making pizza and just need to grab some oregano and cheese."

"Oregano's in aisle three, on your left, in between cardamom and cinnamon," Joanne told her.

"You okay?" Mona looked at her more closely.

"Fine. Your mom and Arlyce are around the corner."

"I thought I saw the boys run through," Mona told her

Leaving Mona and June beside the baking supplies, Arlyce maneuvered to the second checkout lane where Joanne had returned to her tabloid. "I'm sorry. It's just you're a good friend and I don't like to see you hurt." She reached across the metal counter and clasped

Joanne's good shoulder.

Joanne looked up at Arlyce and returned a small smile. "I know."

Arlyce stuffed the packages around the baby in the wagon and paid for the groceries. "Trapper! Hunter! Fisher! Come here! I need you to help carry this back home!" She handed each boy a shopping bag and held the door for them.

"You ever need help, you call me," Arlyce said to Joanne. "See you later," she called across the store.

"See ya!" Mona hollered back. June waved.

Arlyce pushed her crew through the doors while Joanne bent over to take a compact from her black leatherette purse with the red fringe. The puffiness had gone down but the bruising was still vivid beneath the makeup. Her violet eyes nearly matched the color of the bruise, making the effect strangely beautiful. She shook her long black hair back behind her shoulders and dropped the compact back into her purse. The conversation with Arlyce embarrassed her. She thought she was doing a better job covering up. She didn't want people to pity her. She hated to think anyone talked about her. There was more going on in her situation than others could understand, she reasoned to herself. Sighing, she picked up the tabloid and turned the page to get a glimpse of Demi Moore's love child with an alien from Mars.

"Kind of looks like Steve, doesn't he?" Mona asked from over her shoulder, pointing at the insert photo of Demi's Martian lover. Joanne had to snicker. With the huge head and protruding ears, Mona was right.

Joanne rang up Mona, then June and felt relieved when they both walked toward the door. Then June paused and turned around. "I'd help you, too," she said in a very quiet voice before leaving the store. Joanne slammed the cash register drawer shut and scowled. She didn't want people feeling sorry for her, she thought while reaching for a bottle of Windex. She didn't deserve their sympathy.

FIVE

FOUR HOURS LATER, JOANNE hung her apron on the nail in the back room and told Bud goodbye. He had come in at three and told her she was free to leave. Gratefully, she noticed it was still light out when she crossed the parking lot behind the store. The brisk air felt sharp in her nostrils and she inhaled twice more, the sensation making her feel alert after the mind-numbing pace behind the checkout. She reached into her purse for her keys and sat on the cracked vinyl seat, the cold immediate against the backs of her thighs. It didn't matter when she went back to her apartment above the bank—he wouldn't be there anyway until much, much later.

Arlyce helped Fisher into his winter coat, snow pants, hat, boots and mittens and shoved her three sons outside to play. She returned to the living room, filling her arms with a Tonka dump truck, five crayons, two sweat socks and a knitted scarf along the way. She tossed the toys into the wooden toy box by the front door and stuffed the clothes into a dresser drawer.

Victoria's bawl caught her halfway down onto a couch cushion and she rose to get her. "There, there," she called as she retraced her steps back up the hallway. "I'm coming."

The baby's diaper changed, Arlyce took up her position on the couch with a hot cup of tea and the *County Post*. Skimming through high school sports scores and obituaries, she stopped short at the police reports. Sure enough, the cops had been called two nights ago to Joanne's house. "At 3:00 a.m. Sunday police responded to a domestic disturbance at 512 ½ Main Street."

Arlyce shook her head and sighed. That woman had to leave for her own good. Picking up her baby, she held Victoria tight against her chest and rocked back and forth, ignoring the television, the buzzer on the oven and the slamming of the back door.

"Mom!" Hunter's voice blared through her thoughts. "Hey, Mom! Trapper's got a golf ball stuck in his mouth. He needs help."

Arlyce set Victoria on the floor and walked wearily to the back door to look at three boys standing with guilt plastered across their rosy faces, the middle one drooling around a full mouth. It would be a long, long spring break with these monsters home all week.

Joanne raised her head off her pillow in a sudden jerk. Frozen in stillness and silence, she waited, concentrating on the sounds around her, sifting through the layers of noise. The cool green numbers on her digital alarm clock read 8:07. She'd only just fallen asleep. Truck on the highway, hum of the refrigerator, hiss of the furnace, faint buzz of the streetlight outside, there. There it was again, louder now. Clump-clump. Was he home?

In the pit of her gut she felt the clenching of muscles, muscles that had relaxed while she slept, muscles that only unbound completely when she was at work in a public place where people's watching eyes offered her protection. Her head felt light and somehow disconnected while she listened.

Clump-clump.

He was home.

She waited, barely breathing, mind full of impulses. Should she pretend to be sleeping? Wake up? Wait until he fell asleep—hope he fell asleep before he reached for her?

"JOANNE!" His raspy shout broke through the silence and the options fled from her mind. Joanne lifted her legs and swiveled out of bed. She prayed he wasn't too drunk ... or drunk enough to pass out quickly.

"You're home!" She strained to sound cheerful, welcoming. It was the first time she'd seen him in a week.

"What's there to eat?" His huge shape turned suddenly black in the bright light from the refrigerator bulb.

"Um, there's leftover spaghetti. I could make up something if you don't want that." She tightened the tie of her robe and then reached up to do the same to her ponytail.

"Make me a steak."

"I don't think we have any."

"What the—make me a hamburger then. A big one, with mayonnaise and butter and ketchup. What else do we have?"

Joanne reached up to grab the skillet from above the stove. It would be so easy to take the cast iron pan and just bash his head in. Her arms flexed for a brief moment.

"Chips? There's some potato salad maybe."

"Good." He shut the refrigerator door and looked at her, eyes narrowed and bloodshot. "Don't forget the cheese. Velveeta. Not that plastic wrapped crap."

"I won't." Joanne turned her back and started pulling dishes from

32

the cupboard. He was in a hungry, irritable drunk mood, not the sort of mood that would land her another black eye—or cracked rib. Getting up in the middle of the night to cook was a small inconvenience when she compared it to a trip to the emergency room over in Northport. Maybe her luck was turning slightly. Arlyce didn't know everything, she thought defiantly. The sudden burst of canned laughter from the television set in the living room reassured her that tonight was going to be peaceful.

It was almost nine o'clock by the time he'd gulped down his dinner and fallen asleep. Scrubbing the bottom of the frying pan with a steel wool pad, Joanne felt the remnants of rage leave her body. This was the first time he'd come home all week. Instead of feeling relieved each morning when she woke up to an empty apartment, Joanne felt more frantic. She knew he was still in town. She'd driven by his job site every day and seen his truck. She knew where he was staying, too. Friday night she woke up, put on her shoes and jacket, and started walking up and down the streets of Bassville, oblivious to the cold. His truck had been parked in front of Grumpy's.

He'd done this before, disappeared for a while, but he always returned. They would fight, she'd scream accusations at him, he'd apologize, they'd end up in bed together, mad and passionate at the same time. And a month later he'd come home drunk and she'd become "Joanne, The Human Punching Bag" again.

The opportunity lay before her, scary and comforting all at once. *If I left*, she reasoned, *there wouldn't be any conflict because he was already gone. But*, the clanging voice of fear interrupted, *you'd be all alone*. There was the possibility that one day he wouldn't come back. Then she'd be alone anyway. Bassville could be a lonely place. *Why stay here? I can go to my daughter in California, if she'll have me.*

She needed to quit this mess, she decided. It wasn't getting any better and it had every chance of getting worse. She should cash in her chips and try her luck somewhere else.

Joanne rinsed the pan, placed it in the drying rack, and grabbed her purse and coat. There wasn't much time—and who knew when she'd feel brave enough again. She had to go somewhere he couldn't find her. She'd have to trust Rhonda would be there for her.

She jogged down the street to Arlyce's, panting for breath by the time she got there. Catching her breath, Joanne knocked twice on the kitchen window before letting herself in the house. Arlyce and June sat at the table knitting, Victoria was in her high chair pushing Cheerios around on the tray. A TV blared from the other room.

"Joanne! Pull up a chair." Arlyce began to wrap yarn around her knitting needles and stand.

"You're busy—I can come back another time."

"Don't be silly. We're just knitting," Arlyce said.

"Loyal's at a town council meeting—it's the long one, the annual zoning meeting. So I had him drop me here with Arlyce until he's done." June patted an empty seat beside her. "Sit."

Joanne sat down in the one empty chair while Arlyce pulled a mug out of the cupboard for her. "We're drinking decaf, but I've got something stronger if you want," Arlyce offered. "And Steve's at the Pub."

Joanne felt ready to burst. "I'm ready to leave him. For real." She announced this breathlessly, looking at the baby's soft, round cheeks instead of at Arlyce's doubtful expression.

"You are." Arlyce's voice sounded skeptical.

"He came back last night—but he'll be gone again. And maybe he won't come back, but maybe he will, but I'm just so damn tired of it. I can't do it anymore. You're right, Arlyce. It's a cycle and I'm trapped until I cut myself loose. He came home drunk tonight and I left when he fell asleep. If I took off tomorrow while he's at work, that'll be the end of it." Joanne took a shaky breath. "But if I don't go this time, I probably won't be brave enough again."

"Good for you!" June leaned over to pick up Cheerios Victoria had thrown over the edge of her tray onto the floor.

"I need your help." Joanne patted her sling with her good arm. "I can't do this alone."

"Tell us what you need," June said.

"I want to move back to California, with my oldest daughter."

"Well, why don't we just get you a bus ticket and you leave town right away?" Arlyce stacked the supper dishes and carried them to the sink. "Before you change your mind."

"I have to get a hold of Rhonda and tell her I'm coming."

"Oh. I see." Arlyce knew Joanne had two beautiful blonde grown-up daughters, but only from a photograph she'd shown her once.

"It's complicated—we haven't exactly stayed in touch. I do have a phone number, though. Can I call her from here? I'll give you money."

"Of course." Arlyce gestured to the phone hanging on the kitchen wall beside the stove. "I'll get this one cleaned up while you call her."

While Arlyce stripped Victoria down to her onesie and wiped her face, neck and hands, she strained to hear Joanne's end of the conversation, but the Duke brothers' latest escapades on TV made too much noise. If Joanne was for real—and she'd never tried leaving before as far as Arlyce knew—they could try to get her out of town tonight. She returned to the kitchen to find Joanne back at the table. "Well?"

"I had her work number. The receptionist said she's on vacation for a week, and they wouldn't give me anything else—no address, no other number."

"You don't know your daughter's address?" Arlyce couldn't believe that.

"I told you, it's complicated."

"So, what do you want to do?" June asked while evenly pouring out the remains of the coffee between their mugs. "Can you head out to California anyway and wait until she gets back in town?"

"I thought about that. The trouble is, I don't have any money." Joanne looked down at her lap.

"You could stay here," Arlyce suggested.

Joanne shook her head. "No way. If he comes looking for me, it puts you and your kids right in the middle of it. I appreciate it, but I need to go somewhere for a week and lay low."

"You can come stay with me," June said.

Joanne shook her head. "I don't want Loyal to know where I am. Men talk. I know he's a good guy, but I don't trust any man when they're around other men."

"Then let's get you a hotel room in Northport," June said.

Joanne bit her lip and closed her eyes for a moment. "I barely have enough money for the bus ticket."

"Oh." The room was silent except for the revving of the General Lee coming from the living room.

"I was going to ask somebody to lend me some money," Joanne mumbled softly.

"How much?" June asked.

"A hundred."

Arlyce tried to keep the shock off her face by frowning. "Wow. That's a lot."

"The bus ticket to California is one fifty and I'll need to eat. And I'll need a bit to get started fresh. I almost have enough for the bus ticket."

"Yes." Arlyce thought about the fifty-seven dollars she still had in her tip jar.

June said, "Maybe Dottie and I could chip in, but that's a lot to come up with on short notice."

Arlyce took a deep breath and considered where one might hide a fully grown woman for a week.

"Here's a thought," June stood up. "Otto Zimm has that ice shanty he leaves by Cooper's Bayou, right? You could camp out there for a week and then I can bring you to the bus station. The weather's starting to get warmer, all you'll need is some food."

"That's not a bad idea." Joanne pursed her lips.

"You just want to lay low until you reach your daughter. It'll be perfect. No one'll look for you there. Otto and his wife went to Las Vegas, so he's gone until next week. Plus it's free, so you can save whatever money you do have for a fresh start."

"You sure it's safe?" Joanne clenched the edge of the table with her hand.

"It's tucked away in the bayou. No one's ice fishing much anymore and it'll be at least three weeks before the backwaters open up. The main channel always thaws first because of the current," June explained. "Can you think of any place more off-grid than that? I can run out food to you. Or have Steve and Loyal do it."

"No men," Joanne said sharply. "He'll tell. You know how men are. No one can know." Joanne reached for the baby and kissed her nose. "Are you listening to your crazy Aunt Joanne?" The baby squealed and grabbed Joanne's nose.

"It'll only be for a week," Joanne murmured. The more she thought about it, the more she liked the idea. It would be safe in the shanty. How did the writer Thoreau put it? "A man is rich in proportion to the number of things which he can afford to let alone." She could let most of it alone, go "live deliberately" and come back stronger for the experience.

"I left my car behind at home, so he'll think I'm still around," she said suddenly.

"That's bad," Arlyce said. "If he thinks you're still around, he might come looking for you. We have to get your car out of town somehow."

"How?" Joanne asked.

"We'll take your car to Northport tomorrow," June said. "We can park it at the mall, by the Sears store. Should be fine there. I'll follow you in the truck and bring you back to town."

"I like that plan." Joanne said.

"You want to spend the night here tonight?" Arlyce asked. "I can make up the couch for you."

"No, thanks. I'll go back home for one last night. Make it seem normal. Besides, no one else is scheduled at Bud's so I need to work in the morning." Joanne stood and eased her coat back over her wounded arm, then pushed her other arm through.

She was so fragile, Arlyce thought, but finally strong enough to do what needed doing. Even if she didn't agree with Joanne's method of doing it. If it was her, she'd call the cops. But then, everyone knew how that would go. Maybe they'd write up a restraining order, but a piece of paper never kept anybody safe.

SIX

THE SUN FINALLY BROKE through and the icicles on the eaves of the Pub began a steady drip-drip-drip onto the ground. Mona wiped down the top shelf liquor bottles and checked the clock. Nearly noon and not a single customer. Arlyce had told her to call if it got busy, but she preferred not to keep Victoria with her mother if she could avoid it. They wouldn't get busy for another two weeks, tops. Mona guessed there might be a small crowd of locals in after work later in the afternoon, maybe a few pizza and burger orders, but not enough reason to bother Arlyce.

After tossing the bar rag into the sink, Mona double-checked the list Steve had left behind. Most of her work was done; she'd save the rest for later. Reaching beneath the register, she retrieved the course catalog for North Central Wisconsin Community College. She paged through until she found the section on Accounting classes. The introductory course met on Monday nights, ideal for her work schedule because they never needed two bartenders on Mondays, not even in the busiest point of the white bass run. But the other class she needed to take, Propagation and Planting, met twice a week, Tuesdays and Thursdays from 3 to 4:30. There could not be a less convenient time, but she'd ask Steve anyway. He'd howl, of course, but maybe it would be okay. He and Arlyce knew in the long run she wasn't going to stick around. This would introduce the idea gradually to them, and then in another year when the farm was making enough money and she could afford to quit bartending, they'd be ready.

She gazed around at the wood-paneled bar, cavernous when empty. The room never changed—two pool tables, dart machines on the west wall, tall tables by the windows overlooking the river and a large TV mounted on the wall between the bar and the pool table, above the doorway leading to the kitchen. The Pub smelled the same—like cigarettes, sour beer and grease—and sounded the same—the hum of coolers and the low rumble of the stereo in the background.

The door swung open with a brisk *woosh* and Mona spun around to see who her first customer of the day would be. Jake.

Her boyfriend approached her with a wide grin. His blonde hair was covered with a stocking cap and his heavy canvas jacket made him look broader than usual.

"Hello, beautiful," he bent down to kiss her. "What are you serving?"

"Nothing yet," Mona clasped her hands around his neck and pulled him in for another kiss. "You're the first person I've seen all day. I didn't think you'd be back until the weekend."

Jake removed his gloves and rubbed his hands together. "It's getting a little warmer out there, but I was stuck sitting inside a building. Chilly when you're not in the sun."

"Do you want coffee?"

"Yes."

Mona went back to the kitchen to pour him a cup and joined him sitting at the bar. "This is a nice surprise."

Jake drank from his cup before grabbing her hand. "I had a visitor at the job site today."

"Let me guess. President Reagan?"

"No."

"James Lofton?"

"It would be cool to meet a Packer player, but no."

"Miss America."

"You're terrible at guessing." Jake squeezed her hand before letting go. "It was Leon Beyer, the owner of Beyer's Construction."

"Oh. Impressive. Or is it? Does he usually visit the job sites?"

"Yes, but he came by specifically to visit me."

"Ah," Mona grinned with pride. "To give you a raise because of the terrific job you do for him every day?"

"Sort of." Jake leaned back and tapped his hands against the edge of the bar. Then he crossed his arms and leaned in towards her. "He did offer me a raise—and a promotion. Project manager."

"Congratulations!" Jake was the smartest, most talented person ever, she thought with pride.

"There's a catch." Jake's expression grew serious. "He wants to transfer me. To Atlanta, Georgia."

Mona's stomach twisted and her smile vanished. "Well." She inhaled. "Well." Tears pricked at her eyes.

"It's a huge step. This is the kind of thing I've worked for. This is what I went to college for."

"But—Atlanta," she whispered. She picked at a frayed tear on the thigh of her blue jeans. Atlanta was states away from Wisconsin. At least a twenty-hour car ride.

"Yeah."

They looked away from each other. Mona broke the silence after a minute. "Do you think you should take it?"

"I've looked at the jobs around this area, nothing big is happening. I thought the Trayson deal would be further along, but that's a year from starting. If I stick around here waiting, I miss an opportunity to prove myself."

"I thought that foundry expansion—"

"Delayed. They shut down their third shift, so they're not exactly going to start a huge expansion anytime soon. The Atlanta project is huge, a paper mill. I'd have steady work for at least two to three years. If building starts on the Trayson place before I'm done in Atlanta, I'd probably have enough clout to transfer back. It would be great security and it's the best opportunity Beyer's has to offer me right now." Jake's face was lit up with excitement.

"Sounds like you can't pass this up. And you deserve this chance." Mona tried to sound enthusiastic but she couldn't help wondering if this moment wasn't the beginning of the end. She'd always worried Jake wouldn't stay in Bassville. Were she and Bassville just a stopping point on Jake's path to success?

"It's not forever." Jake squeezed her knee.

She pressed her lips together. What next? Would he ask her to come with him? And if he didn't, what would that mean? She couldn't think of what to say. Instead she leaned her head against his chest and felt his hand cup the back of her head. They sat like that for a while before Jake cleared his throat. "This felt like good news until I had to tell you."

"It is good news. They like you at your job, that's great news." Mona slid down from her bar stool and gave him a peck on the cheek. "Not sure how much my bosses like me, I never got offered a promotion."

"Baby, you're already at the top of your game. Where else could you go here?"

"True." Mona reached across the bar and snagged a napkin to wipe her nose. "I'd have to own the place if I want to climb the ladder of success here, and God knows I don't want to do that."

SEVEN

MAW ENDED UP PAYING his sons thirty bucks each to clean out the stock room, but he reckoned a guy had to spend money to make money. He surveyed his shop from behind the cash register. Every bin was stuffed with packages of hooks and sinkers and bobbers. The racks were loaded with lures and the boys had strung fishing line across the ceiling to hang what wouldn't fit on the shelves or racks. It looked festive, he thought, with strands of bobbers and lures dangling from the ceiling. Sure, they'd be a bitch to get down later when he needed to sell them, but they were out of the way for now.

Peg had put her foot down when they'd come across the parking lot hauling boxes. "No, sir," she'd said, meeting them at the door with her arms crossed on her chest. "You're a packrat of the worst kind, if I don't draw the line here my house will be overflowing with all of your crap."

She was right, he knew. But it was a small setback. The boys followed him back to the bait shop with boxes balanced in their arms. Maw called a couple of distributors to delay deliveries and they piled all the old products everywhere they could.

Gazing through the door at the swept and cleaned out stock room, Maw tried to imagine what a laboratory would entail. Tables, he decided. And scientific-looking equipment. Anything with wires and dials and buttons.

"Maw?" Peg's voice broke through his thoughts. He pressed the intercom to answer her. "Yeah?"

"I've got to run to town, you need anything?"

"I'm coming with you," he said. "Hold on."

Maw moved down the main aisle of Fleet Farm feeling like he did as a kid when he got an Erector Set for Christmas. In Plumbing Supplies, he'd piled twenty yards of rubber tubing into his shopping cart. He'd also snagged electrical wire, PVC piping and metal ducts. Maw steered his shopping cart toward Housewares where he knew Peg was searching for some kitchen do-hickey.

Spying his short, wiry wife in front of a shelf of blenders, he sped up his pace. The loose cart wheel banged out a faster rhythm while he charged down the aisle towards her. She was a good woman and no-nonsense, he thought. Kept him steady and did her part to keep the business moving. "See anything you want?" he asked when he caught up to her.

She cocked an eyebrow at the contents of his shopping cart. "I'm all set." She tucked a short brown curl behind her ear.

Maw pointed to the packages of tube socks in her cart. "Are those for me?"

"Did you need socks?" she asked. "They're for the kids."

"No, no, I'm good." He followed her towards the check-out lines.

"What are you building?" she asked.

44

"It's complicated. I'll tell you all about it in the car."

On the ride home Maw explained the plan.

"That's the most ridiculous idea I've ever heard of," Peg declared.

"Why?"

"Maw, you can't convince people you're genetically engineering minnows in your bait shop."

"That's the thing, Peg, I already have!"

"You *say* you have, which is fine."

"God, it's sexy when you use fancy words."

"Maw, I'm serious," Peg rubbed a ChapStick over her lips and held out the tube to him. "You cannot take this any further."

Maw brushed away her offer with his hand. "Too late. I'm taking it further. Besides, nobody watches these things and takes them seriously. I'll just dazzle this guy with my mumbo-jumbo. What's the worst thing that could happen?"

Peg blew out an exasperated sigh. "Every time you say those words, something worse than what I can imagine actually happens."

Maw shook his head. "No. The worst—I've given this some thought—the *worst* thing that could happen is if an actual scientist says I lied. Okay, fine. But what are the odds of an actual scientist even watching this show, and then what are the odds they'd complain—because what I'm doing is *for entertainment value*. Nobody will take this seriously anyway."

"Then why don't you just say so? Why go through the charade?"

"Because people want the charade. They're curious, but not truly. It's like when you take kids to Santa's workshop at the mall. We know there's no Santa, but it's the fantasy—the *what if there is* that gets everybody intrigued. So all the people, even the grownups who know better, lean down to get a better view of the mechanical elves pounding their hammers against toy wagons. That's what I'm doing."

"You're an elf?"

"Missing the point, Peg."

Peg set her lips into a firm line before getting in her final word on the matter. "When this goes south, let it be known right now in this moment that *I told you so.*"

EIGHT

Friday evening, after leaving Joanne's car in Northport, June and Joanne arrived at Arlyce's house. "I told Loyal I was coming to help you with the kids tonight because one of them's sick. He won't expect me home until nine-thirty. Looks like you've been busy," June gestured to the laundry basket overflowing with quilts and canned food on the living room couch. She turned to Joanne who paced the living room with a duffel bag on her shoulder. "Every other day one of us will come out to check on you," she told Joanne. "Not every day, someone might notice if a car went down that back road too often. The forecast will be mild, but bundled up with the quilts you should stay cozy at night."

"One last thing," Arlyce produced a flashlight from the cupboard beneath her kitchen sink and handed it to Joanne. "That should do it." Arlyce gave Joanne a fierce squeeze around her shoulders. "Good luck."

Joanne whispered, "Thanks," and followed June outside.

Joanne got in the passenger side and waited for June to get settled in the driver's seat before speaking again.

"Thank you. I really mean it."

"Don't thank me yet, you haven't seen that shanty." June started the engine and pulled out of the driveway, piercing the dim night with the truck's headlights. Above them, the moon waned, casting long shadows over Main Street. The icy river glistened in the light, a long white snake twisting past the snow-covered banks.

The car's tires crunched across the snow and slush as June drove through the woods. The sound made Joanne cringe. Surely any noise would raise the alarm, announce her arrival. June, however, kept steering down the rutted path with a grim expression. "It's a good idea to bring you here at nighttime," June said suddenly. "We haven't passed a single car, so no one will know where you are until we get you to the bus station. That's the trouble in a small town," she mused. "Everyone recognizes everyone else, you can't even go to the neighbor's for a cup of flour without ten other people knowing about it." After a couple minutes the river came into view through the trees and June pumped the brakes while they slid a few feet before stopping. She turned off the engine and gestured towards the cluster of ice shanties off the shore to their left. "Home sweet home. For a week, anyways."

Joanne followed June around the back of the truck and the women loaded up their arms with laundry baskets and boxes. Walking through snow drifts and past towering pine trees, they approached the river's edge.

"I know it's frozen, but let me go down first to be safe," June said. She set her basket and boxes on the ground before approaching the ice. The only sound was their breathing and the creak of the trees as the wind pushed them back and forth. June knelt down and scooted down the bank until she reached the frozen surface of the bayou, where the ice would stay thick until April. Joanne hadn't heard even the faintest cracking noise to indicate the ice giving way. June turned and gave her a thumbs up. "Slide those things my way!"

Joanne shoved the bundles and basket down the slope and followed behind. Her eyes adjusted quickly in the night, the moon and starlight reflected off the snow and ice making it easier to see than she'd expected. On her feet again, she hefted up her share of the blankets, food, flashlight, extra batteries, radio, books, magazines and first aid kit. They walked past two shanties before Arlyce stopped and turned the latch on the third. The door eased open. Joanne peered into a space about eight feet by four feet, furnished by a couple of buckets, tip-ups, auger and two lawn chairs folded and propped against the wall. The shanty's only window looked towards the woods.

"Wasn't it locked?" Joanne asked June.

"Sure it was. But I came out here this morning and cut the lock off. Otto'll think he lost it, so long as nothing's missing, he won't care."

June surprised Joanne. She picked the right person to help her, she thought. Resourceful and smart. She smiled at her. "Right. So can I lock myself in?"

"Yeah, but that's a bit of a trick," June said. "The door pulls open, so you're going to have to brace it shut using the handle—there's a board in that basket of blankets that should fit. I didn't test it out, yet." She placed the basket on the metal floor and the boxes atop the two overturned five-gallon buckets. She dug out a sturdy board, about two inches thick, and handed it to Joanne. "I'll step out, you try it."

Closing the door behind her accomplice, Joanne shoved the end of the board through the door's latch and it slid sideways, tumbling to the ground. She picked it up and opened the door. "I think it'll work if I find a way to keep it in place. Maybe I can brace it against one of those empty buckets and it'll stay up. I'll figure it out."

"Crazy to think that next week you'll be in sunny California. Fruit trees and sunshine."

"Yeah." Joanne set her duffel bag on the ground.

"You must be excited to see your daughter," June said.

"It's been a long time."

"I can't imagine—I get to see Mona almost every day. Are you two close?"

"Not like you are with your family. But Rhonda will take me in. She's got a good job and a nice apartment. She'll put up with me for a little while so I can get on my feet." Joanne inhaled sharply. "No choice," she mumbled.

"All right then." June looked around. "What else do you need?"

"You've done so much. Thank you." She also knew the sooner June returned home, the more normal everything would appear.

"I'll be back tomorrow. Then Arlyce will take a turn." June scowled and dug in her pocket. "Take this," she said, and shoved a Buck knife into Joanne's gloved hand. "I grabbed it out of my son's old hunting gear. Just in case. I'll try your daughter's number before I come out here again. We'll get you on that Greyhound before the week is over."

Joanne wrapped her fingers around the knife and blinked back tears.

"Behave." June hugged her for a moment and left the shanty, her rubber boots rhythmically crunching across the ice, then up the slope where her tread grew to a whisper through the snow. The car's engine wheezed a few times before turning over, and Joanne watched the headlights swing past the trees and tracked their glow the woods dimmed to blackness.

She was really alone.

NINE

FRIDAY NIGHT THE BASSVILLE PUB was packed for the end of the season pool league party. The Rat River Boys had set up by the back door, and were tuning up their instruments and checking their microphones. Steve slid a pitcher of beer and a small stack of paper cups across the bar to Spade before he picked up the phone to dial Mona's number.

"Hello?"

"I hate to bug you on your night off, but it's crazy down here."

"I can be there in twenty minutes."

Steve hung up, relieved that he wouldn't have to handle the crowd alone. The pool league party was always a busy night—the teams would save their winnings all season and splurge on mixed drinks and shots instead of drinking tap beer like on a regular night. He'd forgotten that it was the Pub's turn to host the party, and when he'd called Arlyce, she said her mother couldn't take the kids.

Mona groaned and reached across the couch to hang up the phone.

"Who was that?" Jake asked.

"Steve. Pool league party tonight. I think he forgot all about it."

Jake lifted his legs off Mona's lap to let her stand up. "Want me to come down there with you?"

She shook her head. "You had to work all day. Come down if you want to, but I don't think it'll be relaxing. Jenny said the Rat River Boys were playing."

Jake scrabbled in the mixing bowl of popcorn resting on his chest. Dropping a handful into his mouth, he shot a glance at the TV where the Badgers were up by three points. "I'll come when this half is over," he said after chewing. "I can't help it, I've got March Madness."

Mona smiled and leaned down to kiss his cheek. "Don't bother. Lock up when you leave."

He winked at her before settling into the couch cushions more comfortably. "Will do."

In front of the bathroom mirror Mona applied mascara and lip gloss while deciding whether to pull her hair into a ponytail or try to pouf the bangs. Poufy. She reached for a comb and ratted the front a bit before combing the ends smooth. Clean shirt and some earrings and she'd be good to go.

The party was in full swing by the time Mona dropped off her purse and coat in the kitchen and walked into the bar. A frantic energy filled the air. She could feel it vibrating into her bones. Weird, it was only the pool league party. Only locals. Unless it was a full moon out, she reasoned, but she thought she'd seen a crescent moon on her way over. Sometimes a full moon could make things a little crazy. There was definitely something in the air tonight. Couples were dancing to *Sweet Home Alabama* and there wasn't an empty stool at the bar. She stepped behind the counter and swiped a five dollar bill from Spade's pile of money while grabbing his empty glass with her other hand. "What'll it be?"

"Rum and Coke," Spade said. "And catch those two bozos on me." He gestured to Scotty Trayson, her childhood friend and his work partner The Pole, a large muscular carpenter nicknamed for his Polish heritage.

The Pole peeled off his stocking cap, his thick shaggy hair was greasy and speckled with sawdust. "Thanks, Spade, you old son of a bitch. I'll have a beer, Mona." He winked at her and rested his huge chapped hands on the edge of the bar.

Steve bustled up beside Mona to load a tray with shots of peppermint schnapps. "Can you clean off the tables by the windows?"

"Sure thing." She refilled Spade's drink and grabbed a tub. Sashaying past a spinning man and woman and avoiding a cue stick positioned to strike, she reached the row of tables lined up against the windows overlooking the river. The energy of the bar reflected against the dark glass. She had to squint to see the silver glint of moonlight on the ice and snow outside. A full moon rose above the trees. She was right. She set down the bus tub and began filling it with empty glasses and cans. She'd just picked up a soda can to give it a shake and determine whether or not it was "dead" when muscular arms grabbed her around the waist and hugged her close. A resounding "Whoop!" made her ears ring as she was lifted off her feet and spun around.

Caught by surprise, it took her a moment to realize she did recognize the voice and the barrel chest pressed against her back. "T.C!" Her heart leaped to her throat before it sank to her gut.

He planted her back on the ground and tucked his chin over her shoulder. His grizzled cheek grazed her skin as he shouted with laughter, "Baby, I'm back!"

She took a step away from him before turning around to stare.

T.C. Barlow. That explained the energy in the air. He stood in front of her, his work boot-clad feet splayed beneath his sturdy frame. His jeans hugged his thighs and a Carhartt jacket made his shoulders look even beefier—if such a feat were possible. And beneath tousled dirty blonde hair, his blue eyes glinted with mischief. A dimpled cheek beneath a couple days' scruff and white, white teeth. He held out his arms as if displaying himself—Look at me!

"T.C." Her voice was husky as she repeated his name.

"The one and only." Charm radiated from his face and he opened his hands towards her. "Looking good, Mona."

"I didn't know you were back in town." She rubbed her palms against the back of her jeans. *Why am I sweating?*

"That's how you're gonna greet me? Two years—you can do better than that, babe." He strode toward her and pulled her close against his body, lifting her off the floor in a slow graceful turn. Mona felt the bar watching and heard a few catcalls and whistles as he leaned in to kiss her on the lips.

A second later she backed away. He gave her a slow grin and reached up to push his hair out of his eyes. "Not here then?"

Mona struggled to find the right words to explain when a sudden movement by the bar made her turn her head. Jake Paulick's tall, lean figure silhouetted by the Budweiser light. His expression was stoic as he turned towards Steve.

Shit.

"T.C. It's good to see you."

"Jake! What the hell, man? I didn't expect to see you here!" T.C. gripped Jake's hand with one fist and pounded him on the back with the other. "Thought you'd be off in some big city by now, making your first million!"

"Still on my way to my first million. How about you, T.C.? What brings you back to this shithole?" Jake thumped T.C.'s back with what looked to Mona like excessive enthusiasm.

"Aw, Alaska's not for me. Great adventure, but there's no place like the Wissipaw River for this guy. Let me catch you a beer." T.C. gave Mona a wave. "I'm gonna catch up with my ol' buddy Jake. I'll catch *you* later." He winked at her and returned to the bar. Jake glanced back at her over his shoulder as he followed T.C. and she wondered when Jake was going to break it to him.

He would break it to him, wouldn't he? On her way back to the bar with a bus tub full of glasses she glanced up at the TV. The second half had started and the Badgers were up by four.

He told. Mona knew the minute she walked past them at the bar. T.C. wore a guarded expression and Jake shot her a triumphant grin. The whole mood had shifted. Good. "Can I get you boys anything?" she asked.

"Beer us both," Jake said and pushed his empty can towards her.

"Thanks, pal," T.C. said. He stared at Mona for a cool moment and then turned his charm back at Jake. "Congratulations again. Mona's a great gal. A great gal."

"Thanks, T.C." Mona tried to get him to meet her eyes but he avoided looking at her. *Okay then*, she thought, *this might be weird between us for a while, but he'll get over it. Besides, we had broken up. We haven't even talked for two years.*

Jake clicked the edge of his fresh can of beer against T.C.'s. "Prost."

The rest of the night dragged along. She felt leaden and empty and forced a false, happy smile on the crowd. Most of the town had come out tonight to run one. Even if they weren't in pool league or fans of the Rat River Boys, the prospect of a party worked its magic on people. Spade, The Pole and Scotty Trayson had stuffed bar rags down the pool table's pockets to convert it to a craps table. Jenny, Sheila and Judi joined the Rat River Boys on stage to add their voices to *We Are*

Family. Then Maw and Peg got the crowd started with a line dance and Steve, feeling benevolent and happy after filling his cash register, ordered Mona to carry around a sleeve of plastic shot glasses and dole out free Peppermint Schnapps—until the bottle was empty.

At two o'clock, Mona helped Steve wave goodnight to the stragglers and they began putting the Pub back together. She wiped down the bar and tables, he stacked the chairs. She washed the glasses, he counted down the till.

"Thanks for coming in tonight. Don't know what I was thinking, putting myself alone on the schedule for the pool league party." Steve tapped a stack of dollar bills into a neat bundle.

"No problem. Looks like everyone had a fun night."

"Sure was something to see T.C. in here, wasn't it?" Steve asked. "He seemed pretty happy to see you."

"Yeah." Mona thought about T.C.'s arms around her, the easy way he kissed her. Jake was a good kisser. She felt bubbles of joy rise in her chest every time she saw him. So why did getting whirled around in a circle and smacked on the lips by her ex-boyfriend leave her feeling so unsettled? She hadn't even thought of him in ages. Mona closed her eyes. *I'm being stupid. I'm tired and just being stupid.* "Yeah," she told Steve, "it was definitely strange to see him back in town."

Steve grinned at her and ran his hand over his balding head. "Didn't take Jake long to set him straight though, did it? Kinda makes you wonder if he didn't get a whiff of T.C.'s being back in town to make him show up here like he did. You know, after you'd turned up to work."

Mona rolled her eyes. "I think he got tired of sitting on the couch like everyone else does at this time of year."

"You need a lift home?" Steve asked.

"No, I drove up." Mona trailed her boss through the kitchen and switched off the lights as she walked outside.

"Mona, I have to tell you something." Steve paused in the doorway. "I actually forgot we had to host the pool league party. I might be losing it."

"They always say the mind is the first thing to go, Steve."

He chuckled and locked the Pub's back door. "Then you better keep an eye on me."

They waved at each other as they got into their vehicles and drove away from the parking lot at the river's edge.

TEN

MONDAY AFTERNOON JUNE PULLED a load of towels out of the dryer when the phone rang. She hurried upstairs to answer the phone in the kitchen and dumped the laundry on the table. It was Arlyce, so June commenced folding towels while talking on the phone, receiver expertly tucked between her chin and shoulder. "I'll put together some sandwiches and bags of cereal, too. I have some jars of applesauce to send along. And a carton of milk. Milk will stay cold enough there without spoiling."

She listened to Arlyce on the other end of the line, then answered. "I'll bring it by tonight. Loyal has a committee meeting in town, he'll never know I left."

The back door slammed shut and June jumped, dropping the phone onto the table. "Shoot. He's back from the barn. I'll call you in a little bit." She replaced the receiver and continued folding the towels. "Loyal?"

Loyal stood at the door. June couldn't believe how her heart pounded. He had to sense something was up. She brushed a strand of hair off her cheek and smiled at him. "Hi."

"Hi." He sat down, holding a sheet of paper in his hand. "Did you hear about this bayou business?"

"No." June nervously piled the stack of towels into her arms and glanced back at the phone hanging on the kitchen wall. How could anyone know about Joanne hiding in Cooper's Bayou? It was impossible!

Loyal rapped the back of his fingers against the paper and held it up as if to show June the words on it. "Walleyes Forever wants to get rid of the culvert on the north end of Dead Run Bayou."

"Oh." Relief swept through June's entire body. "You think that's a bad thing?"

Loyal snorted. "If you don't fish it's a bad thing. Just saw the DNR application this morning. They want to restore the water flow through the bayou by replacing one culvert with three."

"That sounds like a good thing."

"Not if you own a house along the bayou. If the culverts go in as requested, it changes the flow of the water. Originally, the bayou was the original river. About thirty years ago, Pete Swenson installed the culvert to give him access to build his cottage out there. Back then the thinking probably was, 'make more land access for cottages.' Now the fishermen want more access to all parts of the river. Trouble is, other people have built along that edge of the bayou by Swenson's place and if they replace the culvert with three, the water flows in and starts taking up their front yards."

"What happens if you remove the culvert?" June asked.

"The fishermen like it, some old-timers who remember when the channel flowed through there would love it, they see it as restoring the natural flow. Meanwhile, there's some rumbling that other people would like to build back in that spot, so more water would mean less land."

"Either way someone ends up unhappy."

"Yep. You can't have land on the river without the river causing problems. You can't enjoy the river if you don't have land to get to it."

"That is a pickle." *Not quite the same trouble Joanne's in, but a problem*, she thought. "What do *you* think?"

"Not sure. I need to find out more. I just came up to go over it with you. Talking with you always helps me think better." Loyal stood and wrapped one arm around June's waist before bending down to kiss her. "Thank you."

As he retreated outside, June did feel blessed to have a good husband. She picked up the phone and started dialing Arlyce as soon as she heard the back door slam behind him.

Scotty Trayson whistled to himself while he unloaded the back of his pickup truck. Tip-ups, a bait bucket, a box of assorted gear and two jig poles sat atop a pile of packed snow. Birds chirped along the harmonious trickle of melting ice and snow. Scotty figured there was still plenty of fishing time left before the walleye run started, followed by the white bass run a month later. He paused to look down the river, catching a glimpse of a cluster of seven ice shanties tucked along the banks through the bare-limbed trees.

The ice was still six inches thick in the bayous and cuts of the river, but he wasn't taking any chances. He grabbed a thick coil of rope from the truck's bed before slamming the hatch shut. Scotty knotted one end around a nearby tree trunk and tied the other end around his waist. On the outside chance the ice would break, he'd be able to pull himself safely to shore. The cold water would be a shock, but the real danger lay in the swift current of a melting river and the huge sheets of ice that still covered most of the surface. A few years ago a man from Northport had crashed through the ice, but what killed him was getting trapped beneath a sheet of ice. The man had drowned face up, his body wedged against a submerged tree by the force of the river, unable to float up for a breath of air because of the layer of frozen water pressed against his face like a glass. Scotty hadn't found the body, Otto Zimm had, but together they fished it out using an auger. The dead man's panicked, blue expression staring up between Otto's feet was a sight Scotty would never forget.

Tethered to a safety, Scotty gathered his gear and walked out to set up a fishing spot. The sun reflected off the snow and nearly blinded him. After dropping his gear to the pocked surface of the iced-over bayou, he unzipped his jacket pocket and pulled out sunglasses. *Better*, he thought, and he brushed a light layer of snow away with a gloved hand. He'd cut a hole here for jigging, then a couple more holes further out for his tip-ups.

He'd nearly finished drilling the third hole through the ice when he heard a thumping sound from a distance. Scotty paused and tracked the echoing sound as coming from the ice shanties. He didn't think anyone else was out fishing today. Those shanties were mostly owned by weekend guys from the city. He squinted at the metal one on the left. It appeared to be rocking gently. Was someone inside?

After a moment he returned to his task and dropped baited hooks through the holes. He shuffled back to his bait bucket and sat on it, his pole poised in his right hand when he heard a man's voice shouting. Scotty looked again towards the shanties. A man walked out of the one he'd thought was moving and Scotty raised his hand in greeting. "Hey!" Something about the guy looked familiar.

The man didn't acknowledge him, but sprinted over to the next shanty and kicked in the door. Scotty stood, focused on what he knew to be a crime of theft or vandalism taking place before his eyes. "Hey!" he shouted louder.

A second later the man reappeared and burst through the door of the third shanty. Scotty lifted his pole, set it safely on the ice and walked along the river's edge towards the shanties. He was halfway there when the man left the third shanty and started running for shore. Scotty started to run after him and had picked up speed after about seven steps when he felt a tight clutch around his waist yank him backwards. *The damn rope,* he realized too late while his body crashed hard against the ice. The man's retreating footsteps faded as he crashed through the snow-covered woods. Scotty heard a car door slam and an engine turn over. The car drove away, leaving Scotty listening to trickling water, chirping birds and his own heavy breathing.

Thinking over what'd he'd seen as he returned to his afternoon of fishing, Scotty decided the man could've been anyone, clad as he was in a tan Carhartt jacket, jeans and baseball cap. He was too far away to recognize, too. *I'll drive over there when I finish up and check things out. If anything's busted up or missing, I'll report it to Joe.*

A couple of hours later Scotty parked along the road on the other side of the river, across from the spot where he'd caught three nice fat bluegills. He followed the footprints in the snow up to the ice shanties standing on Cooper's Bayou and peered inside the first one. Nothing but the usual stuff, augers, buckets, lawn chairs, tip ups. The door the stranger had kicked in hung crookedly from its broken hinges. A check inside revealed the same assortment of fishing gear. Pulling the door shut and adjusting it within the frame, Scotty thought about how the man had left empty handed and concluded he probably hadn't stole anything. The rest of the shanties looked undisturbed. *What was he doing then? If this was his shanty, he wouldn't've run off.* He considered the remaining shanties for another moment and decided he'd definitely let Joe know what he'd seen. *For whatever it's worth.*

ELEVEN

JOANNE GLANCED OUT THE window of the ice shanty. It was growing dark and she needed to get herself settled in for the night before she couldn't see anymore. She felt tempted to use the flashlight June had given her, its glow would definitely make the nighttime less scary, but a lit-up ice shanty would look suspicious. Earlier today when she'd heard footsteps crashing through the woods and shanty doors slamming open, she'd felt horrified. She'd crouched in the corner beneath a blanket and prayed the door would hold. Then somebody had called out and chased him away—she was safe for now. But would he come back? She felt pretty sure she was alone out on the river, except for the fish, deer and raccoons, of course. But no point in risking it. One more week and Rhonda would be back in California and she'd be able to call her.

She gathered up her spoon and the empty can of pork and beans she'd eaten for supper and slid them into a plastic shopping bag.

She slipped on her winter jacket and loaded her toothbrush with toothpaste. Outside the shanty she walked to the riverbank where she brushed her teeth and spat. Joanne tilted back her head to see the first stars overhead. She'd tuck in and read beneath the covers with the flashlight. Arlyce had loaded her up with a stack of books and some magazines. The Mary Higgins Clark mysteries were no good, she'd decided. Too creepy under the circumstances. But that Danielle Steel one about the woman with the horse, that was a good read. She imagined herself as she read it, riding horseback along a mesa in southern California. Her face would be tanned from the sun, hot west coast sun, not chapped and red from freezing Wisconsin weather.

Joanne retreated to the shanty, propped the board through the door latch and braced it atop an upturned bucket to lock herself in. She curled up in her nest of quilts and an old Army-issue sleeping bag. June and Arlyce had taken good care of her. When she got herself settled in at Rhonda's she'd get a job and repay every dime. She wouldn't miss anything about Bassville. To think she'd come here with such high hopes, crazy in love and believing she'd live happily ever after in this town. And even Arlyce and June's kindness, while appreciated, well, they made Joanne feel like scum. She was stupid and helpless and weak. She knew how people in town pitied her; she always noticed the flicker of relief when they'd see her without a black eye or other injury. Everything would be different in California. Hell, she'd even get a job that didn't involve a cash register.

She pitched a tent of blankets over her head and knees. She switched on the flashlight and started to read, losing herself in the fantasy of riding bareback beneath a vast western sky.

She'd turned the page with a whisper of sound when the steady crunching of feet on snow caught her attention. She switched off the flashlight and held her breath. Deer sometimes walked through the woods, but this sounded different. Her whole body tensed while she concentrated on listening. Crunch-crunch-crunch-crunch. The noise stopped.

Joanne's heart was ramming against her breastbone. She crawled her left hand free of the blankets and felt around for the knife lying on the floor near her bed. A branch snapped and she tried to calculate how far it was from the shanty. More crunching. She inhaled, feeling dizzy from holding her breath, and the air rushing through her nostrils sounded so loud. She tried to breathe through her mouth.

If he was out there again he'd get in. If he got in he'd kill her. She knew it. She needed to get out. Out of the shanty, out of Bassville. Just because he hadn't found her yet didn't mean he wasn't looking. She knew he would be. She was so stupid to think she could get away. She was so stupid not to get further away. She should've just taken money from the till at Bud's and bought a bus ticket to California. What a dope to play by the rules.

The noise of feet on snow continued past the shanty and faded into the distance. Tears leaked out of Joanne's eyes and she clenched her teeth against her sobs. She peeked out the window to see the shadow of a deer disappear into the woods.

TWELVE

J AKE AND MONA SAT next to each other on his couch watching a movie Tuesday evening. She tried snuggling in beside him, but he'd lifted his arm and said, "I'm sorry, but it's cramping me up to sit like that tonight."

She'd slid over to the far end of the couch. "Sorry."

They sat like that for a few minutes and Jake reached down and pulled her feet onto his lap. "This is better."

She looked over at him. Ever since he'd seen T.C. kissing her in the bar he'd acted weird. Like he was pulling away. But he might be pulling away because of the Atlanta job, getting ready to make a clean break. Wouldn't that be her luck? To break up with the first boyfriend who had moved out of town, then fall in love with the second boyfriend who had moved back to town just to watch him leave, too, right when the first boyfriend returned. She groaned.

"You okay?" Jake asked.

Mona took a deep breath. If she learned one thing from watching Jenny it was to *not* act dramatic. Stay cool. She turned to smile at him. "I'm great." She reached over and rested her hand on his forearm. "Couldn't be better."

"Did you hear about the culvert business over in Dead Run Bayou?"

Mona nodded. "Dad had a meeting about it tonight. I'm not on the planning committee. They're supposed to report on it at the next board meeting."

"Do you have an opinion yet?"

She shook her head and grinned at him. "You know how I am. I like to hear all sides before I reach a decision."

"I've been thinking this might spark some new development along the river."

"How's that?"

"If they knock out the culvert, houses along the east shore will probably need to move or be rebuilt. I know for a fact my place will be in trouble. If they do nothing, I heard Swenson wants to fill in that wetland behind him so they can improve the road to his place. Improving the road means it could become more desirable to build back there." Jake shrugged. "Just seems like either way you cut it, something will change."

"If they knock out the culvert will you sell your place? Or rebuild right here?" She glanced at the wood-paneled wall behind them as if she could see beyond to the garage and flat ground that ran to the road. It seemed like enough space that he could stay put.

"It depends on how much they'd offer me. There'd have to be some compensation to property owners. Might be worth it to move, but without numbers in front of me I couldn't say."

"Huh." Mona considered this while chewing on her lower lip. Jake was always so logical, she loved that about him, he didn't make too many decisions with his gut. He liked to sit back and consider all the parts before staking a position on anything. She narrowed her eyes and asked, "Are you thinking of going into the house-building business?"

"Naw," Jake laughed. "I've got a good thing going with Beyer's right now."

"But if you worked for yourself you wouldn't have to move. Unless you wanted to." Mona knew she should stifle the bubble of hope rising in her chest right then, but she couldn't help herself. "Might be worth exploring anyway." She paused to let the idea sink in before continuing. "I know every day I go to the farm I feel a lot different about work than when I go to the Pub. It's a pride thing. The greenhouse will succeed because of *me* and it makes everything I put into it matter more."

Jake leaned his head back and closed his eyes. "Don't know, babe. The Dohills have a pretty solid grip on the market around here."

"They don't do *all* the work on a house, do they? They contract parts out."

"Yeah. The basement work and the framing. There's parts," he conceded. He opened one eye and gave her a grin. "Really? This is your ploy?"

"What?" She struggled to keep an innocent expression on her face. "I only want you to feel the sense of satisfaction of working for yourself. Is that so bad?"

"Not at all. Thanks for the suggestion." He reached over for the remote control and turned off the TV. "Speaking of work, it's getting late."

Mona reached for his hand. "Let's go to bed then."

"You sure you don't mind me staying over tonight? I have to get up pretty early."

She shook her head. "It doesn't bother me. I just roll over and go back to sleep when your alarm goes off."

"Your shower does have better water pressure than mine," Jake said. He rested his forehead against hers and brushed his fingers against her cheek. "We'll work through this. I just need a little time, that's all."

Steve caught himself checking the time again. Nine o'clock. The bar was almost empty. Dob, Scotty and The Pole had come in after they got off work, his only customers since lunch. He'd close early and maybe make it home before the kids were in bed.

"Otto would be tickled to hear about this. I kind of wish he was in town," Dob was saying.

"Hear about what?" Steve asked.

"Walleyes Forever wants to replace that culvert and open the water flow back to Dead Run."

"I like that idea, too," Scotty said. He adjusted his faded baseball cap over his curly hair and leaned back on his bar stool. "More river is never a bad thing."

"Used to be a real pretty spot back there," The Pole added. "Remember when we were little, Dob? We could walk across the boats parked in that spot every spring during the white bass run. It ran clear and deep before they built it up. My grandpa said it was the main river channel before Swenson bought that property and bound it up. That culvert acts like a dam."

"What do you think will happen if they bust it up and let the water back through?" Steve asked.

"Swenson will lose his front yard," Dob said. He leaned forward on his beefy forearms and clasped his hands. "What do you suppose? There's about seven-eight cottages back there that would get flooded out."

"The amount of water wouldn't really change, though, right? I mean, if you moved water back through there it would have more room, so in some sense the flow would have to decrease." Scotty doodled on a napkin. It looked to Steve like he was drawing a map of the river, a twisting snake with little circles and trees along the edges.

"Seems like the east side might benefit. What's over there?" Dob asked. "Farmland. Schmidt's farm I believe."

"Yeah, that's right." The Pole's booming laugh echoed through the nearly empty bar. "Ever hear of a farmer complaining he got extra land? Schmidt would love to see that culvert removed. He probably lost a couple of acres when it went in."

"Speaking of the river, I don't think I told you what I saw yesterday, Steve."

"What's that, Scotty?" Steve folded his arms across his chest and leaned forward against the bar.

"I was fishing Cooper's Bayou—caught three nice bluegill, by the way—and someone was busting into those ice shanties parked off the shoreline."

"What do you mean, 'busting in?'" Steve asked.

"Don't know. I heard banging and looked across. There's some man trying to bust through the door of a shanty. He goes in, comes back out, starts shoving his shoulder against the next shanty door."

"Burglar?" Steve asked.

The Pole scowled. "That's what I told him. He's a hero, probably stopped some asshole from making off with everyone's fishing gear."

"He didn't take anything," Scotty said. "That's the weird part. The guy left empty-handed. It seemed like he was looking for something, though, the way he went along checking each shanty."

"You go after him?" Steve asked. Scotty wasn't tall and muscular like The Pole, he had the typical farm kid build, lean and wiry but tough as forged iron.

"Tried to," Scotty said with a sheepish grin. "I yelled, then started running after him. Kinda forgot I'd tied myself to a tree in case the ice broke. I ended up yanked back onto my ass."

The men burst into laughter. The Pole swiped the edge of his eyes with a calloused knuckle. "Still kills me, the picture of Scotty in my mind. Charging forward like a dog tied up in a yard. 'Yipe!'" The Pole feigned choking with his hands around his neck, tongue out.

Scotty gave The Pole a friendly shove. "I didn't tie myself around my neck. The rope was around my waist."

The Pole chuckled again and flipped down the brim of Scotty's baseball cap.

"You call Joe and report it?" Steve asked.

Scotty nodded while adjusting his cap again and jabbing a sharp elbow into The Pole's arm. "Yeah. I called the Cop Shop. They took down my statement, but no one else had called anything in. They probably won't catch him. I didn't see his vehicle and from a distance he could've been anyone—even from around here—with jeans and hat and jacket. Sun was in my eyes and the glare off the ice made it hard to see."

The Pole's teasing smile faded into a grim expression. "Every year someone comes here to discover their summer cottage was broken into—stuff stolen or vandalized. I suppose it's usually teenagers or kids, bored and looking for some trouble."

"Some areas are easy pickings, too. Cooper's Bayou is pretty remote. No cottages for at least a couple of miles. Seems like you'd have to know those ice shanties were there. You can't even see the river from the road, isn't it just an old logging path that goes back to the water?" Dob asked.

"Yeah," Scotty said. "I thought of that, too. Only a local would even know about getting to those shanties—or a guy who has a shanty there."

"Even if it was someone who fishes there, why bust up the doors of the other shanties?" Dob shrugged his broad shoulders. "Doesn't make any sense. If you wanted to borrow someone's gear, you'd just use it and return it."

"It was weird." Scotty said. "This round's on me, Steve. Catch yourself, too." He slid his pile of money forward a couple inches and gestured to the three cans of beer on the bar.

After Steve cracked open the tabs of three beers and refilled his mason jar with Diet Pepsi, he pulled a barstool around to his side of the bar. Settling in for what he hoped would be the final round of the night, he contemplated grabbing a deck of cards or dice cup. *No, he reasoned, that'll just keep me here later.* "You guys still working up at the hotel?"

The Pole shook his shaggy head. "Not right now. Sue and Judi want to add a deck overlooking the water, but not until the weather gets better." He took a swig from his can and wiped his moustache with the back of his hand. "Hopefully not until fishing season dies down. It would be a pain in the ass trying to build that with all the traffic through there."

"I roped in these clowns to help me with a job near Loon Lake. This couple bought an old barn and wants to make it a restaurant." Dob gestured towards the Pub's back windows. "They want us to install a view through the old barn doors like you have. The hayloft will be seating, main floor seating and kitchen, and outdoor patio seating. Place will be huge when it's done."

"Don't know how I'd feel about eating in a cow stall," Steve mused.

"I thought that, too," Dob admitted. "But we're building over the foundation and sealing the walls. When we're done, it'll probably be more sanitary than this old place. And the electrical will be up to code, too." Dob gestured to the wall behind the cash register where Steve had plugged in adaptors so beer signs, the cash register and a cooler could draw.

"Someday I'll get you in here. Just never seem to have the time." Steve realized how ridiculous that sounded in his nearly empty bar. "Or the money," he added.

THIRTEEN

WEDNESDAY AFTERNOON JUNE DROVE slowly down the rutted path and prayed the car wouldn't get stuck or coated in mud because that would be difficult to explain to Loyal. She was not a skillful liar. She also didn't relish a five-mile trek back to town on foot. Adding to her worry was the "check engine" light that had illuminated on the dashboard as she'd turned onto the county highway. She could hear a grumble from the engine that did not sound healthy. Getting stuck would be one problem—but breaking down? That would be worse.

Easing past the tall, bare trunks of pine trees made her feel small, like an ant. She finally reached a clearing and she stopped, turned off the engine and took a deep breath to calm her nerves. Opening the door, her ears were tuned to every sound around her. The creaking of the trees, the wind's moaning, the crunching snow beneath her feet. She stopped for a moment to assure herself that she was alone. *Silly. Of course the only person here is Joanne.* June forced herself to shout.

"JOANNE? IT'S ME, JUNE!" Her voice sounded hoarse to

her ears. "HELLO?" She saw one shanty door was left open. Had someone come out to fish since Monday?

A moment later a shanty door swung open and Joanne stepped out and waved at her. "Over here!"

June grabbed the two shopping bags from the back seat of her car and side-stepped her way down the shore to the flattened surface. It never stopped feeling strange to her, walking *on* water. Knowing that beneath her feet swam living creatures, muffled in their own strange world. It was, she thought, almost biblical. Walking like Peter across to where Joanne stood waving to her.

The shanty was colder than June had anticipated. Joanne shut the door behind her. It was a small space, one corner full of bedding like a nest. Otto's tip-ups and poles were neatly lined up against the wall by the door. Joanne had set up two lawn chairs in the middle of the shanty and gestured to one. "Have a sit."

June tried to act like this was normal. She'd never even visited Joanne in her own apartment, she only really knew her from across the checkout aisle at Bud's. She determined to act like Joanne was her equal, this wasn't a mercy mission. She was a friend paying a visit. A friend who happened to have brought a few days' worth of food and reading material and a plastic bag with dampened washcloth and soap so Joanne could give herself a sponge bath.

"Home sweet home," Joanne said while she settled herself into the webbed lawn chair nearest the nest of quilts on the ground.

"Are you warm enough?" June asked.

"Yes. This shanty's airtight."

"Anyone come out here?"

"Someone was out here Monday afternoon. I'm pretty sure it was him, searching the shanties. He only got to the first three when someone across the bayou yelled and scared him off." Joanne's voice quavered. She took a deep breath.

"Did he come back?" June looked around the shanty that suddenly seemed less safe. "Maybe we should get you out of here."

Joanne shook her head. "I thought someone did the other night, but it was just a deer." Joanne hunched forward and rubbed her hands together. "I don't think he'll be back. He didn't find anything so he'll look somewhere else."

"What made him even think to look out here?" June wondered aloud.

"Who knows. But I'm probably safer now that he's ruled out looking here."

"I brought you some supper." June reached into one of the bags she'd set by her feet and pulled out a sour cream container on top, pried off the lid and passed it across to Joanne. "Chili. It's still hot." She dug around in the bag and produced a spoon.

"Mmmm." Joanne shoveled in several bites before sitting back in her chair. "Can I tell you how good this tastes? Plus it's *hot*."

June smiled. She'd left the crock pot going all evening so she could bring Joanne something warm. "I stuffed a few magazines in here, too. *Redbook, Good Housekeeping* and *People*. And some books. One's by John Steinbeck."

"Thank you. All I do is read or walk in the woods. I don't like to wander off too far, but if I didn't get out a little I'd go nuts."

"I tried your daughter's work again today. Arlyce and I take turns calling. She's still not supposed to be back until Monday."

Joanne nodded and took another bite of chili.

"I called the Greyhound station today, though. Turns out it's a three-day journey. We can get you on a bus Friday, you'll arrive in Sacramento on Monday."

"Oh God," Joanne let out a whimper. "That's two more days."

"It's already Wednesday," June said in the voice she used to soothe Mona and Sean when they were sick or injured. "I can pick you up first thing Friday and we'll get you on that bus." She pulled her chair closer to Joanne's and put her arm around her shoulder. "You can hold up for two days."

"I know." Joanne sniffed. "I know. I didn't know how long it would take to get out of here. I'm so happy." She stared down at June, her long eyelashes damp with tears. "Thank you. I will repay you."

June hugged her. "You pay me back by staying safe. Start fresh. Don't end up with another jackass."

Joanne pulled back and wiped her nose on the back of her hand. "I promise. After all of this, no way will I turn back."

An hour later June left the shanty, bringing back with her a small load of Joanne's laundry to wash. On Friday she'd bring Joanne to the Greyhound station in Northport and buy the bus ticket that would take her to a safe harbor. Arlyce had chipped in twenty-five dollars and June drew a hundred from her savings account. When it came up, as it would when Loyal read the monthly statement, she'd explain it. By then Joanne would be far away, history as far as Bassville was concerned. Loyal wouldn't mind. He'd probably be mad about the secrecy, but he'd be glad for Joanne, too.

She buckled her seatbelt and turned the key in the ignition. Nothing but a click. *Shit.* Her breath clouded the air and the windshield began to fog over. June banged the sides of her fists against the steering wheel and tried again. She double-checked the gear shift and toed the gas pedal the third time and nearly wept with gratitude when the car started. *If I can get home,* she prayed. *Let me get home.*

June turned off the logging path and south on the county highway towards Bassville. The woods darkened suddenly as thick clouds covered the sun. A few miles up the road June drove past a single truck headed north. The sight made her jump and she twisted her neck to watch it pass. *No. That could be anyone's pickup truck. Two more days.* She accelerated towards home.

FOURTEEN

Maw was not a handy man. He could fix a faucet in a pinch, change the oil in the Buick, but he had little instinct for tools and parts. He pushed back from the table where he was trying to run rubber tubing from a metal box. The tubing had mashed apart and he couldn't get it to loop upwards and across to the aquarium.

It had to look like the minnows could swim from one end of the apparatus through the tubing into the aquarium. Maw looked back at the drawing he'd sketched in pencil. Inspired by the laboratories featured in old *Twilight Zone* episodes he'd watched as a kid, he envisioned a room filled with bubbling beakers, coiled tubing and large metal control panels with flashing lights. So far all he'd managed to do was rig up an old keyboard in front of a glass panel back lit with strands of Christmas tree lights. The effect was cheap and homemade.

"Maybe it would be easier if you just came clean."

Maw spun around at the sound of his wife's voice. "You startled me."

"Sorry. You look deep in thought." Peg lifted the end of the rubber tubing that hung over the edge of the aquarium and wound it around her hand a few times. "Can't you just tell the story of how you raise minnows and market them? Do you have to make such a production of it?"

"They're looking for showmanship and I'm a guy who always delivers." Maw set down the pliers he'd been working with and held out an open hand. "Come on. Give it back."

Peg lay the tubing across his palm. "You're making a fool of yourself."

"I'm in the planning stages. All creative genius seems foolish at first. Everybody thought Edison was nuts before he got that first light bulb illuminated. Henry Ford was a laughingstock. So was Einstein."

Peg cocked her head to one side and folded her arms. "Do you see me laughing at you? No. You see me getting nervous because the walleye run is probably a week out and you're in here playing make-believe instead of actually running the business that feeds your family. I'm not laughing, hon."

"I know, I know. Give me two more days and I promise I'll get back to regularly scheduled programming around here."

"Forty-eight hours. Don't push it, Maw."

"I won't." He watched her leave the room and then set the tubing down on the table. Maybe if he used more metal components. He held a piece of metal ductwork alongside the keyboard. It seemed to help, anyway. He'd get the boys to start scrapping for metal parts at the salvage yard up the road, Maw decided. That was the problem. He wasn't thinking *big* enough. Rigging up some little tabletop lab— how stupid! Of course it would look handmade and cheap. But if he pulled in some pre-built parts and arranged them in a completely random way—say a carburetor connected to a muffler and then strung it all together with the tubing and tanks—that would actually work.

"You wanna *what?*" The old man who ran the salvage yard scratched the back of his neck and adjusted his stocking cap.

"Just borrow some parts. I don't want to buy anything, just use it for a couple weeks and return it."

"I'm not gonna borrow you parts. How'm I supposed to know you're gonna give 'em back? And besides, I already sell *used* parts. You can't borrow and give back *used* used parts."

Maw took a deep breath and mentally dialed up his charisma a few notches. He realized that one man's trash was indeed another man's treasure. "I completely understand. That's exactly why I only want to borrow the parts. I'm not going to actually use any of them. I'm just *displaying* them for people to look at. They won't even be set up in any kind of working order." Maw smiled and hugged his younger son closer to him with his right arm. "See, my son here has this art project for school. He's actually competing at the state capitol with a bunch of other schools. It's an art and science fair and he's demonstrating the beauty of unseen parts. Now, I can hardly tear apart the family car and go without wheels for two weeks while he's working on this project."

Maw turned around and gestured to the three acres of rusting graveyard of auto parts. As far as he could see were rows and rows of cars and trucks. Some had their hoods popped open, others had been stripped down to the frames. Stacks of tires, torn out seats and tetanus-inducing towers of corroding metal were stacked against the corrugated fence. The smell of oil and gasoline made him feel dizzy if he breathed in too heavily. "We just thought maybe you could loan us some parts for his school project and then we'd bring them back when he's done."

"I'll even clean them up for you, mister," piped up a thin voice.

Maw looked down in surprise. His son took up the role as if he'd rehearsed his whole life. "We just figured, well, if I win this contest I get a hundred dollars and someday I'd really like to go to college. It's my big break and I don't want my mom and dad to sacrifice more for me than they already have. I could take your oldest parts, whatever you feel is truly junk."

"And we promise to return it," Maw added, giving his son's shoulder a squeeze.

The salvage shop owner squinted up at the sky for a moment. A black tomcat leapt from the smashed-out side window of an old bus and prowled down the packed dirt path. The man wiped his grease-stained hands down the front of his jacket and cleared his throat. "Never could say no to kids. School's important, son."

Maw's boy nodded soberly.

"But I want it all back. I'm weighin' it before you take it outta here. You prob'ly won't use any of these parts, but you ain't takin' them to sell for cash neither."

"No, sir."

"And I want twenty dollars deposit."

Maw reached into his jacket pocket and deftly separated one of the three twenties he'd come prepared to spend on junk parts. "I sure appreciate your generosity." He tousled his son's hair.

"Yer boy's a chip off the old block, isn't he?"

"He really is," Maw agreed.

FIFTEEN

Mona trudged back to the kitchen with a bus tub full of dirty dishes. Wednesday's lunch rush had been unusually busy today with a large construction crew working on a highway project a few miles up the road. A dozen men had taken seats at the bar among Dale and Spade, and unable to reach Steve or Arlyce, Mona had to fry up all the burgers herself. The bar was now empty as she loaded the plates and silverware into the dishwasher trays.

After tying off the bag of buns and starting a load of dishes, Mona returned to the bar. She'd wash up the glasses by hand, she decided. She'd just finished wiping down the bar's laminate surface when the door blew open.

"Hey there, good lookin'," T.C. greeted her with a wide grin. "Still making lunch?" He straddled a bar stool and tapped his fingers against the edge of the bar like a piano player.

"Sure," Mona told him. "All alone today?"

"Yep. Just got done helping the Dohills with a side job. I'll probably get something regular lined up soon, even though I like getting paid cash."

Mona slid him a menu which T.C. ignored. "What do you want to drink?"

"Pepsi's good. And a burger, please. With fries."

"You got it." Mona snapped the tab back on a can of soda she dug out of the cooler and set it in front of him. "I'm working solo, so I've got to go back and make your lunch." She was two steps away when T.C. leapt off his seat and started following her.

"I'll keep you company."

It felt strange, she thought, to have him to familiarly close. And alone. Not like they hadn't spent hours together alone in the past, but it had been awfully long ago. And they weren't a couple anymore. She pried a raw hamburger patty from the stack in the cooler and slapped it on the grill while T.C. perched on the stool Arlyce kept next to the counter.

"Medium well," he said.

"I remember."

He'd slid off his jacket and leaned forward on the counter, his biceps pulling the sleeves of his T-shirt tight. The silence hung between them while the burger sizzled. Mona took her time, setting the French fries in the fryer before going over to the dishwasher. His presence made her self-conscious which confused her. She was with Jake, why should T.C.'s being here matter?

"I can sort that silverware for you," T.C. offered.

"It's okay." She moved the rack of steaming hot forks and knives to the stainless steel counter to cool before dealing with them. "I've got all day." What if Jake turned up and found them alone back here, she wondered. *He might get the wrong impression, but obviously I have to talk to T.C. if he's back in town. Bassville's too small for us to avoid each other.* But what should they even talk about?

Mona grabbed a plastic basket from the shelf above the grill and lined it with a sheet of red-checked wax paper. "You planning to live with your parents for a while?"

"Yeah," he said. "This fall I'm starting school at the tech."

"You are?" Mona's eyebrows curved up in surprise. "For what?"

"Utility lineman. I'll be done in less than two years."

"Are there lots of jobs?"

"Loads. And the money's good, too."

"That's cool." She turned the patty over and placed a slice of cheese on top of it.

"I can travel if I want. They send linemen all over the place when there are storms and such. But the guy I talked to said there's plenty of work around here, too, with all the new developments. I'll make almost as much as I did fishing."

"That's terrific."

"I'll be able to buy a nicer boat. Remember the *Lana Lee*?"

"Yeah." The *Lana Lee* was T.C.'s old bass boat he'd bought from his uncle. He'd sold it back when he moved to Alaska. They'd fished and waterskied and even spent the night on it a few times, anchored to a sandbar in the river.

"I'd like to buy her back, but my uncle doesn't want to sell her. The marina has a sweet wake boat right now that I could pay for in cash."

"Sounds like you're doing well."

"You eat lunch yet?" T.C. asked suddenly.

"No, I usually grab something later in the day."

"Well, I'm happy to buy you a burger or whatever you're hungry for."

"That's nice of you, but I'm good."

T.C. ran his hand through his hair and frowned. "Look, we should talk and now's as good a time as any. We're alone and I don't want to have this conversation in front of an audience."

His dark blue eyes always made her melt a little. She thought she'd be immune after almost three years, but it turned out she wasn't. Mona felt her stomach do a little flip when she met his gaze. "Okay." *Talk about what, exactly?* She leaned her hip against the counter and crossed her arms.

"When I decided to move back here from Alaska, it wasn't just because of work."

Mona nodded. Her throat felt dry.

"I missed you, Mon." T.C. folded his hands and looked up at her. "We had a good thing and I know I walked away from you, but I needed to see what else was out there." He gestured towards the door and gave a frustrated sigh. "I guess this was selfish of me, but I expected you to be here for me when I came back."

Mona nodded again. What on earth could she say to that?

T.C. reached for her hand and grasped it in his rough, calloused one. "I am sorry for everything I put you through."

"I know." Her voice came out in a raspy whisper. She cleared her throat and pulled her hand back. "I didn't expect you to come back."

"I wanted to surprise you."

She smiled weakly. "Surprise."

He laughed. "Guess I was the one who ended up surprised. Jake's a lucky guy. I just wanted you to know that."

The acrid smell of burning meat reached her nostrils and she turned to see the dark smoke rising from the grill. "Shit. I'm sorry."

T.C. grinned and walked towards the cooler. "Do over." He reached in and pulled out two patties and tossed them onto the grill.

Mona lifted the French fries out of the fryer. "At least the fries are fine." She shook salt over them and dumped them into the paper-lined basket. "Ketchup?"

"You read me like a book."

T.C. started sorting the silverware into the trays, ignoring Mona's protest. She finished making the two burgers and plated them. "You want to eat these in the bar?"

T.C. shook his head and grabbed one, taking a wolfish bite and chewing. He leaned back on the stool and swallowed. "I gotta tell you, I ate a lot of burgers out in Alaska, but none of them taste like the Pub's."

"I bet you say that to all your waitresses," Mona said.

He picked up the other burger and handed it across to her. "Eat. Lunch is on me."

Mona took a bite. She usually took a bowl of soup or chili and a slice of toast for lunch. "Thanks," she told him.

He took a swig out of his can of Pepsi and then slid it across to her. "Go ahead."

Automatically, Mona took a sip before realizing what she'd done. She set the can down and slid it back toward him. "So, you're here for good then, huh?"

"Yep." He gave her a sly look. "Bad timing, eh?"

She didn't have a good answer to give him other than a noncommittal shrug.

"That's not the worst response you could give me." T.C. wiped his chin with a napkin, crumpled it in his hand and finished his soda. After washing his hands in the sink he turned back towards her. "What do I owe you?"

"What do you mean?"

"For lunch?"

Mona flushed. "Oh, um, ten should cover it."

T.C. reached into his back pocket and pulled out his wallet. He thumbed out a twenty-dollar bill. "Keep the change."

"Thanks."

He bent his head low so their foreheads almost touched and

grabbed her elbows. "I did miss you. I am not going anywhere. I will leave you alone if that's what you want."

"Okay." She could barely breathe with him so close to her. Did he mean to kiss her—to mark some sort of official ending between them? She could kiss him goodbye right now. On the cheek it wouldn't mean anything but goodbye, but then again it might mean something else. And there was Jake. Jake who was solidly decent and smart and funny and kind. Kissing T.C. would be a betrayal. T.C. shoved his hands in his jeans pockets, but remained where he stood six inches in front of her, only a few inches taller than her. Mona stood still.

T.C. waited a long moment before kissing her lightly on the forehead and walking toward the door with a wave. "Later then, Mona!"

She brushed her forehead, slick with grease from the fryer and sweat from the heat. *Shit.* She was *not* going down that road again, no matter what. Even if things fell apart with Jake, T.C. was history— no matter how much her knees felt like jelly right now. She sat down on the stool feeling as crumpled as the napkin T.C. had left on the counter.

SIXTEEN

June had finished pulling Joanne's laundry out of the dryer when Loyal came into the kitchen. She heard his boots thumping across the floor above her head and she called up from the basement, "Down here!"

"Darn belt broke again on that tractor," Loyal's voice drifted down the wooden steps and into the bowels of the basement. "I have to run to Fleet Farm."

She'd planned to drive over to Arlyce's to pack a suitcase for Joanne to take on the bus ride to California. "You have to do that now?" she called back. They'd coordinated the plan with knowing Steve would be at the Pub and Loyal would be in the barn.

"Did you need the truck for something?" He opened the basement door and stood at the edge of the steps.

The trouble with keeping secrets, June thought, was keeping them secret. If she told Loyal a reason for needing the truck, she'd have to actually do the thing she said she was doing because he'd ask her about it. She couldn't ask Loyal to drive her carrying a basket of Joanne's clothes to Arlyce's, he'd be suspicious. "The car's having engine trouble. The check engine light came on this afternoon when I was coming home from town and I need you to look at it."

"I suppose I should look at it in case it needs a part. No point in driving to town twice."

"And I promised I'd give Arlyce a hand with something." She paused, knowing exactly the tone that would bend Loyal to her will. "I guess I can call her and tell her I'm coming over later ..." she trailed off expertly and waited.

"I could drop you off on my way to town and pick you up on my way home. Won't take me more than an hour and a half," Loyal offered.

That was a reasonable solution, but not with all of Joanne's clothes in tow. "No, Sweetie. I might be a few hours. We're, uh, we're making programs for the fireman's auction. Is Mona here? Maybe she'd let me use her car."

Loyal's boots disappeared and June heard the scrape of a chair across the linoleum overhead. "I guess it can wait. I'll look at your car. Take the truck. I might take the car, otherwise I'll run in when you come home."

Great. Except he was sitting directly between her and the door and she had a stack of folded clothes in a laundry basket to sneak past him. June eyed the small window above the dryer. Working quickly, she folded the clothes into a plastic garbage bag and slid them through the window, onto the slush-covered yard. She relocked the window and mounted the stairs. "I just have to grab my purse." She patted Loyal on the shoulder as she walked past him.

Upstairs, she bundled the money she'd hidden in her jewelry box into her pocket. Her heart pounded. It would be much easier to simply explain what she was up to, but Joanne was so afraid what might happen if Loyal walked in to the Pub or Bud's and said anything. She had promised Joanne to keep everything secret—at least until she was safely out of town. Confident he could read the guilty flush on her cheeks, June rushed through the kitchen to pull her plaid wool coat off the hook by the back door. "I bet you'll still have time to head to Fleet Farm if I get home early?" she said over her shoulder. She shoved her feet into the winter boots sitting in a tray beneath the coat hooks.

Loyal had poured himself a cup of coffee and was settled in with the newspaper. "I'm going to thaw out. Then I'll check your car."

"Thanks again." She pecked his cheek, grateful for the sports scores absorbing his attention, and walked outside. Running around the corner to the basement window, she grabbed the bag of clothes off the slush-covered ground and hugged them to herself as she jogged back towards the truck. June glanced at the window to see if Loyal was watching her. His head was still bent over the paper.

Driving across the bridge, June looked down at the river through her rain-spotted window. The weatherman's forecast was right, mild temperatures and a couple days of rain had started the thaw. The Wissipaw had begun to break open and the weakest ice in the middle where the current ran fastest had already melted. Huge gashes of black, swirling water revealed themselves through the flat surface of the ice. They had to get Joanne out of that shanty. June knew the ice in the bayou wouldn't melt away as quickly; lack of current and sunlight would play in their favor, but still the prospect of a flooding river sweeping the shanty away was a scary thought. Or worse—the ice cracking open while they crossed it. She pushed the thought aside and turned on the truck's radio.

She parked beside the curb at Arlyce's house and entered.

Midafternoon, the boys were still at school. "Arlyce?"

"Coming."

June removed her coat and placed the bag of Joanne's clothing on the couch. She picked up toy cars, blocks and action figures while she waited, tossing them into a wooden crate in the corner of the tiny living room. A moment later Arlyce appeared, carrying Victoria on her hip. "Did you get through to Rhonda?" June asked.

Arlyce shook her head and stubbed out her cigarette in the ashtray on the coffee table. She set Victoria on the floor and adjusted her bra strap beneath her T-shirt. "I keep leaving messages with the receptionist. Maybe you should try, I think she's sick of my voice." She walked into the kitchen and returned with a memo pad with a scrawled phone number. "It makes me nervous to send Joanne out there on a bus without anyone knowing she's coming, but she can't stay out on the river any longer. It's too dangerous."

"I know. The ice has started to melt."

"Yeah." Arlyce pursed her lips. "Plus I heard Scotty filed a police report. He was fishing back in that bayou a couple days ago and saw somebody busting into the ice shanties, thought they were stealing gear. He told Steve he scared them off when he yelled over to them."

"Who was it?" June's hands clutched her knees.

Arlyce shook her head, her dangly earrings swinging against her thin cheeks. "No idea. Scotty couldn't see. He said he looked in the shanties and didn't see anything missing. I don't know if Joe went out to check or not."

"Rats. We have to get her out of there." June stood and took the piece of paper from Arlyce. "Her clothes are in that bag on the couch. You pack and I'll call her daughter's office."

Arlyce dumped the plastic bag's contents across the couch cushions and began refolding each item neatly, blouses and blue jeans stacked up with brisk efficiency. June picked up the receiver of the wall phone next to the fridge and began dialing.

After two rings, a young woman's voice answered. "Bernstein, Small and Sons."

June cleared her throat. "Hello, I'm looking for a Rhonda Graff."

"She's out of the office this week. May I take a message?"

"Please," June decided a new tack. "My name is June Butterfield, I'm an attorney representing her mother's estate. It's urgent that I speak with her. Do you have a phone number where I might reach her?"

"I'm not permitted to give out personal information." The woman's voice had a sing-song quality, June knew she'd recited the line before.

"I understand," June pressed. She took a deep breath to keep the tremble out of her voice. "This is an urgent matter, her mother has taken very ill and the hospital needs me to get in touch with her next of kin."

"Oh." June could detect the hesitation in the receptionist's voice.

"I realize this request is unusual, but I really need to speak with Rhonda about her mother's situation." June recalled the audacity of Axel Foley in *Beverly Hills Cop* and waded in deeper. "I *could* get a police warrant, but that will make more trouble for you on your end." She held her breath.

"Okay." June heard papers shuffling and then the voice continued. "Rhonda's home number is …"

"Bingo!" June cried triumphantly a minute later, waving the piece of paper above her head as she returned to the living room. "I faked a medical emergency and got it!"

"Did you call it?" Arlyce asked from where she sat stacking Joanne's clothing into a small blue suitcase.

"Well, no," June felt deflated. Her ruse was genius and Arlyce was not responding with any enthusiasm.

"Call it!" Arlyce rolled together the cuffs of a pair of socks and stuffed them along the edge of the case. Victoria crawled over and offered her mother the Matchbox car she'd been chewing on. "No, thank you," Arlyce told her daughter and ruffled her hair with calloused fingers.

June dialed Rhonda's number, feeling light headed. She realized she'd been holding her breath and inhaled. After nine rings she took another deep breath. Wouldn't twenty rings turn on an answering machine? She counted. Fifteen. Sixteen. Seventeen. After twenty fruitless rings, she hung up.

"No answer."

"Damn," Arlyce said. "Well, we can always keep calling, even if Joanne's on her way."

"That's true," June agreed.

"Okay, all of her clothes are packed. I added a pack of gum, extra toothpaste and a washcloth."

"I've got money for her bus ticket. What do you think about bringing her to the bus station tomorrow? She could probably hang out there okay until Friday afternoon.? It's only one night."

"Be warmer there than out in that shanty," Arlyce said.

"Yes." June looked down at her friend who knelt on the floor beside the suitcase.

"Safer, too," Arlyce added.

"Yes." Between someone trying to break into the ice shanties and the ice breaking up, they had to move her.

"You have enough money?" Arlyce asked. She zipped the suitcase shut and stood it on its side.

"Yes. I took it out of the savings account we set up when Loyal's mother died."

"I can give you some after my next shift at work. My tips are cash, Steve won't know."

June reached down for the suitcase. "Don't worry about it. We'll figure it out later."

Arlyce followed June to the door. "Tell her good luck from me," she called.

"I will." June shoved the suitcase across the seat and climbed into the truck after it. The rain was falling harder now and she turned up the speed of the windshield wipers before heading down the street. Everything would work out okay, she told herself, trying to calm the rising anxiety in her chest. She shifted the gears and tried to avoid looking down at the water while she crossed the bridge.

SEVENTEEN

WEDNESDAY NIGHT MONA WALKED into the Bassville Hotel and found Judi waiting for her in the lobby. The slim woman with long auburn curls and warm brown eyes jumped up and gave Mona a quick squeeze on her elbow. "I look forward to Girls Night Out every week. You save me, Mona." She blew a kiss to her mother, Sue, who waved at them from behind the desk.

Sue and Judi Linske had bought the old hotel three years ago and had fixed it up. Within a few years the fifteen-room hotel had morphed from money pit to moderately profitable. The Pole and Scotty were just starting to build a back deck that would overlook the Wissipaw River. Judi planned to move the beautifully veneered bar to the back of the building and convert the old bar area into another room.

Mona and Judi splashed through the puddles and hopped into Mona's car.

"Is Jenny coming?" Judi asked.

"No, she's catting after Beau tonight."

"Fool," Judi declared. "Who misses margaritas and movie night for some stupid guy?" She wrapped her wool scarf more tightly around her neck.

"Any guy," Mona agreed, "but especially Beau." Judi had become her second best friend since she'd moved to town and Mona had invited her out with her group of friends. With the exception of April and May, when everyone was too busy catering to fishermen, the two women managed to have a Girls' Night Out every week. Usually they were joined by a couple others, including Jenny, but Mona relished the time spent alone with Judi. Their conversation always became less superficial and Mona appreciated the wisdom the slightly older woman offered her.

Once a month they headed to Northport where they always ate at the same Mexican restaurant and hit the multiplex at the mall to watch a movie. Judi held up a page from yesterday's newspaper. "Tonight's choices." She cleared her throat dramatically and began to read. "*The Purple Rose of Cairo*, weird; *Mask*, inspiring but depressing; *Certain Fury*, violent; *The Hit*, looks predictable; and *Vision Quest*, stars Matthew Modine."

"Not that your commentary had *any* influence on my decision, but I vote for *Vision Quest*. I love that song Madonna sings in it."

"That was my first choice, too!" Judi fake-squealed.

Mona laughed. "I am dying for a margarita. And a chimichanga."

"Chips and guacamole, baby. Nothing less for this chica. By the way, I heard a little rumor the other day. Your ex is back in town?"

"Yeah." Mona grimaced. "T. C.'s back, and I thought Jake would have a fit. T.C. showed up at the Pub and was acting like we never broke up. Naturally Jake arrived just while he was trying to lay one on me. Awkward doesn't begin to describe it."

"Everything okay now?" Judi adjusted her seat back a bit and turned toward Mona.

"I think so. I was worried, but by the end of the night they were bellied up together like a couple of old drinking buddies. I mean, they did go to school together and played football and all that. It's not like they're strangers."

"No regret or second thoughts about T.C. then?"

"No. He's a good guy." She cut a sly look over at Judi. "Why? You interested?"

Judi grinned and shook her head. "No, ma'am. I've got my Mr. Right. Right in Chicago."

"How is Will these days?" Two summers ago when Chicago's hit DJ Dave LaMay rolled into town and made Maw's Minnows famous, Judi had met William Donne. Will was Dave's manager and he'd fallen hard for the hotel owner. They'd been dating ever since, long-distance phone calls, Hallmark greeting cards and weekend visits kept them connected.

"Good. We're planning a vacation together in July after things slow down here."

"Where are you going?"

"New Orleans. I think it will be interesting—I never went anywhere like that before, and it's kind of a relationship test. See how we travel together, get along for five days all alone."

"What happens if you pass?" Mona asked.

"One of us moves. Probably me, though Will's said he'd be open to coming to Wisconsin. I think he's getting tired of cleaning up after Dave and babysitting him. He has radio experience, so he could look at getting a job with one of the stations up here."

"He's cute," Mona said. "Maybe he could do TV news."

"Maybe. We have options. The biggest question is the hotel and my mom. I feel torn about leaving her."

"But ultimately the long distance thing has to end."

"Yeah. My gut tells me we'll end up together, though."

"When do you know for sure?"

"Why are you asking?" Judi tilted her head.

Mona turned on the Northport Mall exit. "Jake got a job offer. Atlanta, Georgia."

Judi sucked in her breath. "Oh, honey," she said sympathetically.

"Yeah. He doesn't know if he'll take it or not. But where does that leave me? If he asks me to come with him, do I even want to? I have my own stuff going here, the greenhouse and my family. But if he doesn't ask me to come, that tells me we're over, right?"

"Not necessarily. Is it a permanent move?"

"He said it's for a project."

"So short-term. Like a couple years."

"Probably."

"Will and I have done fine for that long. It's work, but it's possible. We talk on the phone. We see each other at least once a month. On the plus side, it makes our time together more special."

"And on the minus side?" Mona asked.

"I miss him." Judi shrugged. "But I don't want to be with anybody else, so I look forward to seeing him the next time. And when we're not together I can really focus on other stuff—like running the hotel and drinking margaritas with you."

Mona pulled into a parking spot in front of the Mexican restaurant. She turned off the ignition and sighed. "I'm really worried about this. I feel like our whole relationship is coming down to this decision. And it pisses me off that it's mostly *his* decision, whether he takes the job or not, whether he asks me along or not. If Beyer's hadn't offered this to him, we'd be making these choices on our own terms."

"That does stink," Judi agreed. "But no matter what happens, you have to know Jake loves you. Be patient with him. Even if he doesn't want you to go to Atlanta, that doesn't mean he won't change his mind. He might leave and miss you so much. And he might still turn down the offer."

"That's true," Mona mumbled.

"Just don't panic. The worst thing you can do is to act clingy while he's figuring it out. I know it's tough, but give him space. He'll figure it out. And I know you want his decision to reflect how he truly feels about you—you don't deserve anything less, sweetie. And neither does he."

Mona sniffed and wiped her nose with the back of her hand. "You're right. This is so damn hard. Thank you for letting me talk about it—and for the advice."

"You're driving me to the margarita bar and to see Matthew Modine on the big screen. Small price to pay for listening to your troubles." Judi wrapped her arm around Mona's shoulder and leaned her cheek against Mona's head. "But now, pay up. Strawberry blended."

Mona followed her friend through the colorfully decorated stucco entrance. *It is good advice*, she thought. *Wait and see.*

EIGHTEEN

A STEADY RAIN STILL HUNG around on Thursday morning and Mona knew her greenhouse was warmer than the Bassville Pub. The chill in the damp bar snaked through the layers of her T-shirt and sweatshirt, and she considered boosting the thermostat. With her luck, she'd forget to turn it down when Steve came in for the night shift and then he'd yell at her. Instead, she bounced on the balls of her feet to keep her blood moving. Mona turned her attention to the small group of patrons.

"Shit!" Grandma Nancy's voice rang out over the conversation around the bar. Frank had tucked a wool blanket over her legs and bundled it between her feet and the wheelchair's footrest.

"You aren't kidding, Nancy," Spade said. "The weatherman couldn't say it better himself."

"A positive deluge," Maw added. "Desultory and despicable."

"Stuck on the "D" section in the dictionary?" Mona asked him.

Maw grinned at her and tapped his coffee mug with his index finger. "Another deposit, dear?"

Mona went around with the coffee pot, topping off the mugs and clearing empty plates into the bus tub she'd stashed on top of a beer cooler. "Anyone else need to order?"

Gene and Loyal were both halfway through their plates of corned beef and hash, and Spade never ate in front of people. That left Scotty, The Pole and Dob.

"Short stack with bacon, Mona," Scotty said.

"Double that, Mona," Dob said.

"Short stack, aren't you two cute?" The Pole teased. "I'll have the corned beef and hash, with scrambled eggs, please. A man's meal." He turned around in his seat and leaned forward to talk to Frank. "I noticed there's a leaky gutter at your place."

Frank looked surprised but nodded affably.

"I can come over there after we get done at Maw's, probably around four or so. Won't take but a few minutes to fix that." The Pole nodded his shaggy head at Nancy and his white teeth shone bright against his dark brown beard and tanned cheeks when he smiled at her. "Last thing you need is to slip on a puddle of iced-over water and break a hip. Who'd push *you* around in a wheelchair, Frank?" He let out a bellowing laugh and Nancy laughed along with him, her eyes sparkling.

"That would be nice of you," Frank told The Pole.

"Listen, I was also thinking, you two like to sit out there on the sidewalk in the nice weather, right?"

"Shit," Nancy agreed.

"There's a couple of old awnings behind Grumpy's. It's shady back there all the time, they've got no need for them. I could take one down and put it up over your front door. What do you think?"

"Shit!" Nancy exclaimed and reached over to pat The Pole's knee with her pale, puffy hand.

"You don't need to do that," Mona said briskly. Since Grandma's stroke years ago, Grandpa Frank had taken on caring for her full-time, but that took its toll on his health, too. Frail and wrinkled, Grandpa Frank dutifully pushed his wife's wheelchair around town, fed her meals and got her to bed. Their first-floor apartment on Main Street didn't require a lot of work, but Mona had noticed a gradual decline over the past few years. "My parents take care of things like that."

"No, no! I think it'll look nice, it's blue-striped and will keep the sun off your heads in the afternoons." The Pole looked over at Frank. "I'll bring it over sometime next week if you want."

"Why that would be mighty kind of you, young man," Frank said. His pale eyes looked moist and he bent his head down to speak directly into Nancy's ear. "Isn't that nice of him? To bring us an awning?" Like most people hard of hearing, Frank spoke louder than necessary.

"Shit!" Nancy grinned.

"You don't need to do that," Mona said to The Pole. "If they need something my dad will handle it."

"It's no trouble."

Mona glared at him. "They don't need your help."

Scotty stepped forward and rested his hand on Nancy's shoulder while looking at Mona. "Suppose I help you with that project. That's how he rolls anyway, you know." Scotty pointed at The Pole with his thumb. "Volunteers to help, then tells me I have to help him, which usually means doing most of the work myself."

Nancy's laughter echoed through the bar and Frank turned her wheelchair toward the dining room where they normally sat for a couple hours each day, enjoying the view and breakfast together. "French toast today?" he asked her as they disappeared around the corner near the dart machines.

"How's that vegetable business going?" Scotty asked Mona.

Mona boosted herself up on top of a cooler and crossed her legs. "Pretty solid. Should break even this year."

Scotty blew across his coffee and took a swallow. "Milk prices keep tanking. I told Dad we should look at trying something different. Maybe we should start selling milk at that farm market. Or switch to raising beef cattle."

"You might look into that," Mona tilted her head and considered this. "I bet you could sell meat there. It's incredible how much zucchini I can hustle on a Saturday morning."

"Who the hell buys zucchini from anyone?" Dob demanded. "We end up with piles of it on our porch. I quit growing it, our neighbors always bring over more than we could ever use."

"You make bread with it?" Spade asked.

"For fuck's sake, listen to you hens," The Pole laughed. "What are we exchanging recipes now?"

"Better than exchanging punches," Mona shot back.

"Hey, I'm comfortable with my manhood." Dob gave The Pole a shove that nearly knocked him off his barstool.

"Don't you dare get into a fight on my watch," Mona warned them.

"Enough about gardening. Let's discuss gambling. They've started a pool on when the river will open up over at Grumpy's," Spade said. "Fifty bucks a square."

"What point of the river?" Dob asked.

"The Sawdust City dam," Spade said.

Dob leaned back and squinted up at the ceiling, calculating this information. "Raining since Tuesday and not supposed to quit until this weekend."

"Yep."

"But it's been cold. Ice is about six inches thick in the bayous yet, but the main channel opened up sometime last night."

"Look, Dob, it's not rocket science. You just put a bet down on the date and time." Spade gave Mona an exasperated look.

"Dob's one of the luckiest guys you ever met, right Spade?" Mona said.

"Yep."

"You honestly believe it's because he *guesses*? He wins too much to leave it up to chance." Mona headed for the kitchen to throw pancakes and corned beef on the griddle.

"He's *lucky*," Spade called after her.

"I'm *smart*," Dob argued.

After taking her grandparents' order in the dining room, Mona finished her cooking duties and brought plates back to the bar. "Short stack, short stack, corned beef and hash."

"Thanks, Mona." Scotty reached for the syrup. "So, guess I'm done fishing for a couple weeks now."

"How's that?" Mona asked just as he raised his fork to his lips. The joke about waitresses having perfect timing was really true, she'd found.

Scotty chewed and swallowed his first bite of pancakes. "Good cakes, by the way." He took a sip of coffee. "The thaw and the rain in the forecast means that ice won't last long."

"You in, Mona?" Spade asked her. "Only fifty dollars you can place your bet on the date and time the river's wide open at the Sawdust City dam. Winner gets $2500. Big money, honey."

Mona laughed and wiped her hands off on a clean bar rag. "Are you placing a bet, Dob?"

Dob nodded.

She looked at Spade. "You think I'm dumb enough to drop fifty dollars into this guy's pocket? No thanks."

Gene turned around in his seat and gazed out the windows overlooking the river. From the Pub it looked calm, flat and grey. "That river's a remarkable thing," he said. "You think about the sheer force of all that water coming through every day and add all that ice just pushing its way through. Remember about ten years ago when the ice floe took out the dock here?"

The public dock near the Bassville Pub had footings two feet in diameter. They were sturdier than telephone poles, but the sheets of ice had piled up on top of each other and then rode down the Wissipaw's fast current. The river crushed the dock like it had been made of popsicle sticks. Mona remembered the pictures of the broken dock in the newspaper. Everyone had stood at the banks of the swirling, angry waters to stare in awe as it tore through town, dragging mini-glaciers in its wake. The river was too dangerous to venture out on for a couple of weeks that year, and anyone who'd left their shanty on the ice or their dock in the water was out of luck.

"Didn't it flood really bad that year?" Mona asked.

"Terrible," Loyal said. "Highest levels since 1924. Imagine if we got that kind of water today. Swenson's place would float away."

"Yeah," Gene said. "What about that culvert business? High water like this would flood anyone who built back in Dead Run."

"How would that work?" Mona asked. "Seems if you build up land around something, the water would have to go somewhere else."

"True, but that doesn't mean the water won't go there at all," Gene said. "The river finds a way. Redirecting the flow is no easy business. When Swenson built that culvert, the river still washed over the road to his place and came up the property. He has to bring in truckloads of fill every few years to repair it. Alois Schmidt lost about ten acres of low farmland when they cut off the bayou."

"So, if they take out the culvert, who benefits?" Mona asked.

"The guy who owns the property south of it. But he'll have to bring in a LOT of fill to make that property viable," Gene explained. "It'll still be a floodplain anyway."

"Think it'll be that bad again this year?" Loyal asked.

"Ice is about the same thickness. If we get lots of rain, it will be bad," Gene said.

"What happens to those shanties that are still out on the ice?" Loyal asked Maw.

"If we get the freaky amount of rain they're calling for, they'll be floating down the river with everything else—or sinking when they break through the ice," Maw said.

"Doesn't Otto have a shanty parked over in Cooper's Bayou?" Scotty asked.

"He does," Dob said. "He's out of town until next week, though."

"Maybe we should pull them up to shore," The Pole suggested. "I've got a winch on the front of my truck. We get a heavy chain and it shouldn't take long. Just line 'em up on the bank there, owners can take care of them whenever they want." The Pole turned to ask Scotty, "How many shanties you figure are back there?"

"Maybe seven," Scotty said. "It'll probably take us three hours to get them all. And I know how this business works," he added, sighing. "You'll send the youngest guy out on the ice to attach the chain to the shanty." Scotty rolled his eyes at Mona. "Always me."

"You be careful if you do that," Gene told his son.

"We'll keep an eye on him, Gene," The Pole said, and wrapped a beefy arm around Scotty's neck, nearly choking him out. His tattoo of a topless luau dancer on his bicep shimmied as he flexed. The Pole tore off Scotty's baseball cap and gave him an affectionate noogie.

"We can't do it today," Dob said. "We have to finish that installation at Maw's. You've got those tanks coming Monday." Dob gave Maw a nod. "Could get out there Saturday or Sunday after church."

"I could give you a hand if you do it in the afternoon," Maw said.

"Peg can watch the shop for me."

"Let's do Sunday," The Pole said. "Things might dry up a little by then."

"Saturday," Scotty argued. "If that ice is thin now, it's gonna be a lot thinner Sunday. I'd rather head back there sooner than later."

Spade shook his head and said to Mona, "Wouldn't even be a problem if these goofy idiots just got their fish like civilized people—you know, I never risk falling through the ice when I go to Bud's and buy fish out of their freezer section."

"Speaking of Bud's," Dob said, "I heard that Joanne hasn't been in all week. I was in there to grab a gallon of milk last night and Bud said she hasn't shown up for two shifts." He looked over at The Pole. "You know anything about that?"

The Pole shrugged. "No clue."

Loyal pushed back from his spot at the bar. "I'm going back to say goodbye to your grandparents," he told Mona. "See you later."

"Bye, Dad," Mona said.

"See ya, Loyal," Gene said and then he turned towards Mona. "I hear Jake got a pretty nice opportunity at work."

"Yes, he did."

"Will he take it?"

"I don't know yet."

Gene took off his glasses and polished them with a napkin. "I figured he'd be busy building things on our land, but that moved slower than we thought it would."

"He might still get something around here."

"True. There always seems to be something new going up in Northport," Gene agreed. "Just a shame he can't work out of his back yard."

"Things happen for a reason," Mona said, but she wasn't convinced.

106

NINETEEN

Maw wiped his hands on his jeans and crawled to his feet. Hands on his hips, he surveyed the room with pride. Now the minnow lab passed for scientific. Various car parts looked unidentifiable after his kids had helped him run tubing and attached some dials and buttons they'd stripped off a couple of defunct remote controls.

Once they'd started hauling in the car parts, his youngest had gone out and returned with four broken transistor radios. Opened up so their colorful wire guts were revealed, they made a complicated-looking series of control panels along the way. He'd scribbled a series of equations on some graph paper and hung it to the wall. More paper, he decided, notes and stuff would make it look busier.

The more to take in, the less attention Boyd Douglas would pay to the details and the devil always lay in the details. Basically, Maw thought while combing his fingers through his beard, baffle 'em with his bullshit.

"Maw!" Peg's voice came down the hallway and he turned toward the door. "You got a phone call!"

Maw hurried towards the shop and took the receiver from Peg with raised eyebrows.

She shrugged one shoulder in reply and returned to the minnow tanks.

"Hello? This is Maw."

"My main man!" the silky voice crooned in his ear.

"Dave! What's shaking?" Maw perched on the stool behind the counter by the cash register. "How's the most dynamic DJ in the Windy City?"

"Rockin' and rollin' hard, friend. What's the fishing forecast looking like?"

"It's a late start this season," Maw admitted. "The walleye run is probably two weeks out, and we're in for a lot of flooding this year."

"So what's that mean for the fish?"

"They like it, but makes it nasty difficult for fishermen. The backwaters will be the spot to anchor your boat, but that means being careful not to get snagged up in anything. That's the trouble with a good flood—all the sh—crap gets pulled in off the shore. Makes it tricky to navigate."

"Okay, listeners, you heard our man Maw, two weeks until the walleye run. And I should mention Maw will be the feature of a documentary currently in production. The new cable channel *Discovery* will run all kinds of programs for nerds, freaks and geeks. If you want a behind-the-scenes look at Maw's minnow business, you'll get a chance to check it out this fall on *Discovery*. Make sure you contact your cable provider to watch Maw's story on *Discovery*."

Ah, Maw thought. *They're using me to advertise this cable channel.* He knew some kind of agreement required Dave to say "Discovery" that many times on the air. But back to him. "And you tell your listeners, Dave, that the most intrepid anglers will have the offensive advantage in our fair backwaters if they swing by my store and buy my specialty minnows. Maw's Minnows, they go after the fish for you!"

"Yeah, you've got the three types of minnows to choose from."

"Four this spring."

"Four? Is that right?"

"I've almost got the bugs worked out. Bit of a wriggler, this one. It's not easy to make the little suckers lie still for testing. Too much anesthesia, they die, too little and they barely slow down. But I've been real busy in my lab this winter developing a brand new breed specially conditioned for deep-water fishing. This minnow can handle water as cold as 45 degrees."

"What do you know. You got a name for this new minnow?"

Maw glanced at his Word of the Day tear-off calendar and grinned. "Pugnacious."

"Pugnacious," Dave repeated. "How do you spell that?"

"Just like it sounds, the qrz is silent, though."

Dave's laughter roared through the receiver.

"So come on up to Bassville. Maw's Minnows, my shop's right by the highway." Maw had a flash of genius and kept spooling out his story. "For a small fee visitors can tour our breeding facility and see up close what goes into our minnow operation. And they can be the first on the river to try our Pugnacious Minnow."

"I almost forgot, is your Bikini Fishing Team ready for the season?"

"The girls have been training all winter. Bodacious bikini bodies don't happen overnight."

"Maw's Minnows, featured this fall on *Discovery*. See your cable provider for details."

When Maw hung up he felt the surge of adrenaline which always accompanied working under pressure and knowing he'd opened his mouth and he had to deliver. In a few days Boyd Douglas would be at his door ready to see the minnow lab. Now he had a brand new breed of minnow to showcase. If anything, that would be a legitimate reason to not have things up and running because they'd just finished a huge project. He could stage some testing exercises. What would some city boy know about spottail shiners anyway? Maw knew minnows, he'd begun understanding them as a kid, wading knee-deep in the shallows with a bucket and net. They were quick, but instinctive and two things got them moving fast—shadows and motion.

What had he told Dave? That it could handle cold water. It was nothing to rig up a fake temperature reading on a tank. Maw rubbed his hands together and hopped down from the stool. He had no time to waste.

TWENTY

Thursday afternoon June found herself examining the Classifieds section of the *Northport Gazette* while she waited for Loyal to return home with the truck. Somehow she felt equally overqualified and underqualified for every job posted. Did she even want a job? She wasn't certain about that. She had no desire to go to an office every day or work in a store. At one point, in college, she'd kicked around the idea of going into teaching, but she didn't feel passionate about working with children. She knew she didn't want to work full-time, and she wouldn't want to work holidays or weekends. Ballpoint pen doodles covered the margins of the newspaper and not a single job posting was circled.

Frustrated at how useless the job postings made her feel, she flipped the newspaper over and started penciling in answers on the crossword puzzle. She was out of sorts because she was nervous about Joanne, she decided. She'd feel better when Joanne was safely deposited at the bus depot.

A blast of cold air reached her before Loyal's voice did. "June?"

"In here!" June folded the paper in half and pushed back from where she sat at the dining room table.

Loyal came around the corner and stopped in the doorway, his eyebrows drawn into a confused frown. "What are you doing sitting in here?"

"Change of scenery. It's a pretty room. We don't really use it much." She gestured at the glossy oak table and hutch filled with inherited crystal and china.

"Huh." Loyal followed her gaze.

"It's nice to have a formal dining room, but with the kids gone, we only use it a few times a year."

Loyal grunted and said, "But we use it for Thanksgiving and Christmas and stuff. Where else would we eat?"

"I don't know," June said. She stood up and ran her fingers along the wallpaper printed with trailing ivy leaves and the heavy drapes by the front window. "Maybe we could still eat in here, but not keep a permanent table set up."

"What else would you put in here?" Loyal asked. "It's a dining room."

"It's just a room, Loyal," June sighed. He was so singular in his thinking sometimes. "It can be anything we choose."

"I don't understand what else you'd do in here."

"Maybe set up a little craft or office space. Maybe a couple of chairs for sitting. Or maybe," June paused for effect. "We could leave the space empty and feel rich because we had the extra room with all of its potential."

Loyal shook his head with an exasperated, "Pfft." He leaned against the side of the door frame and shrugged. "I'm sure you'll figure it out. Just remember we need to have room for everyone on the holidays."

"Don't worry. I won't jeopardize any major holidays. What's the news from town?"

"Not much. The river's going to jam with ice soon. Couple of guys were talking about getting out to Cooper's Bayou to pull those ice shanties off before they break through. One of them belongs to Otto and he's out of town so we're going to pull it for him."

Panic fluttered through June's chest. "Oh my. When were they planning to do that? Is the river that dangerous already?"

Loyal nodded. "With the rain we've had, yes. Things will melt faster than normal, and when the conditions are just right the ice will dam up. Remember about fifteen years ago when the ice floe took out all those docks?"

"I do. When will you help take out the shanties?" June fought to keep the nervous pitch out of her voice.

"Sounded like Sunday."

"Oh." June stood. "Are you hanging around for the rest of the day? I promised Dottie I'd head over and help her with something."

"Yeah, you can take the truck. I'll have that vaccum hose replaced this afternoon. Won't take more than an hour, so your car will be ready when you get home." He reached for the newspaper and began unfolding it.

June was halfway to the back door when she heard Loyal say, "Take care on the back roads, though. This rain makes it pretty slick out there."

It didn't matter that she hadn't grabbed the suitcase full of clothes for Joanne. They could bring it to her later, June thought. Her heart pounded while she leaned forward to wipe the film off the windshield with her gloved hand. She didn't know which was a more terrible thought: Joanne crashing through the ice or someone finding her in the shanty. Crashing through the ice, Joanne decided. But, she tried to calm herself, the bayous melted last, and no one planned to get the shanties out until Sunday. It was only Thursday. Three days. If it was more dangerous, they'd get out there sooner.

She tried to get a good view of the Wissipaw through the trees lining the riverbank. It still looked mostly ice-covered to her, and she was driving alongside the main channel. If the channel was running wide open, then she'd have a reason to worry.

Deciding, however, did not stop the fear clenching her heart and making her hands sweat.

Removing one glove at a time with her teeth, she kept a spare hand on the steering wheel and pumped the brakes for the turn. Alongside the ditch the piles of snow had hardened and looked dirty. Would the ground thaw as fast as the water? Getting mired in mud on her way back to the bayou would be tough to explain to Loyal. No, she shook her head at her own stupidity. The snow cover would insulate the ground and keep it frozen.

Finally she reached the access road and tried to keep the truck's tires on the most iced-over spots on the rutted path. Bouncing along, she stared ahead through the trees, but it would be a minute before she'd see the river. The truck's tires heaved over branches and slopped through mud, finally she saw the brightness through the bare tree branches ahead. It was gratifying to see no fresh tracks in the snow, Joanne was still safe. No one else had come out here lately. She checked her rear view mirror and saw the black mud left behind the truck's tires. Yes, she'd definitely see the tracks if another car had driven out here recently.

June parked in an open spot between the trees where she'd have plenty of room to execute a Y-turn to drive out. Gingerly, she stepped out and tested the ground with her boot. Soggy, but still pretty frozen. She stepped across to the riverbank, looking for any sign of disturbance on the ice. It all looked calm to her, though it was hard to see with the pelting rain. She blinked her eyes to clear them. "Joanne!"

No answer. She reached the slope and knelt, her hands grabbed a branch to keep steady while she crab-walked down to the frozen bayou. The steady drum of raindrops hitting the ice and trees echoed down the river. The noise was loud enough to muffle the sound of her boots scraping down the route she'd chosen to get to Otto's shanty.

"Joanne!" she yelled again when she stood up and started walking towards the metal shack. Her ears burned from the cold and she knew her cheeks and nose were bright red. When she got close enough to see the corner, she saw the door swinging open. "JOANNE!"

Reaching the little structure, she realized before she could see all the way inside that it was empty. June spun in a circle, frantically looking in the trees—had she gone to relieve herself? The woods, the river, the seven standing shanties were deathly still.

Inside the shanty she saw the pile of bedding, a book lying face down atop the pile, and the hunting knife on the floor near the door. The floor was wet, from feet or blowing rain June could not tell. Backing out slowly, she took a couple of deep, gasping breaths. "Joanne!" Her voice sounded tiny against the rain and the woods.

Puddles of water had formed on the ice; there was no way to guess which way Joanne might have gone. June began walking along the bayou, her stomach lurching when she passed the last shanty and faced nothing but the glassy surface of the river. Four holes had opened up further towards the main tributary since she'd last been out here. She stayed close to the shoreline while moving further out—was the ice thinner or thicker at the edges? "JOANNE!"

Desperation forced her along while she checked over her shoulder, hoping to see Joanne emerge from the trees. Had she taken a walk? Or did something worse happen?

She'd gone about fifty yards when she caught a glimpse of something bobbing inside the third farthest hole. *Please be a log—a duck—anything.* Trembling legs brought her closer as she warily tested the ice with each step, listening for any cracking to warn her into retreating.

The dark form moved gently up and down. She was about twenty feet away when she saw the black tendrils snaking from one side. Not grass—hair. Instantly June recognized Joanne's back, clad in a puffy winter coat. She was floating face down, but June advanced, hoping for the best, her breath catching in her chest. June fell to her knees and crawled closer, gasping back her fear.

Lying on her stomach, she pushed herself across the ice towards Joanne's body, yelling out to her the whole time and praying for her to move. June reached out to grab her by the sleeve and pulled. Nothing. Scooting her knees beneath her so she'd have more leverage, she plunged her arms in the freezing river and reached beneath Joanne's shoulders. The angle was too awkward, the river's current too swift. She strained back but it was impossible to move her. Joanne's body was stiff to the touch and her coat had frozen to the sheet of ice. Despite this, June reached wet fingers out to check her neck for any pulse.

"JOANNE!" Sobbing, June released her friend and buried her face in her hands. She remained by the body for several minutes trying to think of what to do. She was dead, but June had to get her free before the river opened up any more and swallowed her. As fast as she could force herself, June half-skated, half-jogged to shore and scrabbled up the bank. She stumbled over fallen trees on her way to the truck and heard the rain, louder now, banging against the metal hood and roof. In her rush, she backed into a tree while turning around, but she didn't stop to check for damage. Alternating one hand between her shirt and stomach for burning warmth while the other hand steered, June sped toward Bassville.

TWENTY-ONE

Trees whizzed by June's peripheral vision while she mentally calculated her options. Approaching the first culvert, she looked for any sign of life at the Longwells' house. No car, no lights. She accelerated and passed it. Another mile to Dottie's. She'd use the phone there.

Wiping her nose on the back of her hand, June pressed on, the speedometer on the Ford hovering at 70 miles per hour. It was stupid to drive so fast in the rain, but she had to reach a phone.

Her hands still burned from cold when she turned onto the gravel driveway that led to Dottie and Gene's green-shuttered, two-story farmhouse. She turned off the engine and ran up to the back door. Without waiting for anyone to answer, she stepped inside Dottie's kitchen after hitting the doorbell once.

It took her several tries to dial the Cop Shop, her hands shook so badly. Jamming her red and swollen index finger into the dial, she took a deep breath and concentrated on the sharp ringing in the receiver.

"County Dispatch, how can I help you?" a woman's voice answered.

Dottie came around the corner holding a dust rag, one hand on her hip. June watched whatever sassy thing she'd been about to say fade from her lips as concern filled her expression. "What's going on?"

June waved her to stay quiet. "I need someone out at Cooper's Bayou. There's a body in the water. Her name is Joanne Graff."

A few minutes later, after she'd finished explaining the situation to the dispatcher, June flopped onto a kitchen chair.

"What happened? You're soaked through! What were you doing out at the bayou in this weather, June?" Dottie poured a cup of coffee and slid it towards June before settling next to her at the table. "Do you want me to call Loyal?"

"No," June reached for her friend's arm. "I'm so sorry. I tracked mud all over your floor."

"It'll clean. Tell me what's going on."

"Don't call Loyal. Not yet." She took a deep, quavering breath and curled her hands around the hot mug. "God, I don't even know where to start. That son of a bitch killed her. I should've gone out there sooner. I should've told Loyal and let her stay in Mona's old room. Or put her in a hotel. I should've—Shit!" June closed her eyes against the fresh tears forming.

"What were you doing out on the bayou?" Dottie's voice was gentle.

"Joanne was staying in Otto's ice shanty until we could get her out of town. She was going to live with her daughter."

"Why would she be in an ice shanty?" Dottie's puzzled expression shifted into one of understanding. "Oh. Oh my gosh."

"I thought we were keeping her safe. She didn't want anyone to know—not even Loyal or Steve. She figured they'd tell him where

118

she was and he'd go after her. Before when she tried to leave … he found her anyway." June dropped her head onto her folded hands. Her shoulders heaved while she cried. Dottie scooted her chair closer to stroke hair. "Shhh. It's okay."

"I need to get back out there," June pushed her chair back and stood. "She's all alone. I need to show them where she is."

"You're not going anywhere alone right now," Dottie said. "I will drive." She reached over to turn off the small TV set on the kitchen counter. "Take this." Dottie handed her a large plaid coat—one of Gene's. "Leave your wet coat here."

Dottie pulled in behind the black and white police car already parked at the edge of the bayou. June jumped out and met Joe, the county cop who took care of most of Bassville's law enforcement problems.

"Did you see her?" June asked. She pulled the collar of Gene's coat tighter around her neck.

"I just got here," Joe said. "Why don't you show me what you found."

Joe had grown up a couple towns over; he had the locals' trust. At age thirty-five, he didn't need to prove himself by acting tough any longer. Joe had a frank, open face and a mellow deep voice which, combined with his mild temperament, effectively diffused most situations. The last time he'd drawn his gun from his holster was to shoot a rabid dog terrorizing a sheep farm. He offered June a black gloved hand and helped her down the bank to the ice. "I've called for back-up, but they won't be here for at least twenty more minutes." He walked a half step behind her, letting June lead him down to the spot where Joanne's body was caught, submerged from the waist down beneath the ice.

When they reached the spot Joe knelt down a few feet from the edge of the hole and removed his cap. Droplets of rain beaded on his somber face and caught in the scruff on his cheeks. He looked up at June with wide eyes. "How do you think she got here? What was she doing out on the ice?"

"The bastard killed her."

Joe's expression did not change, which June felt was to his credit. She knew he'd answered his share of calls to break up domestic disputes. But when Joanne never wanted to press any charges—out of misplaced loyalty or embarrassment—his hands were tied. Once, June knew, he'd been booked overnight on a charge of drunk and disorderly. That had resulted in Joanne ending up in the emergency room the following night. She'd told the doctors she'd fallen down the stairs, and who could argue with her?

"What exactly did you see?"

Here was the rub, June knew. Dottie finally reached them where they stood on the ice, panting for breath. June had not seen anything. All she could do was hope some piece of evidence brought justice.

"Arlyce and I helped Joanne move out here, to Otto Zimm's ice shanty, temporarily. She was going to leave, but she needed to sort out with her daughter before she could head to California. We figured that by staying out here she'd be safe ..." June gulped back a sob.

Joe stood and patted her shoulder. "Take your time. It's okay." He waited patiently for her to continue talking.

"Her daughter lives out of town, we needed to reach her so she'd know Joanne was on her way, so she wouldn't end up homeless when she got there. We'd bought her a bus ticket and she was supposed to leave town tomorrow morning." June took a deep breath. "Otto's out of town, so we helped her stay here where no one could find her. We were afraid that he wouldn't let her leave if he got wind of it, so she was laying low here since Friday. Arlyce and I took turns checking in on her, bringing her food and stuff."

"Did she seem depressed or despondent?" Joe asked.

"No. She seemed excited about a fresh start at her daughter's place. She talked about getting a job and was firm about how leaving was the right decision."

"Did she seem at all confused?"

June frowned. "What? No! She was determined to do what it took to leave that bastard. She was thinking clearly for the first time in a long time if you ask me."

"Had she been drinking while she was out here? Self-medicating a little?"

"If you're trying to insinuate that she killed herself, forget it. Joanne was never that much of a drinker, you know that. What I think happened—" June ignored the hand Joe raised to stop her. "What I think happened," she repeated firmly, "is that he came out here and found her. I know he's been looking for her. Ask around, it's true. In fact, I heard that Scotty saw someone out here earlier this week checking in all these shanties." June waved her arm toward the line of shanties parked on the ice. "He probably came here, found her, and chased her out here on the ice and shoved her through."

Joe squinted his eyes at the shanties.

"I know you're not going to find any footprints in this weather, but I guarantee he was out here," June insisted.

"Are you planning to get her out of the river?" Dottie asked in a tremulous voice.

"Yes, as soon as some help arrives. Let's head back towards shore." He led the way. When they neared the shanties, he slowed down and asked, "Which one was she staying in?"

Wordlessly, June pointed and they walked up to it. Joe looked in the door and then walked around the entire structure.

"Did you see the knife on the floor? I think she was trying to defend herself. He probably overpowered her before dragging her outside." Spasms of cold gripped her suddenly and her teeth started

121

to chatter. "You need to track him down and find out where he's been in the last twenty-four hours."

Joe grimaced. Before he spoke, the hollow wail of a siren announced the arrival of an ambulance and another squad car.

"You've got to believe me." June pleaded. "Joanne didn't kill herself and this was no accident. There's no reason she'd have started walking down the river since I saw her yesterday. I came here to get her because I heard the river had begun breaking up. Tell me why you think she'd walk out towards open water."

Joe shook his head. "I don't think she would, June, but murder is a serious accusation."

TWENTY-TWO

I T TOOK LESS THAN five minutes to extract Joanne from the ice once the EMTs arrived on the scene. Expertly they wrapped her torso with a strap and with a terrible sucking sound the river released her. The men unceremoniously dragged her ten feet across the ice before dropping the rope and unhooking her body. Joe rolled her over onto her back. June covered her own eyes before gathering courage to peek at Joanne's face.

Pale, swollen and blue lips. A scrape along her forehead and cheek were the only visible injuries aside from the previous black eye that had faded to light bruising. Her pallor contrasted starkly against her slick black hair. Dottie sank to her knees and reached over to pull a strand of hair that was caught between Joanne's lips. She brushed Joanne's cheek with her fingertips and murmured, "Oh, Joanne. Poor Joanne."

June watched water drain from Joanne's body and clothes, from her ears and hair and nostrils.

"Of course the coroner will examine her, but cause of death is probably drowning," Joe said.

June whirled on him. "She was killed." Her rage bubbled up and she clenched her hands, no longer cold now. Her entire body felt burning hot. "She was killed and you know it."

Dottie reached up and wrapped an arm around June's knees. "Sweetie, it's okay. They'll figure this out."

"No, Dottie. They'll say it was an accident or that she killed herself and Joanne will never get any justice." June glared at Joe. "And God knows she'd been through enough."

Joe took off his cap and rubbed his hand over his blonde crew cut before pulling it back down over his ears. He stepped toward June and calmly met her gaze. "I promise I will try to find out everything I can. You have my word."

"I hope you nail him, Joe."

As they crossed the ice back to the truck, June saw two policemen carefully searching each of the shanties and taking photographs. The EMTs had loaded Joanne onto a stretcher and were bringing her back to an ambulance that would drive silently back to the station. No need for sirens. They were long past any reason to rush.

"June?" Dottie stopped walking before they ventured up the riverbank.

"Yeah?"

"Let's just … let's give her a moment here, okay?"

June nodded and Dottie grabbed her hands, bowed her head and prayed with a shaking voice. "Dear Lord, we ask you to protect our sister now. Give her the comfort and security of your love in heaven. Give her justice on earth. Help Joe and give him wisdom. Forgive us for not doing more while there was still time. Lord, we ask you to bless Joanne."

124

June squeezed Dottie's hands. "Amen." She dropped them and started up the riverbank.

Dottie brought June home. "You're sure you don't want me to come in with you?"

"No. Please, tell Arlyce what happened and tell her that I'm coming to talk to her as soon as I get cleaned up."

Dottie reached over to pat June's thigh. "Scotty'll drop your truck off as soon as I track him down. Love you." Her face was pink from the cold and creased with concern.

"Love you, too."

June trudged into the house, her limbs feeling impossibly heavy. She kicked off her wet boots and peeled soaking socks from her feet. She tipped the boots upside down over the kitchen sink and watched water pour out. More than anything she wanted to strip naked and wrap herself in bed under layers of blankets, but that wouldn't be fair to Arlyce. Or to Joanne—what right did she have to feel so horrible? *She* wasn't dead, but was she to blame? Joanne wouldn't have been in that shanty if it wasn't for her.

Upstairs, June stood in the shower, the water turned as hot as she could stand it. Her tears mixed with the shampoo and got rinsed down the drain. She let the water run until it started turning cold, having depleted the reserves of the hot water heater. After towel-drying her hair and getting dressed, she ventured downstairs. What a total failure, she kept thinking over and over. She hadn't protected her.

In the kitchen she brewed a pot of coffee, only for the comforting smell. She had no taste to drink it. June watched the yard for the truck to pull in. She should probably talk to Loyal, she realized after a few minutes of staring at the barn. How to tell him?

The phone rang, jolting her into movement.

"Hello?"

"That son of a bitch found her, didn't he?"

Arlyce's anger burned through the phone line. June sat at the table, stretching the phone cord to its limit. "I think that's what happened," she agreed.

"Dottie filled me in, but I want to hear it from you."

"I was going to come over there. I'm waiting for Scotty to drop off the truck."

"No, you stay put. Hunter's home sick from school today and Victoria's got more green snot dripping out of her than you'd think possible for someone with such a small head. I'm their mother and *I* want to wear rubber gloves around them."

"Okay." June leaned her forehead against her fist. "So today Loyal told me that the ice floe was expected to be really bad this spring with all the rain. The guys planned to pull the shanties off the ice because of flooding and the open water. I worried that Joanne might either …" June inhaled sharply to stop the sob in her chest. "Sorry. She'd either go through the ice or get found."

"Oh my God."

"I got out there and she wasn't in the shanty. I started walking towards the end of the bayou and that's where I found her. There were a few holes in the ice; she was caught at the edge of one of them. I tried pulling her out. She was already dead, but I tried."

"Oh, honey." Arlyce's gravelly voice was soft.

"Then I had to leave her and get help. I drove to Dottie's and called the police. Dottie drove me back and we found Joe already there. They got her out using ropes. It was awful. She was so pale, she was face down in the water, so I couldn't see her face until they got her out. I don't know how she fell in, if he pushed her or chased her and she fell through, but she was facing the bayou, caught under the sheet of ice by her waist somehow. I just saw her floating there.

I didn't even know what she was until I walked closer. At first I thought she was a log."

"How was the rest of the ice?" Arlyce asked.

"What do you mean?"

"How close could you get—you said you tried pulling her out."

"I did. I crawled over and grabbed her under her arms and tried pulling, but she was stuck to the ice. The hole was too big for me to go on the other side and reach her."

"And the ice held you? You weren't afraid of falling in?"

"I was scared, but I never heard it crack or anything. I was more scared of slipping in because of the rain."

"Do you think she was trying to leave?" Arlyce asked.

"I thought of that, but why walk out toward the river on the ice if you're trying to leave? I mean, unless someone was chasing you, you'd walk to the shore and up to the road. That direction on the water doesn't lead to anywhere."

"No footprints? Oh, sweetie, no no no! Don't put that in your mouth. I'll be there in a minute, Hunter!"

"With the rain almost all the snow is melted in the woods. The ice just had puddles. No one will find any footprints, I don't even think it's possible."

"He had to have killed her. Like you said, June. He either pushed her in or chased her and she fell through."

The two women were silent for a minute. "I feel like this is all my fault," June said. "We failed to protect her."

"Don't blame yourself. You—*we* were trying to help her. Listen, I have to go, the baby just got into the pantry and dumped over a bag of flour. I'll call you again later."

"Okay. Let me know if you need anything."

"We should tell Rhonda," Arlyce said suddenly.

"I have her number. I'll do it."

June hung up and stared out at the back yard. The sky was getting darker, Loyal would be in for supper soon. She dumped out her full mug of coffee in the sink and grabbed a frying pan. He'd complain, but grilled cheese and a can of tomato soup would have to satisfy.

Loyal shook his coat out before hanging it on a hook. "It's a mud pit out there," he said to June. "I'm starving."

"Dinner's almost ready." She was slicing an apple while the soup heated on the stove.

"Where's the truck?" Loyal asked. "You're home but there's no truck in the driveway. Did you run out of gas somewhere?"

"No." June set down the knife and apple and braced her hands against the countertop. She bent her head and let the tears roll down her cheeks.

Loyal walked over to the stove and took a spoonful to taste. "Is this it?"

"I made grilled cheese. They're in the oven."

"Okay." He went to the sink to wash his hands and then he looked at her. "Are you all right?"

June shook her head and kept her eyes tightly closed.

"Hey? What's going on?" He put his hands on her shoulders and turned her around and then wiped her cheek with the edge of his sleeve. "Did something happen to one of the kids? Your parents? I just saw Mona and Frank and Nancy this morning at the Pub. They seemed fine. Was there an accident?"

June kept shaking her head and leaned into his chest. He placed his hands on her back and held her close while she squeezed out the last tears. How could she have any tears left to cry? After a minute she spoke.

"The Pole killed Joanne."

128

TWENTY-THREE

A GATHERED CROWD AT THE Bassville Pub was busy speculating who would win the payout from the Sawdust City contest. Mona watched with an amused grin while Spade decided how he'd spend his winnings and Dale ribbed him about his calculations, arguing that no one could scientifically win besides a Dohill. They'd taken the midday times for the end of next week, after the rain ended and maximum flooding should drain into the river basin. This mixed with a feisty debate over blocking boater access for more development, or allowing more river and less development, and combined to create a boisterous scene.

Snuffy burst through the door and announced, "The cops just pulled Joanne out of Cooper's Bayou."

All conversation ceased as heads turned to where he stood in the door, rain dripping from his hooded jacket onto his beard.

"What's that now, Snuffy?" Dob asked. Bassville's homeless oaf was loveable, but sometimes prone to spreading crazy rumors.

Snuffy approached the bar and wiped his hand over his face. "It's a deluge out there. I just ran into Joe the Cop at the gas station. He told me someone found Joanne's body out in the bayou. She fell through the ice."

"What the hell was she doing out on the ice?" Spade asked.

"Is she okay?" Mona asked. She hadn't seen Joanne in a couple of days, rumors had floated through the bar that she'd disappeared, which sounded crazy to Mona. How could somebody disappear?

"She's dead."

Mona gasped. "Oh." She took a step backwards and her hands fluttered to her chest.

"Told you that ice wasn't safe," Dale told Scotty. "When it stops snowing and starts raining, you gotta get off of that river."

"Who found her?" Scotty asked.

Snuffy shrugged off his jacket and slung it over an empty stool. "Joe didn't say. I don't think anyone was fishing in this crap today. Otto's out of town and nobody came by for bait. I usually sell to the guys who have shanties out there."

"Shit." Dob turned to his brother. "How old was she? I remember when she started working at the grocery store—what was that? About six-seven years ago?"

"She moved here with The Pole. Remember? They met in Branson, he was in that fishing competition and then she followed him up here," Dale said.

"Where was she from?" Mona asked. "I mean, I always thought she was from here."

"No," Snuffy said. "She's from—where's she even from?"

"Branson?" Dale said.

"I heard she had grown daughters who lived out west somewhere," Scotty said. "One of them visited her a couple years ago."

"I kind of remember that," Dale leaned forward on his elbows and resumed biting the end of a cocktail straw. "Tall, pretty blonde girl. Met her when Joanne brought her up to the Luau Lounge for dinner."

Mona couldn't believe she'd known Joanne for so long without really knowing her. How had it never occurred to her to wonder who her family was? She was just Joanne, who worked at Bud's. She'd come in sometimes for drinks with The Pole, and of course everyone talked about how he treated her, but she was, Mona realized, essentially alone. Did she even have any friends? What did she do besides live in the apartment down the block and work a cash register?

"Does The Pole know?" Scotty asked.

Dob and Dale exchanged a look.

"What?" Scotty said.

"Where is he anyway?" Snuffy asked. "You two are like Velcro, always stuck together."

"I stayed at the farm today. Mom and Dad had to bring Angie to a doctor appointment." Scotty leaned forward and looked over at Dob and Dale. "Was he working with you guys?"

"We were finishing the wiring in that new warehouse over towards Northport. The Pole never called us looking for work today." Dob shrugged and looked at his brother. "Think he might've been at the hotel?"

"Maybe he's in the river, too," Dale suggested. "Did anyone check?"

"Shit, when's the last time anybody saw him?" Snuffy asked. He pointed at the glass of beer in front of Dob and nodded to Mona. "Nobody's at Grumpy's. Been deader than a doornail all day. I haven't seen his truck around either."

Everyone turned to look at Scotty. His eyes grew wide and he held up both hands defensively. "I honestly have no idea where he's at. Would the police have found him? To tell him about Joanne?"

"Or question him," Mona said in a quiet voice. Everyone turned to look at her. "I mean, we all know he beat her up." She fiddled with the soda gun before meeting Scotty's incredulous expression. Suddenly she felt mad. Sure, nobody ever talked about it, but why? Because they were polite? Or because they didn't want to get involved? "Come on," she said with a defiant tone. She crossed her arms and stared back at Scotty. "There's no reason she'd be out on the water alone, she'd go out there with somebody. Joanne only went anywhere with The Pole. If they were together, the police would want to know what happened. If they weren't together, they'd be looking for him … for all kinds of reasons. I mean, he's next of kin, right?"

"Were they married?" Dob asked.

"I don't know," Scotty said.

"Weird to think how you can know someone for so many years but not really know much about them," Spade mused. He rattled the dice cup in his hand as if to suggest a game. When no one said anything about dice or Joanne, he slouched over his can of Pepsi.

"How's it work if they weren't married?" Snuffy asked. "Would her kids come get her things and sort out funeral arrangements?"

"What if they can't find her kids?" Mona said while passing him the glass of beer. She shook her head at him when he started digging in his pants pockets for money. She always spotted Snuffy a beer, just like she always gave him a ride if she saw him hoofing it along the side of the road. Snuffy winked and nodded at her before tipping the glass. "What happens then?" She paused, considering how alone Joanne was. "How long do they wait?"

"No clue," Dob said. "But the ground's froze anyway and I think all the graves they dug last fall have been used up. They'll probably store her in the county morgue until the ground thaws."

Mona pointed at Dob's can of Bud Light and raised her eyebrow. Dob nodded and gestured to catch the bar a round. "How's that work anyway?" she asked. "How do they know how many graves to dig before winter and how do they know where to dig them?"

"Good question," Dob answered. "I think they have an average, someone keeps track of it from year to year—probably Doris Lobermeyer at the town hall. They pre-dig a few, but if you want to get placed in a particular plot, like a family grave, you have to wait until spring."

"That happened to our grandma," Dale explained. "She died in December. We had the funeral and pallbearers at church, but then we put her in cold storage until spring. We waited until April to pop her out of the freezer and bury her next to Grandpa."

"God, that sounds horrible." Mona scrunched up her nose.

"Is it?" Dob shrugged his beefy shoulders. "I mean, they're dead. It's not like they know."

"People have some weird ideas about death," Spade said. "I want to be cremated and my ashes scattered at the front door of Caesars Palace."

"That makes sense. The ultimate sacrifice at your holy place." Dale chuckled.

"I don't think it's legal to scatter ashes just any old place," Scotty said. "And ashes aren't exactly ashes. They're more like clumps."

"Don't care," Spade insisted. "You'd do it for me, wouldn't you, Mona? If I left money for you in my will? You'd fly out and drop me in a little pile by the front door of Caesars Palace."

"Sure," Mona said. "And then when I'm done some street sweeper will push you into a bin and you'll end up in a garbage dump on the outskirts of Las Vegas."

"Ah, but he'll be dead and not know any better anyway," Dale reminded Mona. "A smart girl would pocket the cash and use ol' Spade there to fertilize your vegetables."

Everyone laughed while Mona reached into the cooler to refill drinks. She took Dob's money and dropped it in the till. It felt sacrilegious to her to discuss death this way. Not with the recent discovery of Joanne. Mona wanted to feel sad, and she was, but she also was aware that she was telling herself to feel that way. What she felt was *bad* that Joanne was dead, not the actual grief like she had experienced when Grandma Butterfield died.

She glanced at the clock. It was almost six, past suppertime. She looked through the windows of the Pub and could barely make out the river through the darkness. The only light came from the two dockside lights at the ends of the piers. Jake's cottage was dark. Where was he? Had he heard this crazy news yet? She wanted to ask him what he thought about all of it. She wanted to hear him agree with her that The Pole was somehow involved in Joanne's death.

TWENTY-FOUR

JUNE HAD WRAPPED HERSELF from head to toe in a blanket on the couch and was watching a rerun of *Cheers* when Loyal came in from his evening chores in the barn. She heard him kick off his boots and run the faucet to wash his hands. It was always a comfort to hear him return from outside, and this made her wonder just how awful it would be to live with someone cruel, like The Pole had been to Joanne. How did that work, exactly? Did she see it coming, a bad mood that made him lash out at her, or was it unpredictable? Unpredictable would be worse, she decided. Not knowing how someone might react, with a kiss or a kick? That would make you a cringing wreck of a person.

Joanne never confided in her how things worked out specifically between them. From the little June'd read, she knew most abused women chose to stay because of low self-esteem. But Joanne didn't seem like a person who suffered from low self-esteem. She was beautiful and smart, and very well-spoken. June had never heard her swear or use poor language. She wore fringed leather, but not booty shorts like Sheila or some of the other younger women around Mona's age who let everything hang out.

What force drew Joanne to The Pole? Had he destroyed her, or was that work done by someone else who'd come before him? There seemed to be some pattern between women who were abused as kids and then again as adult wives or girlfriends. God forbid Mona ever got messed up like that. She had to trust that she and Loyal had provided a strong enough example and raised her right to prevent that from ever happening.

Besides, June reflected, Jake was a good guy. And T.C. was a good guy. Mona had solid judgment—worrying about *that* was borrowing trouble, as her mother used to say. June grimaced. Now her mom could just say, "Shit," and it was kind of funny because it was still a perfect thing to say.

Loyal came in the room and leaned over to kiss her forehead. "You doing okay?"

"Mmm-hmm."

He sat in the easy chair across from her and released a groan.

"Are you all right?"

"Just a little sore. Had to help Lobermeyer with the hoof care today. One of the heifers didn't cooperate."

"Sorry I didn't get supper going."

Loyal rubbed the back of his neck. "I wasn't that hungry anyway."

They sat silently for a moment; the radiator hissed from the wall.

"You did a brave thing, trying to help her," Loyal finally said.

Tears welled up in June's eyes. She couldn't believe she hadn't withered dry yet. "I should have handled it differently."

"Naw. You did what you thought was best."

"I shouldn't have kept it secret from you."

"You respected what she wanted. Joanne wanted to hide, keep her situation secret. You were trying to do things on her terms."

His words, his attempt at comforting her felt like rain in the driest part of August. Her hands unclenched slightly and her shoulders unbound a notch. "Loyal?"

"Uh huh?"

"Come, sit here by me." June sat up, scooted over on the couch and held up the edge of her blanket. He unfolded his tall body from the easy chair and crossed the room, and she reached her arms around the familiar strong form of him. "How are you such a good, kind man and then someone like The Pole is not?"

Loyal leaned his greying head against hers and exhaled. "I don't know. He was bad to Joanne, but then he's good to other people. Maybe he was good to her once, too. I don't understand it."

She stroked her fingertips along his grizzled cheek. "I don't know how people can ignore how he treated her, yet still buy him drinks and fish when he beat her up all the time." June paused. "I don't know how I could have ignored her."

"I guess people just focus on the good parts of a person and forget the bad."

"Aren't some things unforgettable?" she persisted.

"Depends on who you ask."

"It feels like men have an easier time forgetting than women. I think if a friend of mine beat up her kids or something, I could never talk to her again, I'd be so disgusted."

Loyal thought about that for a moment before replying. "But if you never talked to her again, would she know why? And how would she change to become a better person if you shut her out? Maybe that's how come people never shunned The Pole."

"I don't agree with that. I think they just didn't want to think about something so ugly. Or worse, they somehow felt like Joanne deserved it—she was too stupid to leave or picked fights with him or didn't stand up for herself."

"I admit, I struggle to understand why she didn't leave him."

June had to confess she didn't have an answer for that. "I just wish I hadn't failed."

"You did your best and you did a lot more than anyone else ever did to help her." Loyal squeezed her knee for emphasis. "What happened was not your fault."

It was good to hear him say that, but June still felt terrible.

TWENTY-FIVE

Mona was glad Steve showed up at the Pub to help her close. "Look, I know it was probably an accident, but I didn't like thinking of you alone here tonight after what happened today," Steve explained when he joined her behind the bar. He took over wiping down the bar and Mona went around switching off the "Open" sign in the window and locking the two main doors. Still no light at Jake's and he hadn't called her either. *He might just be caught up at work.*

When she finished stacking the bar stools Steve waved her off. "I'll mop in the morning. Drive home safe."

"Thanks," she called over her shoulder and zipped up her jacket, stuffing her tips into her pocket and pulling free her car keys. Joanne's death spooked her, made her aware of her vulnerability as a woman. Even though it was only ten o'clock, she felt weary like she'd worked a double shift. She opened the door of her car and was about to get in when a deep voice startled her.

"Hey, Mona."

The sharp edge of the car door jammed her funny bone when she turned and she gave a little yelp of pain. The Pole stood three feet away from the front of her car. *Where had he come from?* She frowned, taking in his wet work boots, Carhartt jacket and cap pulled low over his eyes. *If he murdered Joanne, would he come after somebody else right away?* Her breathing grew harder.

"Just getting done with work?" He grinned at her, his teeth white in his thick beard and his black eyes shining. Everything about him seemed menacing.

"Yep. Steve's in there now, bunch of other guys, too. But Steve's about to bring out the garbage," she added as a warning.

He nodded and turned his head to look up at the lone light shining above the parking lot. "It's been a long day. Time for a cold one."

"Where have you been all day?" The question burst out of her before she could think better of it, but she had to ask.

"Working up in Northport."

"Really?" Her voice sounded incredulous.

"Yeah. Why?" He crossed his arms over his barrel chest and stared at her.

"People have been looking for you—I think."

"Huh. I coulda swore I told Dob and Scotty I wasn't coming to the job site today. Anyway, you have a good night." The Pole started to lope off across the parking lot when Mona spoke up again.

"Did the police find you yet?"

The Pole turned toward her, now backlit by the huge light at the end of the dock, Mona couldn't read his expression. He was a tall shadow looming between her and the building. "The police?"

"Haven't you heard?" Mona knew she'd stepped into it, up to her ankles, and she wasn't turning back now. "They found Joanne in the river."

The Pole took a stumbling step away from her, then another. The rain splattered against the blacktopped parking lot around their feet. "Found Joanne?"

"Yeah."

The silence spread thickly between them and Mona wondered if he did kill her.

"I should go." He took off running, his long legs pulling him around the corner of the building.

Joanne was his girlfriend, Mona thought. Would he run to the police or run and hide? If he disappeared, would she be in trouble for talking to him—possibly tipping him off to escape the police? Rain trickled down to her scalp and she ducked into her car.

She started the engine, and flicked on the windshield wipers and headlights. As she drove down Main Street towards her house, she looked for The Pole and his truck, but saw neither. She had to believe if he was somehow responsible for Joanne's death, the police would figure it out.

At home, Mona made a beeline for the shower. The film of cigarette smoke and fryer grease coated her skin and hair, making it hard to leave work behind her at the door. Once showered, she pulled on sweatpants and one of Jake's college sweatshirts that she'd raided from his closet. Ensconced in cotton fabric and smelling like lilies of the valley, thanks to the bath products her grandparents gave her for Christmas, Mona filled a cup of water and put it in the microwave. Ninety seconds later, she dropped a peppermint teabag into the boiling water and picked up the phone to call Jake.

He answered on the third ring.

"Hey. How was your day?"

"Good—busy—good." He sounded distracted.

"Did you hear Joanne is dead?"

"What? She's not very old—how did she die?"

She had his full attention now. Mona settled back in a chair. "They found her in Cooper's Bayou—she fell through the ice."

"Wow. I didn't think it was that thin already. That's so sad. She was a nice person."

"I think I was the one to break it to The Pole."

"How's that?"

"He came by the Pub when I was getting off work. He ran off after I told him. Do you think that means he was involved? It seems really strange that she'd be on the ice by herself. Unless she was at work they were always together."

"That does seem strange, but if he was with her he'd have gotten her out. The Pole's smart about stuff like that, and strong, too."

Mona sighed. Even though it felt better to process this with Jake, she really wanted to talk in person. "Did you want to come over?"

He hesitated. "I've got to get in really early tomorrow morning."

Mona glanced at the clock, "It's only ten-thirty."

His sigh echoed in her ear. "It's been a really long day. I wouldn't be good company. I'd probably fall asleep on you."

"Oh. Okay." She knew she was becoming clingy instead of giving him the space he needed to make his decisions, but the idea of losing him—she didn't want to go there. *Relax*, she told herself. *He's just tired. It's only a weeknight. No big deal.* "No big deal."

"Thanks for understanding. We'll do something this weekend, maybe dinner out at Pine Tree?"

"That would be nice. Get your rest."

"I will. Talk to you later. Love you. Are you sure you're okay?"

"Yeah." She spoke the words—"I love you, too"—into the receiver but suspected he'd hung up before he'd heard.

Switching on the TV, she settled into the couch with her tea. She steeled herself against thinking the worst. Judi had counseled her to give Jake space to figure out what he wanted. She knew she didn't want him to feel obligated to her, or trapped by neediness if she panicked about him leaving. Enough people married and divorced because they'd coerced their partner into the deal. No, she'd be patient, like Judi suggested. If he loved her, he'd either choose to stay or ask her to leave with him.

TWENTY-SIX

Maw leaned across peg and shut off the alarm clock while knocking a stack of catalogs and magazines to the floor. "Sorry," he mumbled before crawling out from the covers and heading for the bathroom.

Opening the bait shop by five o'clock was necessary, but painful. He finished getting showered, dressed and combed before brushing his teeth. A quick examination of the back of his head confirmed that he was not getting bald like his brothers had, and he shot up a quick thanks to God for getting good genes. He might have gained forty pounds since his prime, but he still had all his hair. He could lose the weight if he really wanted to. The thought comforted him.

On his way through the kitchen Maw grabbed a strawberry Pop-Tart, which he held between his teeth while sliding his arms into his winter coat. He always dialed the thermostat down to 57 degrees in the bait shop, so the first hour at work was pretty cold. Crossing the gravel parking lot, Maw noticed the pinprick lights of stars overhead. A clear sky! He hadn't seen that in weeks, he guessed. He paused to admire it for a moment before unlocking the door and turning on the lights.

He'd just stepped behind the register when his phone rang. "Maw's Bait and Tackle, home of the Pit Bull Minnow."

"Just checking to see if you're open," the voice said. "How safe is the water?"

"The river's starting to open up in spots, but if you stay out of the main channel, ice fishing should be good through the weekend."

"I heard in the news a lady drowned."

"A lady drowned?" Maw asked. "Here?"

"That's what the news said. A Bassville woman, discovered in Cooper's Bayou."

"Then I wouldn't fish this week if I were you," Maw said reluctantly. "Another week and you can get a boat in the river. Don't take your chances."

After hanging up, Maw switched off the "Open" sign in the window and walked back to his "laboratory." Who died, he wondered. He couldn't think of any women who'd be out fishing alone. Otto Zimm kept a shanty out there, but he was on vacation with his wife. Unless a local came in, he'd have to wait until the Pub opened in a couple of hours and then head into town to get the scoop.

June woke up with a jolt and slowly rolled over to see the numbers on her bedside clock flip to 8:47. Loyal's side of the bed was empty, he was milking cows. She didn't have to get breakfast for him for at least another hour.

Her heart still pounded hard in her chest at the memory of the dream. She was walking—if one could call it that, the surface of the ice slick with rain—towards Joanne. Joanne kept raising an arm and looking at her and June drew closer and closer to where she'd fallen through a hole in the ice. The sound of splashing water filled her ears and she tried to move faster, but when she got close enough to grasp Joanne's hand, her friend sank beneath the surface.

In her dream she dove across the ice, sliding to the edge of the hole, yelling "Joanne!" Her throat felt raw as though she'd actually been screaming. Had she been snoring? June swallowed hard and winced. The dream had left her feeling despair that she couldn't shake. The cold black river swallowed Joanne and left no trace, not even a bubble. She tried to remember the way Joanne's face had looked. Was it panic-stricken? No, June realized, it was calm. She'd simply bobbed up and down in the water, raising her arm and waving it towards June, silently gesturing for help.

What did it mean? Maybe it meant she'd failed and Joanne was dead. It was her fault. But how? She'd tried her hardest, she'd done all she could. June tossed back the covers and stuffed her feet into her slippers. She made the bed, straightened the bedroom, changed into jeans and a sweatshirt. She was halfway down the stairs to start making breakfast when she paused, hand on the railing and foot midway between the ninth and eighth step. Perhaps her dream meant she needed to pay closer attention. Joanne had never yelled for help. In real life she'd never made any visible appeal to her—or to anyone else as far as June knew, until the very end. But everyone knew she needed help. Maybe that was the message, she thought. In order to save somebody, you have to be aware of their suffering and just get in and give them a hand. You don't wait for them to start yelling because by then it's probably too late.

June resumed descending the stairs and with each step she took inventory of the people in her world. Mona didn't need any help, really. She was self-sufficient. Loyal was fine, she'd always helped him more than he needed. Sean only needed her support from the cheering section, she sent him cards at college and let him know she believed in him. But he was off being successful at college and lining up his future career. Her parents? Well, they needed her help, but she did pitch in every week. She brought them shopping, cleaned their apartment, managed doctors' appointments. And they knew she would do more if they asked, but she also didn't want to insult what little sense of independence they had by hovering too much.

Arlyce? Well, she could babysit the kids, she supposed. Or bring over the occasional casserole to cut her some slack. Dottie didn't need anything now that their farm had sold and Angie was in remission. She only needed companionship, which June gave her each week at Stitch 'n Bitch. Who else?

June pulled out a frying pan and opened the fridge to grab a carton of eggs. Snuffy, who was technically homeless although he lived at Grumpy's, could probably use a hot meal and someone to run his laundry. But aside from him, no one she knew directly *needed* anything from her.

Maybe her nightmare was a sign, she thought. She lit the front right burner with a match and watched the flames flare up in a perfect circle. She needed to figure out who wasn't making any noise but desperately needed help. Who was quietly struggling?

The thought burned in her while she finished making breakfast— toast, eggs, applesauce. She waited at the table with a cup of coffee and allowed the idea to simmer. She'd felt discontented and restless for some time now but the past week had given her life meaning. That sounded audacious, but it was true. She'd felt purposeful. She'd gotten out of bed each day thinking about something beyond herself and her household. She'd gone from fretting over what the bathroom scale said and scouring the grocery store flyer for coupons to doing something that mattered. Helping Joanne mattered. She needed to keep doing something like that, she thought.

While she refilled her coffee cup, she saw Loyal leaving the barn. He strode towards the house and June thought about how he never seemed to doubt his place in the world. His purpose was to keep the farm running, and that looked different every day depending on all kinds of things—the weather, illness, prices. Mona now shared that purpose, even though it looked different than Loyal's vision of the farm, but together they'd work it out. She'd never cared much about farming. It was their family's livelihood, but she didn't get involved beyond feeding hired workers when they cut hay and occasionally lending a hand in the barn when Loyal needed it.

But now she had some resolve. June lifted her chin and greeted her husband with a smile. "Good morning."

He leaned in for a kiss after he removed his coat and boots. Then he washed his hands at the sink. June served up their plates and joined him at the table. "I think I know what I want to do."

"About what?" Loyal asked around a mouthful of eggs.

"With my life."

Loyal raised his eyebrows.

"This afternoon I'm going to Northport and apply for a position at the women's shelter."

"Why do you want to do that?" Loyal asked. "This isn't about Joanne, is it?"

"It is, but not in the way you think," June told him. "I've felt so alive this last week. I hated sneaking around and keeping things secret, but I felt like I was finally doing something really important and useful by trying to help her. I want to keep doing that, even though Joanne is beyond helping. I mean, I'll do what I can to make sure Joanne gets justice, but there are lots of women like her."

"I don't know, honey," Loyal began but June interrupted him.

"Don't tell me I don't have time or I'm just reacting emotionally. I've felt useless ever since the kids moved out. All I do is keep house

148

and how hard it that—keeping house for the two of us? I certainly have time on my hands to do something *useful* and it will make me happy. I don't want there to be another Joanne, another woman dead because she didn't have anywhere to go. I can clean rooms or answer the phone at the shelter. Maybe I'll even get a little legal training and be able to offer some counseling." She put her hand on his before he could speak. "I'm not saying I'll do this right away, but for goodness sake, Loyal, I'm only forty-six. I've got plenty of life left in me and I'm not going to spend it sitting around here knitting sweaters."

Loyal shut his mouth and swallowed. He turned his hand over and grasped her fingers in his. "Are you sure this is a good idea? I do depend on you. You are useful here."

"Aw, Loyal," June sighed. "I can do what I do around here in my sleep. You matter to me, it isn't that. I just need something to make me feel like I have a reason to get out of bed in the morning. It's not a midlife crisis. I spent the first chunk of my life as a student, then I was a mother—but now what am I? Nothing. A wife. What does that actually require of me? I want to do something meaningful and help others. What happened with Joanne is going to haunt me." June thought about telling Loyal her dream, but that probably would not help her cause. He put no stock in things that weren't real.

"I'm starting by volunteering at the women's shelter. It won't cost anything but gas to drive me there. Maybe over time I'll get a paid position. Maybe I'll even get a shelter opened up here, in Bassville. Or maybe I'll just publicize the issue of abuse and educate women about their choices."

"Those are some big goals," Loyal said.

"I know. I plan to live at least another thirty years. I've got time."

His eyes crinkled at the edges and he shook his head. "It this is what you really want to do, how can I stop you?"

"You can't. But I prefer to do this with your support."

"Can we leave the dining room a dining room if you do this?" Loyal asked.

June lightly punched him in the arm before digging her fork into her scrambled eggs. She wasn't giving up on that project either, but one thing at a time.

Across the yard Mona walked in to check on her plants. While watering flats of seedlings, she noticed that another row of pepper plants had started to wilt. Inspecting the leaves, she didn't see any fungus, mold or traces of bugs. Maybe she'd bring one into the Farm Services office and see if anyone there might have an idea.

She'd nearly finished her morning chores when the greenhouse door banged open and Jenny plopped down in one of the lawn chairs. "Holy shit!"

"And good morning to you," Mona said. She watched Jenny pick up the barn cat that had trailed her in from the yard and start scratching behind its ears.

"Did you hear they found Joanne dead in the river?"

"I did. It's awful. What's the latest?"

"They brought The Pole down to the Cop Shop for questioning. Guess he was there for about an hour, then he went home. Sheila said she saw his truck parked behind the building and the lights on."

"Well, they must not think he's responsible if they let him go."

"Or they're waiting until they have enough evidence to arrest him," Jenny said.

"Yesterday people wondered if he hadn't fallen through the river, too. I was shocked when he showed up in the parking lot at the Pub."

"Wait a minute—*you saw him?*"

"Yeah, I was headed home about ten o'clock when I saw him. I talked to him."

"Holy shit. What did he say?"

"Well, it seemed like he didn't know what had happened to Joanne. I told him they found her in the river and he took off running. I didn't know if he went running to or away from the police." Mona sat across from Jenny in the other lawn chair.

"Huh. Could swear Sheila said they brought him in for questioning, but maybe he went there himself."

"That would make him seem less guilty."

Jenny nodded. The cat on her lap rolled over and offered its belly for scratching. "Are all your cats this weird?"

"That's not my cat." Mona could understand the cat's attraction to Jenny, however. She had the longest fingernails, painted dark purple today, and those nails were going to town on the cat. She decided not to mention the ringworm and fleas a barn cat carried, Jenny would freak out.

"It's a terrible thing to think about—dying like that." Jenny repositioned the cat so she was back to scratching its ears and neck.

"I know. I think she'd have died fast because of how cold the water was. Maybe she went into shock and didn't really feel anything."

"God, I hope so."

"She was always so nice." Mona propped her feet on an overturned bucket. "Every time I'd go into Bud's she was friendly. And she had a pretty smile."

"I always felt sorry for her. I mean, getting beat up all the time. How terrible. How desperate would you have to be to put up with that kind of crap?"

Mona shrugged. She couldn't understand it either.

"Remember when she was in the hospital for a week?"

"When her pelvis was cracked and her leg broke?" Mona asked.

"Yeah, that's the one. She said she was in a car accident, but no one ever saw any wrecked car. Obviously she was lying, but why would you lie about someone breaking your legs? Still, everybody just went along with her story, including me."

"That's the million-dollar question," Mona said.

"Speaking of questions, has Jake popped one yet?" Jenny leaned forward eagerly.

Mona pulled her lips into a tight line. "No."

"He should, you guys have been together almost a year. What's he waiting for? If he's moving for his job, it's the perfect timing! What do you think you'd do in Atlanta if you moved there with him?"

That was the million-dollar question, Mona thought. She also thought how nice it was just to sit and talk to Jenny when she was acting normal and not psychotic. Why couldn't she always be this way? "I don't know. I haven't really thought about it."

"Liar!" Jenny pointed a finger at her, her bracelets jangling up her arm.

"Yeah," Mona wrinkled her nose. "I am. I have thought about it and I honestly don't know. Would I try going to school? Get a job? I don't even know what kind of job I'd get—I don't want to work in a bar or a restaurant, but could you see me working in a store?"

"You could be a secretary," Jenny suggested.

"I feel like that would get boring."

"Why? You'd have weekends and nights free!"

"Yeah, but you'd be stuck in an office all day looking at the same people all the time."

"You're stuck behind the bar all day."

"True," Mona agreed. "But at least the view changes. The river looks different every season."

"You want to get out of the bar anyway," Jenny pointed out.

"I know." Mona said. "I guess I want to leave the bar on my own terms, not because I *have* to move. I planned on getting this greenhouse business running and then quitting there. I actually filled out the registration form for a couple of classes at the technical college."

"If you get a job at a clothing store like The Limited you get a great discount. They have malls in Atlanta, right?" Jenny tugged on the edge of her leather jacket as if to demonstrate the power of a good employee discount.

"Probably, but I don't want to work at someone else's place. I like the farm because I helped build it. It's mine, I have control over how I run it, what I do here. I might not do all the dairy stuff like Dad, but maybe I will. I just really like it here."

Jenny narrowed her eyes at Mona. "You didn't want to leave with T.C., either. You're just too chicken-shit to leave town."

Mona knew Jenny was right, but it wasn't fear keeping her here, was it? "Would you move? I don't see you packing up a U-Haul to chase your dreams."

"Don't need to." Jenny boosted the cat off her lap and started brushing fur off her coat. "I'm living my dream."

"What's that? Working at the mall and chasing Beau?"

"When he's ready to settle down, I'll be right here," Jenny said. "Did I tell you what I've started doing?"

"Oh no—what?"

Jenny gave her a smug grin before announcing, "I have a storage unit where I've started putting things for when we move in together. I picked up some really cute rugs and towels. I've got an entertainment center, lamps ..."

"Jenny!" Mona exclaimed. "Does Beau know about this? Geez, you two aren't even together right now. I don't think that's such a wise idea."

"Of course Beau doesn't know, he doesn't need to."

Mona closed her eyes and imagined a vision of Beau hogtied in an apartment, trussed up like the angry boss in *9 to 5*, kept prisoner among matching throw pillows and vases. "Good grief." Jenny was really crazy. Certifiably nuts.

Jenny stood to leave. "You should offer to help Jake shop for his new place when he moves. Guys appreciate a woman's touch, and if you pick out all his stuff, he'd have a really hard time letting some other woman take over your territory. My advice is to make your move now before he gets out there and loneliness hits, and he's going out for cocktails with the airline stewardess in apartment 9-B. You'll regret it if you don't stake your claim."

Mona waved Jenny off. Judi had advised her to wait it out for the best outcome. Totally opposite advice from two friends. The choice wasn't hard, though. She was not going to worm her way in like that. She had too much pride to play that game.

Later that morning June stopped in town to check on her parents and fill up the gas tank. She was waiting for the attendant to give her her change when The Pole walked through the door. He headed straight for the back cooler where he grabbed a can of Pepsi and then he turned and looked at her. "Hi, June!" he greeted her with a big smile.

She turned back to the attendant trying to decide how to reply.

The Pole took up a lot of space, physically and with his personality. He started chatting up the attendant and leaned in beside June, his bicep as big around has June's head. She ignored his presence and held out her hand for change.

"What's the matter? Everything okay out on the farm?" The Pole asked. His voice sounded concerned and June inhaled deeply before answering.

"Yes. It's fine." She paused. "You seem well. Considering."

"Considering what? Joanne? It tears me up. I haven't slept since they told me last night. I gotta plan her funeral, but I don't even know where to start."

June stared at him coldly. Tears glistened at the edge of his eyes and he bowed his shaggy head. She studied him closely, his tanned skin was lined with wrinkles above his beard, which was flecked with grey. He was a good looking man, but evil to the core.

"She wasn't real religious, you know, but I think it would mean a lot to do a church funeral. I think the priest over at the Catholic church will do it." He swiped at his eyes with his fingers.

"Really?" June asked in her most sarcastic tone. "You really expect people to believe you feel *bad* right now? You killed her."

The Pole frowned and the attendant froze, holding June's three dollars and sixty cents a few inches from June's hand.

"You did. You did! Even if the cops can't prove it, you know you did and *I* know you did. You drove her to it—you probably found her out on the ice and pushed her through because you knew she was leaving you."

"What are you talking about?" he asked, his voice raising.

"You are a murderer." She spat out the accusation.

The door chimed again and Judi walked in, digging through her purse, oblivious to the drama unfolding in front of the cash register. Judi pulled out her wallet and smiled warmly at everyone. "Hi there! How's it going?" She gave The Pole a sympathetic squint of her eyes and put her hand on his forearm. "If you need anything …"

"He doesn't need anything," June said, fury making her hands tremble. She grabbed her change from the attendant with a brisk "thanks." June pointed her finger at The Pole's broad chest. "You are responsible for that poor woman's death. It is your fault." She glanced over her shoulder at Judi and added, "He doesn't deserve anyone's pity. Joanne deserved our pity, for being his punching bag all those years. This man?" June jerked her chin up to dismiss him. "He's worthless scum."

She fled the gas station so rattled she could barely get the key to turn in the ignition. Her face felt hot and she knew the whole town would talk about the scene she'd just caused, but she didn't care. She'd call him out every time she saw him. To do anything less would be cowardly. What did she have to be afraid of? No, Joanne was dead, she owed it to Joanne to hold The Pole accountable as long as he hung around Bassville. Even if he hadn't killed her, the way he treated her was the reason she was out on the bayou. But June believed in her heart that The Pole was directly involved in Joanne's death. No other explanation made sense.

TWENTY-SEVEN

FRIDAY NIGHT MONA SET the table and lit candles she'd placed around the kitchen. Candlelight was a good accompaniment to spaghetti. Garlic bread toasted in the oven, filling her house with an aroma that made her hungry. A bottle of wine chilled in the fridge. She tossed salad greens from her greenhouse with dressing and portioned it into two bowls. Jake would arrive any minute for date night.

With nothing left to do in the kitchen, she headed to the bathroom to touch up her lip gloss and pouf her bangs a little more. Nothing had changed between her and Jake, they were on the same path to nowhere, but his job offer gave her a sense of urgency. It was, she determined, time for him to shit or get off the pot. Was she prepared to end it if he didn't move things forward? She didn't want to, but what would happen if he moved?

One option was to follow him, but she wouldn't—couldn't. She didn't want to leave Bassville and she definitely would not leave without the security of a wedding ring. Moving in with Jake held no promises, not that he'd offered that, but she planned to hold out for the real deal.

The other option was to stay together but live far apart. Could they make a long-distance relationship work? Phone conversations cost money and Mona didn't know how often they'd see each other until that job wrapped up. Judi made it work with William and they'd been doing it for two years—but their distance was only three hours of driving, not eighteen. It wasn't as though she wanted to be with anyone besides Jake. Life would be so much easier if he didn't take the job—or if Beyer's Construction would offer him something local and he wouldn't have to move at all.

Wishful thinking. She stared her face in the bathroom mirror. What did her future hold?

Jake. She hoped it involved Jake. She'd hold out and wait for things to move at his pace because she didn't want him to decide under pressure and regret it. That would be the worst outcome of all, she knew.

The doorbell rang once and she heard Jake's boots on the floor. "Hey, Mona! Smells delicious in here!"

She took a deep breath and went out to greet him.

After the supper dishes were washed and put away, Jake followed Mona into the living room where they sat on the couch. "TV?" she asked.

"I'm good," he said and leaned back into the cushions. "I'm stuffed. Too bad it's so wet out there or we could go for a walk." He held out an arm, inviting her to snuggle into his side. She did, and inhaled the clean smell of him.

"It's so crazy about Joanne drowning in the bayou," Jake said.

"Does anyone know why she was out there with the ice being so thin?"

"No. In fact it sounds like she was alone out there. I wouldn't be shocked if The Pole had anything to do with it. Did I tell you I saw him that same night?"

"What?"

"Yeah, it was kind of weird. I was leaving work and he came through the back parking lot. He acted surprised when I told him Joanne was dead—and then he ran off. I didn't know if he ran away because he was guilty or because he was upset."

"Did you feel afraid?" Jake asked.

"I did. I mean, he's always been nice to me, but the way he treated Joanne makes me nervous. Especially now that she's dead."

"I hate talking about it." Jake shifted into the couch cushions and rested his arms around her shoulders. "Let's change the subject."

"Why do you hate talking about it?" Mona wanted to know.

Jake shrugged. "Anything like that—a man hurting a woman— it's not right."

"I feel like nobody talking about it makes it okay that he did it."

"I never thought of it that way."

Mona brushed her fingertips along his forearms. She didn't know what else to say and she didn't want to wreck the night fixating on something depressing.

"Did you hear the latest about Maw?" Jake asked her.

"What's that?"

"He's going to be in a documentary. Some guy is making a movie about his bait shop and how he makes his minnows."

"No fooling? Where did you hear this?"

"Beau. He was in there the other day and said the kids were pulling everything out of his back stock room to stage a laboratory where he'd demonstrate the minnow-breeding process."

"Wait a minute," Mona said. "Minnow breeding process? I thought

Maw sold regular golden shiners."

"He does. But he tells everyone they're special, right? So this movie is supposed to show how that happens."

"This sounds pretty shady if you ask me."

Jake chuckled. "It is. I'm pretty curious. All I know is that Beau said he had set up wires, old car parts and pipes to make it seem like a science lab."

"So, it's like a play or something."

"Yeah, only I don't know if the movie people will appreciate it or not."

Mona shook her head and grinned. "Leave it to Maw."

"Think it'll be as nuts around here as it was last spring?"

"I do. And I'm ready for it. The way I figure it, I've got one more fishing season to work until I can make a living off the farm venture."

"I'd love to look over your business plan sometime," Jake said.

"Business plan?"

"You know, the numbers, the projected sales, all that stuff."

"I don't really have one."

"What do you mean?" Jake asked, his voice higher with disbelief.

Mona shrugged. "I just guesstimated things."

"You can't plan your future by *guessing*," Jake said.

"Huh," Mona said. *That's an interesting thing for you to say.*

"Seriously, you need to write down all your expenses and your revenue streams and do the math. Don't you want to know for sure when you can quit the bar?"

Stay on target, she reminded herself, *he's talking about your business, not our relationship. Totally different things.* "I never wrote a business plan before."

"I'll help you. It'll be fun. I took a couple classes in college. How about this weekend? Pull all your paperwork together, the accounting and receipts and everything, and we can go over all the parts."

"Thanks."

They sat for a few moments listening to the rain on the roof. Finally Mona spoke up again. "You know," she said slowly, "a lot of planning for the future is guessing. Take us, for instance."

Jake sat very still. "Go on."

"Well, you're still deciding about your job, right? And I'm sitting here waiting. I guess we'll be together, but I don't really know for sure how this is going to work out between us. What you decide for work could change things a lot for us."

"I realize that," Jake said quietly. "You're being wonderful—supportive and patient while I figure it out. I guess—there's that word again, huh? I guess I need a little more time. Leon Beyer wants to know by the end of next week." Jake gently took Mona by the shoulders and turned her to face him. He looked into her eyes with a sincere expression. "I love you. The next step here is a big one, I'm not ready for it yet. But you have to believe that I love you."

Mona nodded.

"So, business plan this weekend. I'll bring my old textbook and we'll get that baby going."

"Okay."

Jake lifted her chin with his hand and waited for her to meet his gaze. "I'm not going to let you down."

TWENTY-EIGHT

AFTER A SLOW, GRINDING weekend at the bait shop, Maw faced Monday with an optimistic eye on the calendar. The river was breaking up which meant fishermen would start showing up. He had faith that Joanne's death wouldn't scare people away; it was a freak accident on ice and had nothing to do with fishing. Pausing in his morning routine, Maw surveyed his reflection on the metallic surface of a minnow tank. He had gotten a haircut two days ago and his skin had a thin line of whiteness where his hair had previously covered his neck, forehead and ears. Maw tugged the front of the white lab coat he'd bought and glanced around the "lab" he and the kids had designed in his former stock room.

Gone were the stacks of boxes, plastic packages of lures, piles of T-shirts. Two long tables stretched along the walls. Maw had taped up a dozen intelligent-looking equations written on notepaper. Two aquariums (one the former home of his daughter's long-dead pet hamster) were up and running. Electrical cords, wiring, tubing and PVC piping were laid out in various patterns, all form and no function. It was time for a test run of the system, he decided.

After retrieving a few golden shiners from the tank in the shop, Maw slipped the first one into an aquarium and practiced his demonstration.

"This is a golden shiner, *Notemigonus crysoleucas*. A typical minnow used for bait in the Wissipaw River, its characteristics include a lateral line with a pronounced downward curve, with its lowest point just above the pelvic fins; and there is a fleshy keel lacking scales on the belly between the pelvic fins and the base of the anal fin." God, he sounded brilliant.

Maw reached for one of the jars lined up on the other table. Inside was a mixture of tapioca pudding and cooking oil. "Inside this jar is DNA from a tiger shark, one of the ocean's most ferocious predators." He'd wanted to go great white, but Peg had talked him out of it. "The hybridization of the shark and minnow create the fierce, fighting minnow sold as bait here at Maw's Bait and Tackle. This procedure is delicate and patented, trademark pending."

Here's the part where Maw used one of his daughter's sculpting tools from her art kit to perform a brief and bloody surgery on a minnow writhing on his palm. He'd read that visual tricks were best performed with a distraction. Blood and guts would distract and make the science look legitimate. The process was simple and tested. In the first aquarium he'd stock minnows in regular water. The second aquarium got stocked with minnows in water spiked with Mountain Dew. The caffeine made the minnows shoot around the tank like crazed hyperactive teenager. He disguised the color of the water by adding food coloring, which he'd explain was the stabilizing chemical that protected the fish.

Previous experiments killed the caffeinated minnows, but that was okay. They stayed alive long enough to sell the scam. He only needed them to look lively for about twenty minutes, tops. The minnow on which he performed the "operation" was a decoy. It stood to reason that he didn't surgically alter every single one of the millions of minnows he sold. He surgically altered one generation, which he then bred and multiplied to create the mighty predator minnow. He glanced at the wall where his sons had created a poster of the "PUGNACIOUS MINNOW FAMILY TREE."

"This is only a simulation of the original operation," Maw went on to tell the imaginary camera crew. "We imparted a small amount of the shark DNA into the minnow's brain." This was the tricky part, he had to scoop out a tiny amount of the tapioca pudding mixture and make like he was "injecting" it into the minnow's head. He hoped the cameras didn't take a close up shot. He opened his fingers to reveal a fully "transformed" minnow, one actually made furious by the lack of water and pain inflicted on it. Maw then closed his fist around the minnow and dunked it in the water. He "palmed it" by sliding it up his shirt sleeve while stirring his hand around and "releasing" the bait. No one could possibly notice no minnow added to an aquarium loaded with fish jetting around in every direction.

"The altered minnow will continue to grow to adulthood under our watch here in the lab," Maw continued. He felt like he made a convincing presentation, he had the pitch down cold. "After it matures, its offspring will inherit the body of a minnow with the predatory instincts of a shark, making it the ideal bait for catching walleye and white bass in all depths of water in the Wissipaw River."

"This process took years to fully perfect, what you witnessed was the culmination of many failures." Here's where Maw rolled up his shirt sleeve, not the one with the dying minnow, his left shirt sleeve, to reveal a nasty scar from a night of teenaged debauchery involving the Dohill brothers, a bottle of peppermint schnapps and cow tipping. He'd gotten tangled up with a fence post and rusty barbed wire. Maw pointed to this scar and solemnly pronounced it "too much shark, not enough minnow in one attempt."

Feeling satisfied with his performance, Maw walked back into the shop and shook the limp, lifeless minnow out of his sleeve and into a garbage bin. He took a swig of Mountain Dew and looked at his to-do list. Later, he thought, and turned his attention to the Word-of-the-Day calendar by the cash register. *Obfuscate. A verb that means to complicate or confuse.* That seemed like a good omen, Maw decided. "I obfuscated the process of designing a genetically engineered minnow. Obfuscate." His voice echoed in the empty shop. "Bring on the fishermen."

TWENTY-NINE

On Monday, June had just finished scheduling a doctor's appointment for her mother when the doorbell rang. Everyone came through the back door. The chimes from the front of the house sounded strange to her ears and it took her a moment to react. She bowed sideways as she approached the door so she could see through the glass. A tall figure dressed in dark clothing appeared blurry but the hat was a giveaway. Joe.

"Hi," she said, swinging the door open and gesturing him inside.

He politely stomped his feet on the mat before following her to the living room where she invited him to sit. "I'm afraid I have news that won't make you very happy," he began.

June interrupted him. "Can I get you coffee or water?" She was the daughter of former bar owners, being a good hostess was ingrained in her.

Joe shook his head and wiped his palms across his thighs. June sat across from him and folded her hands in her lap.

"We searched the entire area and found no evidence that Joanne was killed. The autopsy report declared death by drowning. All of the evidence—fingerprints and so forth—indicate that she was alone at the time of death. We did find a flask in her jacket pocket. Brandy. That may have been a contributing factor, but we have to conclude her death was accidental." Joe shrugged his shoulders apologetically. "I know you want Adam to be held responsible, but if she was depressed or scared and under the influence …"

"Baloney." June spat the word out. "He was there."

"June, he came to the police station later that evening. He reported to the officer on duty that your daughter told him about Joanne's death."

"What? No, that's not right."

"The Po—Adam said he'd been in Northport much of the day and produced receipts that prove his claim. One from Fleet Farm was marked 9:32. You can't fake a cash register receipt, June. I went to his place this morning and he was able to show me all the items he'd purchased." Joe gazed down at the carpet. "I'm sorry. There's absolutely no evidence that he was anywhere near Joanne when she died and we can't arrest someone on suspicion. The truth is, Joanne was probably suicidal, maybe had drunk too much and that may have impaired her judgment. We have to conclude it was an accident."

June shook her head. "What? An accident? No. No no no."

"This could go either way, you know. The evidence leans towards suicide. I'm trying to be kind here, June. You gotta appreciate that."

She leaned back against the chair cushion and closed her eyes. It felt like someone had stomped on her chest and squashed all of the air out of her lungs. She opened her eyes and stared hard at Joe. "What about the battery? She'd had a sling on her arm, you saw her face with the black eye. Can you pin that on him?"

167

Joe shrugged. "What's the point?"

"What's the point?" June's voice rose. "The point is that he's a bad man and needs to be held accountable for what he did. He hurt her and even if he didn't directly attack her, it was because of the way he treated her that she ended up out on that river. Her blood is on his hands."

"She'd have to file a report accusing him of battery," Joe said in a quiet voice. He unfolded his hands and spread his fingers wide apart. "It's kind of late for that."

"Shit. So what then?"

"Joanne's death is ruled an accident and that's all."

"So The Pole gets to walk away like nothing happened."

"He was really upset when he came to the station the other night. He was crying, June."

"Pfft. Crocodile tears."

"I don't know. He seemed genuinely sad."

"It's an act. He's a good old boy that everybody loves, but the truth is he's a creep. Fine." June stood. "You don't want to hold him accountable. That doesn't mean other people can't."

Joe remained seated on the couch and shifted in his spot. "That's the other thing."

She cocked her hip and crossed her arms, waiting for whatever other bad news Joe needed to impart.

Joe squinted at the ceiling before looking up at June. "Um, Adam dropped by the station this morning."

"Uh huh."

"He shared with me that you accused him of murdering Joanne in front of customers at the gas station."

"For Pete's sake, Joe. Judi was the only other customer, and the kid working the register. So what? What? I can't exercise my right to express my opinion?"

"I'm just saying you probably should back off talking to him in public."

"Why?" June sat up straighter and waited.

"Look, he didn't do anything official. I asked him not to and told him I'd talk to you. The thing is, he has a legal right to file a report if you harass him. And if he files enough reports, he could accuse you of harassment. That's a misdemeanor."

"And what do you classify punching your wife?"

Joe exhaled a long sigh. "I know what you're saying and I'm not saying I disagree with you. The trouble is, Joanne's dead and she never filed any charges against Adam. He's not dead and he could file a complaint against *you*. I don't want to see this escalate, June. You're a good person, don't go looking for trouble." Joe stood and tugged at his jacket, which had ridden up his back while sitting on the couch.

"I'm not looking for trouble. I'm looking for justice." June realized she sounded like a cartoon superhero, but she kept her icy expression. She was serious and Joe had to know it.

"Be smart, that's all I'm asking." Joe held out his hand and June shook it before following him to the door. She shut it behind him and sank to the floor, right there on the carpet, and she hugged her knees and screamed.

How was this fair, she thought. *Joanne's a real victim—beaten and now dead, but everyone seems eager to just sweep her body under the rug and move on like nothing bad ever happened. I call out someone on their bad behavior, their obvious bad behavior—no secret about The Pole's treatment of Joanne. Hell, there were enough police calls to his address in the newspaper to prove how awful he was. And yet somehow I'm the bad guy? I'm the bad guy for calling him out?*

She pictured Joanne's face, gaunt but hopeful when she talked about moving to California. She imagined what it must have been like to live so isolated from everyone, embarrassed that the person you lived with treated you terribly and deemed you too dumb to leave or even—this was worse—even *deserving* of such abuse. June shook her head. She had two choices. She could do what Joe wanted, shut up and act like nothing ever happened. Or she could keep speaking the truth.

June thought back to a course she'd taken in college. The class learned about political dissent, specifically in Chile. The professor, a short, stout man who wore wire rimmed glasses and bowties, repeated the same phrase over and over throughout the semester: "Silence is compliance." Those three words had never left her memory. She'd repeated them to her kids when they were little and came home with tales of school bus bullies. *Saying nothing is the same as going along with the bad behavior.*

Her choice was easy. What was the worst thing that could possibly happen to her? Joe already told her, it was a misdemeanor charge. Big deal. Joanne dying was a way bigger deal.

THIRTY

Mona dumped a tray of pepper seedlings onto a pile of compost. She had misgivings about this decision. Whatever was wrong with the seedlings could infect the compost heap and keep spreading among her other plants, but she was pretty sure it wasn't a disease or a pest. The fact was, peppers required a certain climate to thrive and her greenhouse wasn't hot or light enough. It would cost more money than she had to install grow lights and keep the heat up against the winter chill, so her dream of raising peppers would have to wait.

She ignored the metaphor poking its way into her mind. "I'd thrive anywhere," she declared to the nagging doubt. "I could live just fine in Atlanta as I do here." *Sheesh. Here I am talking to myself now.* She turned the compost over with a small pitchfork and watched the police cruiser back out of her parents' driveway. Was something wrong with her grandparents? She couldn't think of any other reason for the cops to visit. She leaned the empty tray against the side of the greenhouse on her way back to the house.

Inside the back door, she called out for her mother while prying off her boots.

"In here," June answered from the living room.

Mona walked in to find her mother on the floor in front of the door. She rushed over and knelt in front of her. "Is it Grandma?"

June frowned at her. "What? No."

"Why were the police here?"

June rumpled her fingers through her hair and scrunched up her face to fight the tears. "It's stupid. It's about The Pole."

"What about him? You know, it was really weird. I saw him at the Pub the night Joanne died. I thought he already knew and he didn't. I couldn't decide whether he was taking it really hard or acting guilty."

"That man puts on a great act."

"What do you mean?"

June ignored the question. "Joe came by to tell me they're ruling Joanne's death accidental." She waited to watch her daughter's reaction.

"Really?"

"She was murdered."

"How do you know that?"

"She was hiding in Otto Zimm's ice shanty until Arlyce and I could get her to the Greyhound station in Northport. She was going to leave him, finally. Joanne was just waiting to get in touch with her daughter so she wouldn't be alone."

"Wait, what? How was she living in Otto's ice shanty?"

"We hid her there so The Pole couldn't find her."

"Why wouldn't you just let her stay here with you?"

"She was too scared of anyone else knowing where she was. She didn't trust any men, not even your dad."

"But they're saying she fell through thin ice."

"Why? Why would she walk further out on the ice when she knew it was dangerous? Why would she even leave the shanty in that rain and walk out onto the river? If anything, she'd walk towards shore. No, she was running away, he probably found her and either chased her out there and she fell in or he pushed her in. I know for a fact she didn't go there voluntarily."

"That's a pretty big accusation, Mom."

"I know, but I know the truth. He was looking for her and he found her. She's dead. It's not a coincidence."

"I don't know—"

"Acting. Same as how he acts nice and friendly to everyone but then goes home and belts her around. This man helps Gene and Dottie roof their barn and bashes Joanne in the skull. He's a psychopath."

"So ... why were the police here?"

June told her daughter about Joe's warning and watched her expression shift from skeptical to concerned.

"I can't believe they'd take me to task for saying what everyone already knows."

"Well, you can't exactly go around telling everyone everything you think."

"Why not? If it's the truth, why not?" June persisted.

Mona had no answer for her mom. She felt tired. The Pole, he always treated her decent, but she didn't like that Joanne got knocked around, that she sat there so silently beside him in the Pub and never spoke up for herself. *But I sat there, too. Whose fault was that?* Joanne could've left him a thousand other times. It was just bad luck that she picked March and an ice shanty.

"The fence seems like a comfortable place to sit, sweetie, but I feel like this is one of those times when you have to pick a side."

Moreover, Mona thought, what was happening to her mother? June never got riled up about anything. Not even when Sean decided he didn't want to come back and work the farm. Even then she was the voice of reason, keeping peace between everyone. Now her mother had a steely look in her eyes, her jaw set like she was ready to fight.

People would forget about Joanne—they always did eventually after someone died. Life would go on, there would be fishing and boaters and town politics and new houses built. In another year no one would talk about how The Pole used to beat up his girlfriend and one day she sank into a river and died, except in late spring when the ice started to break up. But that didn't mean Joanne *should* be forgotten.

"I hope they aren't letting him make the funeral arrangements," June said suddenly. "We've been trying to call Rhonda and find out what she wants to do."

"Who's Rhonda?"

"Joanne's daughter."

"Wait—how do you know her daughter?"

"I don't. Joanne planned to move in with her and she gave me and Arlyce her number so we could call and tell her Joanne was coming. The police probably notified her and her sisters, but I feel like I should call her, too."

"What else have you been up to, Mom? Geez, I thought you were holed up trying new recipes and knitting sweaters."

"Nope." June stood and brushed off her pants. "I'm applying to volunteer at the women's shelter in Northport."

Mona actually felt her mouth drop open. "Wow." She stared up at her mother. She looked like she always did, sturdy, her hairstyle a conservative bob, frosted to conceal the grey. As far as she could recall, June didn't express strong opinions. This declaration felt shocking. Mona examined her mother for other signs of change. She wasn't dressing younger, which was something that made Mona and her friends nuts. Seeing middle-aged women suddenly wear trendy clothes made them come off as desperate. It was more dignified to settle into one's age. Everything else her mom did was solidly *her*. She knit, baked, sold raffle tickets for the Ladies' Auxiliary. This volunteering in Northport business surprised Mona.

"Are you sure that's a good idea?" Mona knew her question was stupid the moment she said it.

"How," June paused for emphasis, "would helping people in need ever be a bad idea?" She scrambled to her feet and left Mona sitting there.

After a few seconds Mona joined her mother in the kitchen. "I'm sorry. Of course it's a good idea. You've always supported me in things, I don't know why I just said that to you." She was gratified to see her mother smile at her. All was forgiven, but things had gotten weird.

THIRTY-ONE

Mona WENT TO WORK Tuesday evening feeling apprehensive. The moon was full and the natives were restless. She felt it in her bones. It would be one of those weird nights. Dob Dohill won the Sawdust City Contest, or as she called it, the dam bet, and sat at the bar lording it over all of the others who'd bought a square. "Six hundred dollars in cold, hard cash. How to spend, how to spend." He kept brushing a stack of twenty dollar bills beneath his chin and grinning at everyone.

"Good question, Dob," Spade said. "How about you start by buying us a round?"

Dob nodded and looked at Beau Longwell. "Do you have any ideas?"

Beau just snorted and shook his head in reply. The goading and boasting and drinking continued for an hour and everyone seemed in high spirits when The Pole walked through the door. Mona watched him approach the crowd at the bar. His shaggy hair stuck out like he'd slept on it—normally he wet it down and combed it when he came out. His flannel shirt was misbuttoned and one side hung lower than the other. His huge work boots were untied and clomped across the floor.

"Hey there," Mona broke the silence. "What can I get you?"

The Dohills shifted in their seats and nodded a greeting at The Pole. Spade raised a hand and Beau clapped The Pole on his shoulder and said, "Hey, sorry about Joanne."

"Thanks, buddy." The Pole slumped onto the nearest empty barstool and looked dolefully at Mona with bloodshot eyes. "Just a beer."

"Catch him on me," Dob offered.

Mona watched the scene unfold. Scotty stared at The Pole wordlessly, Maw asked how he was getting on, Jake echoed Beau's condolences. The Pole nodded and accepted their words. He seemed sad, possibly remorseful, but in Mona's mind the jury was still out. She was glad to see some of the men reluctant to chum up to him, reading their standoffish behavior as condemnation of The Pole's treatment of Joanne.

"What do you suppose made her walk out onto the water like that?" Maw asked.

"I don't know." The Pole stared at his chapped and calloused hands clasped together on the bar.

"No, how could you?" Scotty said. Everyone looked over at him. His eyes were round and he continued speaking. "I mean, you hadn't seen her in a few days, right? You were shacked up with that lady you met at the Beach Club up in Clearwater and then when you did finally go home, she was gone."

The Pole cocked his head. "Why are you saying this, Scotty?"

"Because it's true. Joanne had left you. In fact, now that I think

177

about it, when's the last time anyone saw her?"

"My mom said she'd seen her the day before she died," Mona said quietly.

"Ah, two days after I'd been fishing in that bayou and saw a man breaking into the shanties," Scotty said. "That was you, wasn't it?"

"What are you talking about?" The Pole asked.

"You made fun of me, but come to think of it, where were you that day when I was fishing?" Scotty pointed at the Dohills. "Was he working for you?"

The brothers shook their heads, but leaned forward, intrigued by the drama unfolding in front of them.

"Yeah. Funny about that."

"I was probably home or maybe on a run for supplies," The Pole said.

"Where were you three days ago?" Scotty asked Jake.

"Working over in Northport all day," Jake said in a mild voice.

"How about you?" Scotty directed this question at Beau.

Beau smirked for a brief second, but then realized how serious Scotty was. "I woke up at Jenny's," he admitted, "then went home until my shift at the Luau Room."

"Funny, isn't it?" Scotty said. "Everyone here seems to recall where they were three days ago except for you." He glared at The Pole. "You knew she was missing and you were looking for her. What happened? Did you find her?"

The Pole pushed back from the bar. "I don't need this right now."

"Come on, Adam. We're not supposed to think it's weird that she's missing for days but you don't mention it to anybody?"

The Pole shrugged. "I don't know. I figured it was a woman thing. She was pissed about her time of the month. But most of her stuff was in the apartment. Why am I telling you this?"

"I'm not sure how to see you," Scotty kept talking like The Pole hadn't said anything.

"Scotty, we know you were close with Joanne, it's okay, man." Maw moved closer to The Pole and placed his drink on the bar. "He doesn't mean this."

"Cool it, kid," Spade muttered to Scotty. "You still have to work with him in the morning."

The Pole gave Scotty a long look before shaking his head slowly. "I'm sorry you feel this way. I am sorry." He stood up and nodded at everyone. "Thanks for the beer, Dob, but I think it's best if I go."

"Hey," Maw said. "Don't leave. It's okay."

Mona crossed her arms over her chest and watched The Pole leave the building. She guessed if she moved to the window she'd see him cross the street and disappear into Grumpy's. "Scotty, that was brave."

Scotty's cheeks flushed red and he twisted the tab off his can of beer. "I don't know about that. I'm just trying to figure it out."

"Buddy, it's a small town," Spade said.

"What happens between a man and a woman is their own business," Dale added.

"Even if the woman ends up dead?" Mona shot back.

"Mona, the cops said it was accidental. What are we supposed to do? Shun him? We're not Amish. We have to let this pass." Maw looked around the bar for agreement.

"I think it's bullshit that we act like it's okay. It's not." Mona crossed her arms in front of her chest and glanced at Jake. He gave her a quick nod.

"What are we supposed to do then?" Beau asked her. "Everyone in this town has their gripe with someone else. I think the best thing is to live and let live."

"I agree," Maw said.

Jake spoke up. "Maybe it's too early for all of us yet. But give it time."

Jake's words made her feel better and she realized how the mood had shifted to serious. "Okay." She reached back for the bottle of ginger brandy that Arlyce favored for sore throats and raised it. "This round's on me." She poured out the peace offering into shot glasses and by the time her patrons were wiping their lips with the backs of their hands, Jenny and Judi walked into the Pub. "Party's here tonight," Jenny called over her shoulder. They were followed by a group of people. Among them was T.C., who grinned at Mona and gave her a big wink. Jake saw this and raised his eyebrows, but didn't say anything.

The jukebox got plugged with quarters and Mona considered calling Steve. She couldn't keep up with the drink orders and watched the dirty glasses fill bus tubs and the coolers slowly empty out. He was probably curled up on the couch with his kids, she thought. Let him have the night off. It was all locals in the bar anyway, she reasoned. They'd understand if they had to wait a while to get served.

The volume grew louder and more frantic as the night wore on. People were dancing, shooting pool, burning off what remained of the steam from being cooped up all winter. Jake ordered a fifth round of shots for his end of the bar, the most Mona had seen him drink in ages. She grabbed another bus tub from the kitchen and made the rounds of the back tables in the bar to collect empty glasses and cans. Suddenly the bus tub was lifted from her hands and set aside and T.C. grabbed her around the waist to dance. He was laughing and singing along to the lyrics. Her stomach did a loop-de-loop when he twirled her in a circle and she joined him in the chorus, feeling grateful for a moment that they could still be friends. After all, she thought affectionately while giving his hand a quick squeeze, he was a good guy.

His expression shifted from joy to fear in an instant and Mona's view of him was blocked, then his curly head jerked back and he let go of her hand. She stumbled back. T.C. fell backwards onto the floor so hard he bounced once and blood dripped from his mouth. He braced himself with both hands and jumped up yelling, "What the fuck!"

Mona watched Jake rear back his arm for another blow and she flung herself in front of him. "No!" She shoved him back with both hands and Jake looked down at her in surprise. "What?" His eyes were glassy and unfocused, his mouth half open. He leaned around her to point his finger at T.C. "If I ever ..." his voice slurred. "You ever touch her again."

"That's enough, Jake," Mona said and tried to steer him in the direction of the kitchen. Two hundred and twenty pounds of muscle, he was immovable even though he staggered a little. "Jake," she pleaded. "Come on."

"No." Jake waved away her hands. "You wanna be with him? Is that it?"

"What are you talking about?" Mona was horrified and embarrassed. She cut a look at T.C., who scowled at Jake. "Jeez, knock it off." Jake gave her a glacial stare in return. Is that what he really thought? That she wanted to be with T.C?

"What the fuck?" T.C. repeated. "You wanna go? C'mon!" He jumped from foot to foot like a boxer and waggled his fingers, egging on the assault.

Jake shoved Mona to the side and the punches rained down on T.C. for a moment until he got the upper hand. Jake fell to the ground after four well-placed uppercuts to his sternum and jaw.

"Enough!" Dob roared through the chaos. Feet scuffled and Credence Clearwater Revival kept singing about the bayou at top volume. "Mona," he commanded, "get back behind the bar. I've got this." Dob grabbed Jake by the armpits and hauled him up and forced him towards the back door. He looked back and shouted at

T.C. "Stay."

T.C. froze and watched Dob push Jake through the door. Jenny followed Mona behind the bar and started unloading one of the bus tubs.

Mona's hands shook too much to crack open a beer for a customer waiting with a ten-dollar bill in their hand. "Shit. I'm sorry." She caught Jenny's eye and pointed over to the customer. "Can you?"

Mona ran through the crowd and out the back door. She reached the parking lot in time to see Dob's taillights turn onto the road. He was probably driving Jake home. What the hell was that? Why was Jake acting jealous now? T.C. lived here, of course they'd have to act friendly—what did Jake expect? How did he get so drunk so fast? And if he expected her to never speak to T.C. again, well, that was ridiculous. She took several deep breaths to calm down enough to return to work. Jenny raised her eyebrows at Mona when she stepped back behind the bar, but Mona replied, "Stay. Please."

In tandem, they finished the night, Mona serving customers, Jenny washing glasses and backing up the bigger drink orders. At one-thirty Mona pulled the plug on the juke box and turned up the lights. Groans filled her ears, but gradually the crowd dispersed, trained to comply with Bar Time.

"Want any help, Mona?" Spade asked. He looked concerned, his large forehead creased and his eyes squinting at her from behind his glasses.

"No. We're good. Thanks, though."

He waved goodbye and left through the back door. Mona took inventory of who remained. A little crew from Sawdust City and a couple she vaguely recognized from one of the downriver resorts. Maw and Dale were long gone, as were most of the other regulars. She started stacking barstools on the tables surrounding them, and after a few minutes they took the hint and left. Mona locked the door behind them. "Toss me a clean bar rag," she told Jenny. She wiped down the bar, stacking glasses and cans and ashtrays on the side. Her body ached and she wanted a good cry. *What was going on with Jake?*

"You want me to restock?" Jenny asked.

"No. Steve can do it in the morning. I'll tell him we were too busy." Mona assured her. "Thank you."

Jenny rolled her eyes. "Whatever. You want a drink before you head home?"

"Yeah," Mona said. "I'd like that." She turned off all of the lights except one above the bar and locked up before pouring herself a stiff whiskey and coke. Jenny gave Mona a sly look and lifted the bottle of Crown Royal from the back shelf. "On the rocks," she said, handing Mona the bottle.

They carried their drinks into the dining room where they could look out the window at the moonlight reflecting off the river's black surface. Mona couldn't see any lights on at Jake's cottage. Dob probably put him straight to bed, she thought. His truck was still in the Pub's parking lot, so he was stranded. Jenny lit a cigarette and leaned back with a groan. "It is way harder to tend bar than to work in the boutique. Seriously, even Black Friday is easy compared to your job."

"Tonight was pretty nuts," Mona agreed. She leaned forward to ease the ache in her lower back.

"So ... that business with Jake and T.C. Did you know he was that jealous?"

"I had no clue T.C. bugged him that much." Mona stirred her drink with the plastic cocktail straw. The ice cubes gently clinked against the glass.

"Didn't they get along in high school? I always thought they did."

"Well, they were teammates, so they must have at some level. I don't remember them fighting at parties or anything like that."

Jenny grinned at Mona. "Then he's just that jealous of your old lover."

"Don't call him that."

"What? *Lover?* T.C. was your loooooo-ver." Jenny dragged out the word and it sounded even grosser to Mona's ears.

"Stop it."

"Fine." Jenny took a drag off her smoke before continuing. "How does it stand with you and T.C? Pretty casual?"

"Yeah." Mona thought about his lunchtime visit—was that only a week ago? It seemed longer than that. "He's a good guy. Our timing was just really bad. I don't appreciate Jake being a dick about it."

"Maybe it's his way of expressing his love for you."

"He's stupid. Besides, if he wanted to express his love for me, there are more effective and less violent ways. He's the one keeping us on the fence."

"Yeah."

"Unless ..." Mona paused. It was a terrible thought. She took a drink and felt the whiskey heat her throat and chest.

"Unless what?"

"Unless he's trying to end it and saying T.C. and I aren't over makes a good cover story."

"Five'll get you ten he wakes up sober and apologizes."

"He's got to apologize to T.C., too. Seriously," Mona protested at Jenny's laugh. "How am I supposed to avoid him? Jake's got to figure it out. How can I not be friendly with a guy who lives in the same town? It's not like there's a million people and we can go other places."

"True." Jenny swallowed the last of her drink and set her glass down. "Maybe I need a new boyfriend to make Beau jealous. Then I'd get him for good."

Mona reached across the table and patted Jenny's hand. "You do that. Let me know how it works out for you." She dumped the night's tips out of a plastic bucket onto the table. "We're splitting this even-Steven." Mona quickly sorted the money and handed Jenny her half—fifty-seven dollars and change.

"Thanks, babe." Jenny stood and swung her purse over her shoulder. "You ready?"

"Yeah." Mona carried their glasses to the kitchen sink and then followed Jenny out the back door. "Thanks again."

Jenny hugged her and headed for her car. "What are friends for, dummy?"

Bassville seemed empty while Mona drove the few blocks to her house. A light breeze rattled the branches overhead and she walked up the steps to her front door when a figure stood up on her porch.

"Hey."

Mona slapped her hands to her chest. "Holy shit, T.C. Don't do that ever again!"

"I'm sorry." He stepped closer to her. "Look, I didn't mean to come between you and Jake," he said. His words hung suspended in the cold air, they looked like smoke.

"It's fine. We'll be fine." Mona could see the swelling of his right eye and cheekbone in the streetlight. "You okay?" Instinctively she reached out to touch it, but stopped short. What was she doing? "I've had worse," he cracked with a quick grin. Then he grew serious and bowed his head. "Do you want me to leave? I will if you want." He stuffed his hands in his jacket pockets. His breath steamed out of his lips in the cold air.

"What? No. Of course you should stay. Bassville's your home, just as much as it's mine or Jake's." *He meant leave town, right? Or leave her house right now? What was he driving at?* "I'll talk to Jake, but I'm sure he was just acting stupid because he was drunk. It'll be fine."

T.C. gave a quick nod. "And we're good?"

"Shit." Mona reached past him to open her front door. She needed to get him off her porch. She didn't want to lead him on, even though it felt really nice to have someone concerned about her. "We've got a long history, T.C. We'll always be friends." Didn't they go over this at the Pub?

He leaned against the door jamb and grinned. "I hope you mean that."

"Listen, it's been a long night. I'm beat. Yes, we're friends. I'll see you later."

She walked into her house and shut the door firmly behind her. A few minutes later she heard an engine start up and headlights glowed briefly through the window.

What a night, she thought. She got ready for bed and flopped onto her pillow, her body exhausted. Unfortunately, her mind wasn't as tired and she lie wide awake wondering what would happen with Jake, what T.C. really wanted from her and why men had to be so darn complicated.

THIRTY-TWO

"P EG," MAW SPOKE INTO the intercom, "can you send over some blue food coloring?"

"Food coloring?" Peg's voice crackled back through the speaker.

He pushed the Call button with his finger. "Yeah. I think a little coloring will make things look more chemical and scientific." Maw watched out the window and a few minutes later his daughter walked out of the house carrying a small bottle in her hand. He met her at the door. "Thanks."

"You've got something in your beard," she told him and turned her heel. Maw dug his fingers through the hair on his chin and felt something grainy. Picking it out—was it sandwich crumbs?—he reflected on the lack of support the female contingent of his household had offered his latest scheme. "Insane" was Peg's word of choice. His daughter insisted that no one with any scientific background would be fooled by his genetics lab. They couldn't understand that none of that mattered. What was important was the publicity. Of course viewers would know the whole minnow operation was a fraud—that was sort of the point. But it was like going to the freak show at the fair. You knew there wasn't *really* a snake man, but you played along because it was fun. And people would still believe that what he did with minnows was somehow special. It was the same sort of technique used in marketing food—why did kids like Happy Meals? McDonald's sold them the same burger and fries on the regular menu, the only difference was the packaging.

Boyd Douglas would arrive in a few hours and Maw had the whole production staged and ready. About ten minutes before the film crew showed up, he'd add the Mountain Dew to the last minnow aquarium, giving the shiners adequate time to absorb the caffeine and move even faster and more frantically than normal. The perception was everything, he thought as he walked into the back store room and uncapped the bottle of food coloring.

He gently tipped the bottle and watched the drops of deep blue dye hit the water, then streak out and dissolve, changing the color in the tank to a more interesting and aquatic shade of turquoise. Maybe he should doctor all the tanks, he thought. He watched the minnows swarm from end to end, their steely eyes as dead as a corpse's.

Maw turned to adjust the beakers and pans and cords he'd lined up on the adjacent table. He stood back to admire his handiwork. There. It looked pretty good. But what mattered more than the staging was his showmanship. He walked back into the shop and stood in front of a cooler, watching his reflection in the glass as he ran through his demonstration. The lab coat was definitely a nice touch, he thought. Maybe he'd start wearing it more often. Peg was having such a fit over the bikini fishing team, perhaps he could move the marketing into a science direction. "Don't leave fishing to chance, let science optimize your catch." Too long and wordy. "Better science, better fishing." Might work. "Breeding the best since 1980." That was better.

He could dress the girls in lab coats, too, over their swimsuits. What guy wasn't turned on by a sexy scientist? Add some fake horn-rimmed glasses and BAM! That might work even better than the in-your-face sex appeal of bikinis. He envisioned the team posed around a minnow tank, holding beakers and test tubes. It definitely had potential.

Maw reached into the cooler and snagged a can of Mountain Dew. Cracking the top, he glanced at the clock. Over two hours to go. He felt too much nervous energy to hang around the bait shop any longer.

Ten minutes later Maw sat in a booth at the Bassville Café, ordering a burger and fries. He glanced outside at the muddy road and dreary sky. The end of March always felt hopeless, like spring would never come relieve them. This feeling was made worse by a couple of balmy 60 degree days at the end of February that inevitably teased people into false optimism that warm weather was right around the corner. But how could he complain? Maw had done steady trade in T-shirts and can coolers and caps throughout the winter. He wasn't at the brink like a lot of other people in town.

Across the street Frank pushed Nancy in her wheelchair towards the Bassville Pub, straining to move her through the slush. "Wait here," he told the waitress who was loading his burger and fries onto a tray with a bottle of ketchup. "I'll be right back."

Maw left the café, crossed the street and hailed Frank. "Let me help you!"

Frank paused and squinted at Maw. "Hi, Maw."

Maw reached across Frank and grasped the chair's handles. "Nancy, how are you doing? Off to visit Mona for breakfast?"

"Shit," Nancy answered.

Maw recognized Boyd Douglas as the kind of man who lacked imagination, which surprised him because he figured anyone who made movies for a living had to be creative. Maw ignored the fact that documentaries sought revealing a kind of truth to people, the sort of storyline that discouraged invention and dissembling. Maw also recognized his reaction to Boyd: intimidated.

Boyd Douglas was one of those timeless forty-ish-year-old men with a smidge of distinguished grey at his temples. His hair was buzz-cut, his stature lean and tall, and his piercing, hooded eyes caused Maw to squirm beneath their inquisitive stare. He wore a blue button-down shirt with the sleeves rolled up enough to display muscled forearms adorned by a military-grade watch. Everything about Boyd Douglas left the impression of precision, from the level bristled hairs on his head to the soles of his desert boots. Equally intimidating was the stack of legal documents Boyd presented to Maw for his signature, which Maw eagerly scrawled his name upon in his excitement to cut to the cameras.

Maw tried to tamp down his fear that Boyd would somehow find him lacking and decide to steer away from featuring him and his shop in his documentary. Standing as tall as he could, Maw resisted the urge to tilt his head back. Instead he stepped ahead of Boyd to make the difference in height less obvious.

"Welcome! I don't know how much Dave told you about the bait shop here, but I figured we'd get started with the grand tour and you can ask questions along the way."

Boyd nodded. A man of few words, Maw surmised. "Okay then." He held out both arms and locked down into showman mode. "Welcome to Maw's Bait and Tackle, home of the Pitbull Minnow! I opened my shop ten years ago, but first I should back up and explain that I was born and raised right here on the shores of the Wissipaw River." Maw paused and nodded towards the crew of three camera and sound men behind Boyd. "You getting all this?" Boyd glanced at his crew and said in a gravelly voice, "They'll get what they need. My work is never staged, Mr. Cooper. Documentaries seek truth, so just act naturally and the story behind fishing and minnows will reveal itself."

This struck Maw as pretentious and silly, but he decided to play along and ignore the crew. He pointed to a picture of himself in a rowboat holding a fishing pole—he'd been about ten years old when it was taken, a thin kid in jeans and a striped T-shirt waving at the camera. "My childhood home was a stone's throw from the mighty Wissipaw. I grew up enjoying all of the seasons she had to offer, from the lazy summer currents filled with catfish and crappie, to the crisp fall days trolling her depths for perch, to augering through the ice in the winter for panfish and, of course, the crazy excitement of the walleye and white bass run every spring. We are, you know, just days away from that excitement. Maybe you'll come back to tape some of that? My store will be packed, wall to wall fishermen from all over the place. The river will be so busy you'll think you were standing in the middle of rush hour in Chicago."

Boyd continued to watch Maw without any facial reaction to his story. This made Maw nervous, but he determined that the best course of action was to carry on as usual, pretend Boyd was absorbed in every word he said. And for all he knew, Boyd was. He might just be one of those inscrutable people who kept a poker face all the time.

"So, I was born here and about ten years ago I opened up this bait shop. My mission was to bring the best quality fishing experience to people coming to Bassville. This building was originally a workshop, I think the previous owner did some cabinet-making. I added the plumbing to make it minnow-friendly." Maw walked back towards the tanks. "In the early days I pretty much sold live bait and a few lures and whatnot. Over time I added inventory, and, as you can see, we have full displays of rods, reels and all the accessories you need to fish. Remington, Penn—it's all here." Maw flung out his arms in a grand gesture towards the racks and shelves of tackle and gear.

"Plus we have our branded merchandise." Maw held up a Maw's Minnows T-shirt and cap.

Boyd didn't even nod. Maw stammered a bit before asking, "What would you like to see now?"

"I think viewers are always interested in the process."

"The process."

"Yes. The process."

"Like, how the minnows are prepared?" Maw asked.

At last Boyd nodded.

Maw gulped. He'd expected some eager kid with a ton of questions, but this man was sophisticated and confident. Suddenly Maw suspected his minnow lab would not impress.

"Okey-dokey. Now, I can't reveal all my secrets, but," Maw led the camera crew down the hall to his laboratory. "The science behind Maw's Minnows is state of the art, but it's really based on Mendel's work, which we studied in high school. All creatures have dominant characteristics. Take the shark, for instance. Its dominant characteristic is being a predator, which includes fast swimming, excellent senses, sharp teeth and an instinct to go after things. The minnow is a herd creature, they travel in swarms and the only overlap is speed, the ability to dart in a different direction really fast, making it tough to catch."

Maw had drawn a Venn diagram illustrating this concept on a large poster board pinned to the wall. He pointed to it while continuing his mini lecture on genetic engineering. "I figured the trick is to make the minnow more like a shark. The minnow's speed is built in, but the predator instinct, that's what had to get added." The camera crew started whispering to each other. Maw assumed they were making sure to get a good shot of the poster so he stepped behind the fish tanks.

"Here's where I started tinkering with the golden shiners. The golden shiner is just your average minnow, nothing spectacular about it, aside from the fact that its breeding period is short and it's the minnow bigger fish are most likely to hit. But look at the minnows in this tank. So sluggish and passive, right?" Maw used a ruler to stir the water in the aquarium as if to prove his point. Some of the fish swam from end to end of the aquarium to avoid the ruler, but most of them floated gently in the water. The immobile fish were actually dead, but weighted so they wouldn't float to the surface, a clever trick his youngest had come up with while they prepped the tank. Maw dramatically sighed. "Sure, it's easy to catch this minnow and drop it in the river on your hook, but a flaccid minnow won't attract attention below the surface."

Boyd Douglas now sat on the edge of a table across the room, his arms folded and eyebrows raised. Maw felt positive he was a hit. He watched a cameraman turn to Boyd, but Boyd simply waved his hand in a circle, indicating his desire to keep rolling.

"A buddy of mine works at UW-Madison in the Biology department. I can't say his name for security reasons, he's working on some top-secret genetic mutations, but he shared some shark DNA with me. The early experiments were a little nasty." Maw rolled back the sleeve of his flannel shirt to reveal a scar on the inside of his left arm. He paused so the camera could get a close up.

"Success came after years of trial and error. Basically, we inject the golden shiner with extracted shark DNA that specifically creates a breeding specimen. Allow me to demonstrate." He scooped out a live minnow and pinned it to the table with his hand while making a show of injecting its belly with a syringe he'd loaded with green gelatin. Then Maw messed around a little with the tubing and liquids on the table, all distractions to dazzle his audience. He deftly palmed the minnow and retrieved the "activated" minnow from a dish of water laced with Mountain Dew. Before sliding the caffeinated minnow into the larger aquarium he held up the new minnow, which writhed frantically between his thumb and index finger. The minnow flew from his grip into the empty fish tank and swam a crazy pattern back and forth, hitting the sides of the tank.

"The breeding stock is the source of our minnows, and we've even refined the bloodlines to produce a better bait, depending on what you're fishing for and conditions." The caffeinated minnow didn't have long, so Maw started for the door. "Follow me and I'll show you how we dip minnows."

He shut off the light on his way out of the room and made it impossible for anyone to linger and look too closely at his lab set up. "Right this way," he said and urged the crew down the hall towards the minnow tanks.

Maw overheard Boyd say, "I hope you're getting all of this," to one of the crew, and he smirked to himself. They were eating out of his hand. He could relax from this point, everything he showed them now would be authentic and honest. He encouraged the men to take the net themselves and scoop out minnows; he demonstrated how a fisherman would hold the minnow and hook it through the back, but avoiding the spine. "Most people think the lips is the best spot to run a hook, but the minnow will die faster because it can't draw water through the gills. Hooking the back allows it to swim freely, you wanna let the minnow do the work for you. Kind of like golf, let the club do the work, right? So you get the minnow on your hook and gently cast it into the water.

"That's another mistake people make. They cast overhead, thinking more distance is better, right? Big mistake. It's physics—more velocity equals greater force, so if you hit a minnow into the water harder, you're gonna kill it. These minnows may be tough, but they're not indestructible. An easy sidearm or underhand cast lets your minnow slide into the water safely, then swim away and hunt your bass for you."

Boyd Douglas held a net above the water and Maw watched him slowly lower it and wait. "Fishing is all about patience. Raising the bait is all about patience, too. Treat your minnows right and they'll treat you right. That's what I'm always telling people. These minnows will catch your fish, that's what they're bred to do. It's literally in their blood. The only way they don't is because of human error; it's never the minnow's fault."

After a few tries, the camera crew had mastered the craft of baiting a hook properly. "Obviously minnows are the main event here, but there's a lot of other bait you can use. Do you want me to show you?" Maw asked Boyd.

Boyd, who Maw now understood to be a man of few words, nodded assent. Maw launched into explanations of grubs and jigs and flies. He taught knot-tying, weighting lines and depth finding. The filming lasted longer than he anticipated, but when Boyd Douglas shook his hand before pulling out of the parking lot at six o'clock, Maw felt he'd done his profession proud. He could hardly wait to see the finished product on TV. Him! The star of a documentary! Could fame and fortune be far behind?

THIRTY-THREE

WEDNESDAY AFTERNOON ARLYCE PULLED a matchbox car out of Victoria's mouth and unbuckled her from her high chair. "Can you sit quietly for a few minutes?" She went over to the phone on the wall and dialed Rhonda's phone number. She'd done this so many times over the past week she didn't even need to look at the scrap of paper where she'd written it down. Her fingers moved by memory from number to number on the dial and Arlyce sat down at the kitchen table with a sigh. The receiver rested in the crook of her shoulder against her ear and she lit a cigarette. How many times had she called without result? She pulled the ashtray closer and prepared to wait for another fruitless twenty unanswered rings.

Steve had been shocked to learn that she and June had been involved with Joanne's disappearance. Like the rest of the town, he hadn't noticed her absence, but came home from his shift at the bar bursting to tell her Joanne had been found dead.

"Arlyce!" he'd nudged her awake with a loud whisper. "You won't believe what happened!"

Arlyce had rolled onto her back and opened her eyes. "What?" It hadn't occurred to her at that moment that Steve didn't know. Of course he didn't know. No one knew except for her and June. They had carried the secret for nearly a week before June found Joanne on the ice. June had gone straight to Dottie, and Dottie called her a couple hours later.

Arlyce was sorting laundry when the phone rang. Upon hearing the news she sat stunned at the table, dropping the receiver to the floor. The phone cord contracted, dragging the receiver a few inches back towards the wall, and then Victoria scooted over to chew on it. Arlyce watched her baby girl drooling her gummy mouth over the rubbery spiral and made no move to stop her. *Joanne dead.* They'd been so close to getting her out of town and now it was like nothing had happened. It didn't even matter.

Her brain and body numbly absorbed this fact and by the time she went to bed she'd reached angry acceptance. The only people she needed to talk to were Dottie and June. It never occurred to her that anyone else would care.

"They found Joanne dead in the river today," Steve was telling her.

"I know." She rolled over.

"It's so sad. She was a nice lady."

Then Arlyce had shot to her feet and started yelling. "So sad? You wanna know what's sad? How that asshole beat the shit out of her and everyone looked the other way. How she was this close to getting out of it when she died. We almost had her out of here!" Ugly tears rolled down her cheeks and Steve's expression shifted from shock to concern.

"Hey," he stepped forward and pulled her into his chest, his thick arms and soft stomach pressed against her. She buried her face against his shirt, smelling the grease and smoke from the bar. "It's okay." He stroked her hair and shushed her.

After she'd calmed down Steve started asking questions and learned what she and Arlyce had tried to do—had done. His reaction had been sweet, but he seemed to feel worse for her than for Joanne. Arlyce couldn't understand that.

Unexpectedly, Arlyce heard the click of someone picking up on the other end. Her spine straightened.

"Hello?" a young woman's voice asked.

"Is this Rhonda Graff?"

"Yes. Who is this?"

"Arlyce Shanski. I'm a friend of your mother's. I have some very sad news about her."

"She's dead." Rhonda's voice sounded flat.

"You know?" Arlyce was surprised.

"A policeman got in touch with me last night. I came home to find a notice on the door of my apartment. It said to call the local sheriff's department. That's how I found out."

"Oh. Well." Arlyce didn't know what her role was at this point, she'd figured on breaking the news to Joanne's daughter, but now what? "So, you probably know how she died."

"They said she drowned. By accident."

"Or not. Anyway, do you need any help? With the funeral plans?"

"Listen—what did you say your name was?"

"Arlyce Shanski."

"Arlyce. Joanne took off ten years ago when I was eighteen. My younger sister was fifteen. She was 'following her bliss,' and that obviously didn't involve us. I only talked to her once a year plus a card at Christmas. She probably loved me. She said she did. But I said goodbye to her a long time ago."

"Rhonda," this confession was breaking Arlyce's heart. She had to explain what she knew. "Your mother was in a very abusive relationship. Did you know her partner? Adam Lewsciewski? I don't know if she *could* have been in more contact with you."

"What do you mean?"

"He belted her around. He broke her leg, gave her concussions, landed her in the hospital on more than one occasion."

"I'm sorry to hear that, but Joanne was a grown woman. She could have left. She didn't have any problem leaving us."

"She was trying to. She was trying to get a hold of you—we'd bought her a bus ticket to California. She was going to start over and we—my friend June and I—we were helping her. She was living in an ice shanty on the river until we could get her on that bus. Joanne didn't want to come out there until she'd gotten a hold of you because she didn't have any money. Anyway, we were hiding her from The Pole—that's Adam's nickname—to protect her when she died."

"The police said it was an accident."

"Yeah," Arlyce said. "It might have been. Or it might have been that The Pole found her."

Rhonda didn't say anything so Arlyce pressed on. "My friends and I are happy to help with any arrangements. What can we do?"

"Whatever you want. Like I said, I told my mother goodbye a long time ago. You handle this however you see fit. My sister and I want no part of this."

"But she was your mother!" Arlyce was certain this was grief talking, maybe anger, but not Rhonda's true feelings.

"In the loosest sense of the word, yes. Look, I have a lot to do, I just got home from vacation. Thank you for trying to help her. I'm sorry it didn't work out."

The dial tone vibrated against Arlyce's right ear while her mind reeled at Rhonda's reaction. She couldn't imagine not wanting to bury her mother. She lifted Victoria off the floor and held her close.

"Baby girl, I hope we never end up like that."

She decided to call June and Dottie. Between the three of them they'd figure out what to do. But no matter what, no way were they letting The Pole near Joanne's funeral.

An hour later June and Dottie pulled up chairs around Arlyce's kitchen table to sort out Joanne's funeral. "I'll call Joe. If it's up to next of kin and Rhonda doesn't want any part of it, then she can delegate the whole works to us."

June dialed while Arlyce poured coffee and Dottie opened a spiral notebook to a clean page. "Was she religious at all?" Dottie asked. "I think we could convince either church to do the funeral, but do you know if she had a preference?"

Arlyce considered this for a moment. "I never saw her with a rosary or genuflect or do any of the other Catholic ritual, so let's start Lutheran."

Dottie nodded and wrote this down. "They might not be willing to do a full service, but I'll ask Pastor."

"What do you mean you let The Pole take her body? Jesus, Joe! He treated her like shit when she was alive. Why on earth would you let him be responsible for her now?" June's face had turned red and she scowled at the floor while she listened to his reply. "Well, we have permission from Joanne's next of kin. If her daughter calls you and tells you we are in charge of handling her affairs, what happens?"

Dottie and Arlyce leaned forward on their elbows.

"*What?* No! No, no, no. You call the funeral home and you tell them under no circumstances is that son of a bitch having any part of her funeral. I don't care if he paid them money, it doesn't matter. You know what? He can do whatever he wants, but *we* get the body. Do you need Rhonda to call or can you handle this by yourself, Joe? Fine." June hung up and whirled around to look at her friends. "Can you believe this? The Pole had the funeral home pick up her body today. I swear to God no one in that police station has a lick of sense."

"What happens now?" Arlyce asked.

"Joe said he'd call Rhonda and if Rhonda consents, then he'll let the funeral parlor know we're taking over."

"What if The Pole objects?" Dottie asked.

"Tough nuts," June declared. "He can do what he wants. Have his own damn party, I don't care. He's not going to be in charge of her final moments."

The other two women nodded and turned open a fresh page of notebook paper. Writing an obituary was a difficult task since Joanne was so private and secretive about her life. "I think it's okay if we write how she'll be remembered by others. There's no rule that you have to include a person's hobbies or jobs or whatever."

June and Arlyce agreed. "Besides," June added, "what matters most is how people remember you. Nobody cares about the dead person's spoon collection or that they were a Packer fan or worked at Zwicker Mills. That's actually pretty boring to read." She thought about how she'd better get busy writing her own obituary ahead of time to make it interesting and how sad it was to read an obituary that summed up a person's whole existence by their job and their spoon collection.

"I'll call the Lutheran church," Dottie said. "Then we should go to the funeral home in person because we'll have to decide on a casket and so forth."

Dottie made a phone call to her pastor, who agreed to host the service in the church and say a homily. He said he'd get the organist to play a few hymns and then he'd lead a prayer at the end. "Short and sweet, it'll be perfect," Dottie said, and jotted down a few hymn titles in her neat script.

The ladies bundled up to drive to the funeral parlor, and Arlyce rode in back with Victoria snugged into her lap. "We don't need to have a visitation," June said. "We're not the family, no one's offering condolences to *us*. This service is honoring her life and giving her a proper send-off, it's not a regular funeral."

"I agree," Dottie said. "I don't even think a funeral luncheon is necessary. People can send flowers to church if they wish, but it's more important for people to gather and recognize who she was."

"With kindness," June added.

"Yes," Arlyce said. "And I hate to mention it now, but how will we pay for any of this?"

"Let's find out the cost first," June said.

Dottie pulled up along the curb and the ladies all noticed The Pole's truck at the same moment.

"He's in there!" Arlyce whispered, as though he could hear her.

"Should we come back later?" Dottie asked.

June was already out the door and heading toward the building. Dottie looked back at Arlyce who shrugged in response. "Okay then."

Inside the funeral home, somber music played quietly in the background as though a service were taking place. Floor-to-ceiling burgundy curtains covered the walls and a huge arrangement of fake flowers made a centerpiece on a round table with a cherry finish. Whoever decorated the interior made it seem grand, wall sconces and carefully placed lighting made the room seem vast. Two offices with glass doors were off of the main room and in the nearest the women could see a stout man in a black suit talking to The Pole. The Pole's back was to the door, his damp hair curled over the collar of his shirt.

"Do we wait out here or interrupt?" Arlyce asked.

"Let him finish," June said. "It won't matter anyway."

They sat down. Victoria began side walking while holding onto the chairs and the women strained to hear the conversation in the office. "What's he saying?" Arlyce whispered.

June shook her head. A few minutes passed and the main door

opened again. Joe walked in and his expression relaxed when he saw them waiting. "Oh, good. I was worried you'd started without me."

"Why are you here?" June asked in a sharp voice.

"I called Rhonda. She gave permission for you to handle her mother's remains."

June nodded at the others. Of course, they'd expected as much.

"However," Joe pointed at the office, "I came down here to mitigate any conflict of interest."

"Hmph." Arlyce leaned back and crossed her arms across her stomach.

"Have you spoken to anyone yet?" Joe asked.

"No, we're still waiting," Dottie told him. She nervously twisted the strap of her purse around her knuckles.

"Okay." Joe sat beside them and another five minutes passed with the slow moan of funeral hymns as background music. June suggested that organ music was depressing and creepy, they would choose something more suitable for Joanne's service. Maybe they'd even allow something unconventional, like the country music Joanne did like to listen to.

The Pole stepped out of the office with the funeral director and froze in his tracks when he saw them. "What's this about?" he asked Joe.

"Adam," Joe stood and held out his palms in a pacifying gesture, "the ladies have the family's permission to handle Joanne's funeral service."

"What?" He scowled fiercely at the women, and because he'd dressed up in khaki trousers and a clean white shirt, this seemed more threatening than if he'd come straight off a job site covered in sawdust and dirt. "She was my girlfriend."

"Yes, but that's not a legally recognized relationship."

"Baloney. We lived together. Her name's on my lease."

"But when it comes to legal status, you have no rights."

The Pole turned to the funeral director. "You already agreed to handle this for me." He turned back to Joe. "I scheduled a mass at the Catholic church."

Dottie gave the women a triumphant look before addressing The Pole. "We've arranged a service at the Lutheran church."

"She wasn't Lutheran," The Pole argued.

"She wasn't Catholic either," Dottie said.

The Pole looked at Joe for help. "I've already organized the service. The funeral's Saturday at eleven, visitation starts at nine."

"That's true," Arlyce said. "But you've got the wrong church. The *Lutheran* church is having her service Saturday at eleven. No visitation."

"What the—Joe? These women have no business with this!"

"Actually, they do. Joanne's daughter gave them permission to handle her remains. As next of kin it's her decision. Now, I can't stop you from having a funeral service or anything like that, but as far as her body goes, these ladies get that responsibility. It's the law." Joe rocked back on his heels, looking pleased with his explanation.

The Pole gaped at them for several seconds. "What do you plan to do with her?"

"I don't see how that's any of your business," June said. She turned to the funeral director. "Can we sit down right now and settle this with you?"

The funeral director looked at Joe, who nodded. "You can make any funeral plans you want with anyone you want, but these women have custody of the remains."

The director frowned and looked over at The Pole who blustered at Joe. "I told you she was after me. I told you she wouldn't leave me alone. You said you'd talk to her."

"I did," Joe said. "And she is leaving you alone, technically. But she's got the legal right to do this."

June and swept past the men and took a seat in the director's office. "Let's get started. I have to get home and make supper in an hour."

The director joined the women in his office after pulling in an extra chair. Victoria made herself happy chewing on Arlyce's jacket sleeve until he offered her a shortbread cookie from a tin in his desk drawer. Outside the office The Pole continued a heated conversation with Joe.

"We lived together! I loved her!"

"But it's not your right to bury her."

"Would you just let anyone bury someone's—look, she was almost my common-law wife."

"You'd have to prove that, and anyway, a child precedes that relationship as next of kin. I'm sorry, Adam. You should've called Rhonda first."

"I didn't even know Rhonda's damn number!"

"I don't know what to tell you ..." the voices trailed off and a door slammed. The funeral director folded his hands and studied the three women seated before him.

"This is highly unusual, but I don't need to tell you that, do I? Adam had suggested embalming and burial in an oak casket with yellow satin lining." He pulled out a color brochure and pointed to a picture of the coffin. Arlyce inhaled sharply when she read the price.

June exchanged a look with the other women before speaking. "We have no money for this. Now," she held up a hand before the director could interrupt her. "We will pay you, but we need to handle this in the most economical way possible. Joanne's daughters are not contributing to the funeral costs. I doubt she even had a life insurance policy. We'll pay you, it might take some time, but we'll settle up with you. What we need you to do is provide Joanne with the cheapest and nicest burial possible."

Dottie held a tissue up to her nose and sniffed. "Sorry. Just got overwhelmed thinking about how this could've been Angie. I'm okay."

Arlyce squeezed her knee and leaned forward. "We got the Lutheran church doing the service, we don't need you to do anything but get the body ready and put her in the ground."

"Jeez, you don't need to say it like that," Dottie protested.

"Sorry," Arlyce muttered. "What's your basic package?" she asked.

The funeral director opened a desk drawer and pulled out a mimeographed page with lists of services and prices. He pointed at the bottom of the page. "We can cremate her remains and bury her with a modest headstone."

June let out a low whistle and Dottie nodded. "Okay, we need to scrape up a bit more."

Arlyce shrugged helplessly and shook her head. "I'm tapped out. We have the money from her bus ticket and whatnot, but how will we come up with the difference?"

June clenched her jaw and nodded at the funeral director. "Go ahead with this. If push comes to shove, can we pay you in installments?"

The funeral director started writing out the invoice. "I trust you ladies are good for it. We'll work something out."

The women left the funeral home feeling a mix of jubilation and sorrow. As they drove back to Arlyce's house they divided up the responsibilities.

"I'll finish up the obituary and get it to the newspaper. June, can you take this list of funeral music and run it over to the church? And go ahead and choose any scripture you want read." Dottie ticked off items on her notebook. "Arlyce, you find something appropriate to wrap her body in and I think that should do it."

"I've been thinking," June said suddenly, "What if we put in the obituary 'no flowers' and instead ask for donations to the women's shelter in her memory?"

"Ooooh, I like that idea a lot," Arlyce said.

"You think he'll really have his separate service the same time as ours?" Dottie asked.

"We'll find out, won't we?" June said. "But it doesn't matter because he's never touching her again. Not even in her last moments."

It was a small victory, but the women agreed it mattered. Even more important, the statement of having a separate funeral from The Pole would force people to face what he had done to Joanne.

"I worry about Scotty, though," Dottie said. "He and The Pole have become so close over the past few years working together. I think he's taking the whole business pretty hard."

"Well, he's got to know what a schmuck he is," Arlyce said.

"It's one thing to know that, but it's another thing to accept it."

"Will he keep working with him?" June asked Dottie.

"He hasn't said. I assume he will, it's a good gig and it keeps him close to the farm, which is nice. If he took a job with a regular crew he'd have to travel all over. That would be tough."

"Can't he just go work on his own? Does he even need to work with The Pole?" June asked.

"It's not that easy. Lot of their jobs require two or more people. And as good as Scotty's become, he's not ready to go it alone yet or hire someone."

"It's so complicated in a small town. Everyone's wrapped up in everyone else's business," June said.

"That's the truth," Arlyce agreed. "It's a lot easier to have convictions anonymously." She didn't envy Scotty's position and she wondered what Steve might be saying about the situation from behind the bar. They had an even more public line to toe.

THIRTY-FOUR

It had been a rotten night of tossing and turning and Mona finally gave up trying to sleep when the clock read 6:00. She had chucked her sweatpants and T-shirt into a corner and took a long shower. Monologues of what she could say to Jake rolled through her mind. She felt mad, scared, hurt, but mostly frustrated. She had done nothing wrong, she thought, while working conditioner through her long hair. T.C. had approached *her* every time and that was not her fault. If Jake wanted to act like a complete moron—worse yet, if he was *looking* for an excuse to break it off—well, she had to get ready for the worst.

Her stomach flipped while she drove through town earlier this morning. Mona had resisted the urge to head over to his place and knock him awake. "Nope," she said to herself, "he can come to me."

Working all morning with the smell of soil in her nose and a prickle of sweat between her shoulder blades helped her feel better.

She decided she'd pack it in around one, have lunch and nap until she had to go to work. Mona was pruning the tomato seedlings when she heard gravel crunching beneath truck tires. She swiped her hand across the glass pane of the greenhouse to clear the condensation. Jake. Instinctively she reached up to fluff her bangs.

While he got out of his truck and headed towards the greenhouse, Mona deposited the clippings into a bucket of compost. She inhaled the earthy smell deep into her lungs to calm down. *Please, don't let us be over. Don't let us be over.*

She forced a smile to greet him, trying to keep her uncertainty under a layer of calm. The doubts and fears lurked on the edge of her imagination while she concentrated on his face. Jake had stubble on his jaw and chin, his eyes looked bloodshot and weary. "Hey, slugger," she greeted him.

He winced and shook his head slightly, as if the movement felt painful. "You busy?"

"Not really. If I do a little every day this is manageable."

"It's nice and warm in here. That wet weather gets in your bones." He shoved his hands in his jacket pockets and hunched his shoulders.

"What brings you here? I figured you'd be working." Mona tried to sound casual.

Jake rocked back on his heels. "Can we sit down?"

Here we go, Mona thought. "Sure."

They sat in the webbed lawn chairs and Jake leaned his elbows on his knees, clasped his hands and bowed his head. "First, I need to apologize to you."

Mona curled her toes and her back stiffened.

"I've been a jealous asshole since T.C. came back to town. I understand you two have history, of course you do. I've gotta quit thinking every time you talk to him or look at him that it means you're in love with him." Jake glanced up at her before continuing.

"If you wanted to be with him, you'd tell me, right?"

Mona frowned. "Of course. But I don't."

"Okay." He exhaled. "I'll grow up. Be patient with me. I'll get over it."

"All right."

"And last night was unacceptable. I could say it happened because I drank too much, but that's an excuse. I am really sorry. I embarrassed you. I embarrassed myself." Now Jake raised his head to look at her.

"Thank you for saying that." Mona nudged his foot with hers. "And I'll try to remember to tell you regularly how much better you are than that bohunk."

Jake sighed and he ran his hands through his hair. "No, he's a better man than I am. I behaved like a jerk."

"Whatever." *He has, but no point in rubbing it in.*

"I have. I've made you wait while I figure out this job thing and I haven't been fair to you. I thought if I hedged on commitment with you, it would be like a test and you'd go back to T.C."

"Oh."

"So, I'm sorry about that, too."

"It's okay."

"You're the best girl-bartender-farmer in the world."

"That's probably the most romantic thing you've ever said to me."

"Really? Sweetheart. My darling. My heart," he teased.

"I bet you say that to all the girls," Mona said.

"Just the beautiful ones." Jake kissed her and for the first time since T.C. had come to town and Jake talked about leaving, Mona felt like they were safe. It would be all right.

"One more thing," Jake said when they came up for air. Mona raised her eyebrows. *Was this it? Was he—*

"I'm not quite ready for the big commitment yet, but I'm almost there. Please be patient with me for a little while longer. I promise,

I'm not jerking you around. I just need a little more time." He dipped his head and looked up at her through his eyelashes.

Mona grabbed both sides of his head and pulled him in for another kiss. "I'll wait."

THIRTY-FIVE

THURSDAY MORNING MAW SAT on the stool behind the cash register in the bait shop and got comfortable with the newspaper and a couple fishing magazines. He'd just taken a sip of his coffee when his eyes got big and he choked, staring at the third page of the *County Post*. He pushed back from the counter and hurried back across the parking lot to the house. Banging through the back door, he yelled, "Peg!"

Peg came around the corner to the entryway, wiping her hands on a dish towel. "What?"

Maw pointed to the newspaper in his hand. "Did you see this? My God, did you see this?"

Peg squinted at the paper Maw held and her lips moved while she read the page he indicated. In bold letters beneath "Obituary" it read "Joanne Graff." The next obituary read "Earl Alois Schneider" and that was followed by another obituary for "Joanne Graff." "What on earth?" she asked. "Why did they run it twice? How odd."

"They're different," Maw said. "Listen. 'Joanne Graff, beloved mother of Rhonda Graff and Racquel Cranfield, and clerk at Bud's Supermarket tragically lost her life drowning in the Wissipaw River.' The other one begins 'Joanne Graff died unexpectedly on March 12. She was 43 years old, the daughter of Marv and Betty Ogden.' They're two different obituaries for the same person! Have you ever seen such a thing?"

"I haven't. What do you suppose?" Peg pulled the newspaper out of Maw's hands and continued reading it.

"Two different obituaries means two different people sent them in to the paper. Can you believe they'd run both like that? Keep reading."

"I'm trying to, but you keep talking."

Maw shut his mouth and waited for Peg to get to the best part. The whole thing was unbelievable. He shifted from left to right foot.

"Two different funerals?" Peg finally asked.

"I know! It's crazy, isn't it?"

"How is that possible? What does it mean? They're almost at the same time, too. Did The Pole not know her religion and want to cover all the bases?" A crease between Peg's eyebrows deepened while she tried to make sense of it.

"Beats me, but they can't be the same funeral twice. Look, they overlap by a half hour!"

"That's weird. Do you think one is a typo?"

"Could be, but the funeral's Saturday, and there won't be a new paper before then, so that's a big mistake to publish."

Peg slowly nodded. "Unless there actually are two separate funerals. That would be weird, but it could happen." She pushed up her sweatshirt sleeves and leaned against the kitchen table on her elbows.

"Why would there be two separate funerals?" Maw asked. Then his eyes narrowed and he said, "The Pole holds one and who holds the other one?"

"I heard June and Arlyce were somehow involved in Joanne's being out on the river. They were hiding her in Otto's ice shanty until they could get her out of town. Rumor was she was going to live with her daughter in California."

"So, the daughter is having a second funeral? That would make sense. She wouldn't know about The Pole's maybe."

"How on earth do people know which one to attend?" Peg wondered.

"Maybe," Maw said, "this is the answer to the age-old conundrum. You just go to the one where you normally go to church. Think of it. The Lutherans don't have to worry about clogging up the pews when the Catholics go up for communion. Nobody has to think about when to sit or stand or kneel or read along with the priest. Heck, each church even has their own version of The Lord's Prayer, so this could be the ideal situation. By the way, do you know if Joanne was Catholic?"

"I don't think she was," Peg said. "But I only know for certain that she wasn't Lutheran because we never saw her at church."

"It would be even weirder if she was Jehovah's Witness or something. Then neither funeral would be appropriate."

Peg lightly socked Maw in the arm. What he said seemed sacrilegious somehow, and the whole business made her uncomfortable. "I think we should go to the visitation at the Catholic church and then attend the Lutheran funeral service."

"Fine by me," Maw said. "I can't stand all that kneeling and their lousy monotone singing."

Peg took a step back from Maw. "Cut it out. If you get struck down for blasphemy, I want no part of it."

214

A similar conversation was taking place at the Bassville Pub where the locals gathered and passed around two copies of the *County Post*. Speculation over why Joanne was having two funerals (Although she wasn't actually having the funerals, was she? Someone was having them on her behalf.) ranged from confusion about her religious beliefs to the possibility that family members disagreed about what to do. Was The Pole a family member, though? Scotty thought not, he'd heard The Pole say marriage was just another form of slavery and no way was he ever getting chained down by any woman.

Gene Trayson walked into the bar and took a spot near Spade. "What's the good word?" he asked. He nodded at Mona who held a coffee mug in one hand and the coffee pot in the other.

"Everyone's wondering why there's two separate funerals for Joanne," Mona told him while pouring his cup full. "The *Post* printed two different obituaries with two difference services. Look." She slid her copy of the newspaper across the bar to him.

"I still say it's because nobody knows what religion she is," Spade said. He idly shook the dice cup and spilled the dice onto the bar. He gathered them up and shook again.

"But how do you know which one to attend?" Dale asked. He sat drinking coffee and sorting his mail retrieved from the post office on his way through town. "Or do you pick based on where you normally go to church?"

"I like that idea," Beau said. "I'll go to the Lutheran one. They've got a faster pastor."

"You can't say stuff like that," Mona said.

"Why not?" Beau asked. "What's the problem?"

"I don't know. It just feels disrespectful somehow."

"They are two separate funerals," Gene's deep voice broke through the conversation and everyone turned to look at him. "The Pole is having one and my wife and her friends are having the other one."

"Why's that?" Scotty said. A concerned expression flitted across his face. He had a bad feeling about what was coming out of his father's mouth next.

"Well, the ladies don't think The Pole has the right to have Joanne's funeral because of how he treated her. Technically, he doesn't have the right because he was only her boyfriend, and that isn't a legally recognized relationship. Arlyce called Joanne's daughter out in California and got her to agree to them handling her remains."

"But why have two funerals?" Spade asked.

"Because anyone can have a funeral, body or no body. The Pole had already begun to make arrangements when the ladies interfered. He felt he wanted to do his own thing, so as a result, there will be two funerals."

"Which one will her body be at?" Scotty asked.

"The Lutheran one. The Pole's Catholic, that's why he went to St. Bridget's. Your mother made plans with St. Peter's at the same time. Churches usually do funerals late in the morning, which is why the times overlap."

"Why no visitation at the Lutheran one?" Beau asked. "I mean, I'm not complaining. It speeds up the whole business." He ignored the dirty look Mona gave him.

Gene blew out a long sigh. "The ladies believe that since they aren't next of kin or family they don't need people to give their condolences. They just want to celebrate Joanne's life and give her a good send-off."

"That's a nice idea. I mean, it's kind of messed up that it goes against The Pole's plans, but the sentiment is good," Spade said.

"I don't think The Pole has any business having a separate funeral," Mona said.

Scotty shot her a sharp look. "Why?"

"Because." Mona ticked off the reasons on her fingers. "He treated her like shit. He doesn't have legal permission to have her funeral.

And I think it's crap that he expects people to give him condolences at a visitation. I never thought about it until Gene said something, but we're supposed to go up to The Pole and say 'sorry Joanne is dead' when maybe he killed her?"

"The cops said it was an accidental drowning," Scotty said. "I talked with Joe about this and he explained why."

"Doesn't matter. She wouldn't have been out on that water if The Pole didn't beat her up. There's no proof he *didn't* kill her either." Mona crossed her arms defiantly.

"Hey, kids, no fighting," Spade said. "Who's up for a game of pool?"

"You can't go around saying The Pole killed her when there's no proof," Scotty said to Mona.

"And you can't go around saying he *didn't* when there's no proof," Mona retorted. "I thought you were with me on this thing—you went after him last time I saw you here."

Spade piped up again. "Why are you acting like this? The Pole's a good guy."

"A good guy? A good guy? Seriously, how can you say that?" Mona put her hands on her hips and looked around the bar with a challenging expression on her face. "He beat up on her. All the time."

"And she stayed with him," Spade said, sliding the dice cup to the edge of the bar. "She could've left."

"From what I heard she was trying to and he didn't let her get very far."

"YOU DON'T KNOW THAT!" Scotty yelled. Everyone's eyes widened and they collectively leaned back, surprised at his outburst. Scotty was the most laid-back, even-tempered person around. He didn't even yell during a Packers game. But he just yelled at Mona, Mona who he'd known his whole life, a family friend and classmate. No one spoke or moved. They waited to see what Mona would do.

Mona planted both of her hands on the bar. Her words came out softly with a tiny quiver. "I can't believe you're defending him, Scotty. You're one of the most decent people I've ever met. At least I used to think so." A deep flush covered her cheeks and her neck.

"I don't need this kind of harassment." Scotty pushed back from the bar and started toward the door before stopping to turn and point a finger at Mona and say, "She could've left. Spade's right, Joanne *chose* to stay with him. But that doesn't matter. You think what you want, I'm not sticking around to fight about it." He looked at the rest of the men seated at the bar. "Anyone wants me, I'll be at Grumpy's—or the hotel." He stalked out the door towards Main Street and an uncomfortable silence grew.

The accusation that Joanne somehow *deserved* to get beat up fueled Mona's rage. She grabbed Scotty's half-empty can of soda and flung it into the bin. She wanted to tear into someone, break something, feel the satisfaction of something crushing beneath her fists.

"I should really get—" Spade was interrupted by Maw walking through the back door.

"Anyone here know why the paper's got two different funerals listed for the same person? And for that matter, why two obituaries?" Maw asked, his voice loud in the thick silence.

Dale shook his head quickly but Maw didn't catch the signal. "What's the matter? Who died?" Maw shrugged off his plaid flannel jacket and threw it over a bar stool.

"Joanne did, that's what we were just talking about," Mona said.

"Actually, we should probably change the subject," Dale said.

"Why? What's the matter? I can't be the only one who thinks it's confusing," Maw said. "Which one's the real funeral? Was it a typo?"

"The Lutheran one is the real funeral," Mona said.

"They're both real," Gene said. He felt tired thinking about how messed up the whole business had become. If Dottie and her friends would've just left things alone. Or if The Pole would've backed off and let them handle the funeral. Without wanting to be, he found himself up to his neck in the middle of it, wife on one side, son apparently on the other.

"They can't both be real," Maw argued. He sat down beside Spade. "I'll have a Mountain Dew," he told Mona and grubbed around in his jeans pocket for change to pay her.

"You up for a quick game of dice?" Spade asked. He slid his wallet out of his back pocket and took out a five-dollar bill.

"No, I gotta get back to the shop. I just told Peg I was running in to grab gas. If I gad around too long, she'll be mad."

Mona wondered why men couldn't just tell women the truth. Maw could've just as easily told Peg he was curious about Joanne's funerals and she'd have let him come to town without a second thought. As Spade explained the situation of Joanne's two funerals, Mona's customers drifted out the doors with various explanations—Gene back to the farm, Dale to meet a client and Beau just snuck off, leaving Mona alone in the bar with Maw and Spade.

"That's crazy. We're going to go to the Lutheran one after the visitation." Maw took a swig out of his can of soda.

"Mona," Spade's voice held a warning tone.

"What? I didn't say anything yet."

"Be cool, kiddo."

"I am." She gave Maw a tight smile. "I think that's a swell idea. Go tell The Pole how sorry you are that his wife isn't around for him to beat up anymore and then head down the street to her funeral service, that he probably isn't even allowed to go to anyway."

"What are you talking about?" Maw asked. "He'll be at the Catholic one, why would he go to the Lutheran one?"

"Exactly. He should stay away from the real funeral," Mona stated.

"You seem wound pretty tight," Maw said, eying her carefully. He took another drink from his can of soda and seemed to suddenly notice the empty bar. "Where'd everyone go?"

Spade shrugged and glanced at his wristwatch. "I gotta go, too. Working second shift this week." He escaped out the back door. *Sheesh*, he thought, *I hope this business blows over fast.* He really didn't have to go to work, the factory was only running one shift these days, but Mona didn't know that. Spade didn't feel like getting in the middle of her and Scotty, choosing one side over another seemed disloyal somehow, so he drove home.

"How can anyone think The Pole deserves people's sympathy?" Mona asked Maw after briefing him on her argument with Scotty. "That's the dumbest thing."

"Well, he did love her, in his way." Maw knew that was a lame offering. He tried to think of an example to support this claim and came up empty other than, "They did a lot of things together."

"Like what?"

"Fishing sometimes."

"And?"

"I don't know. I think they might have hunted together."

Mona blew out her cheeks. "He screwed around on her, beat her up, treated her like shit. I have a hard time understanding why everyone's all 'Poor Adam.' Joanne's the one to feel sorry for."

"But she's dead," Maw said. "Funerals are for the living."

"It's not right."

Maw could see that Mona was dug in and he didn't feel like trying to convince her she was wrong. He sat back and gazed around the empty bar. "Well. I suppose I better get back to the ranch."

Mona waved him off. She seethed at Scotty and the general unfairness of the whole situation. It was wrong to blame Joanne for getting hurt by someone. Sure, she should've left, but she probably had her reasons for staying. Besides, she was trying to leave and that's what mattered.

As she wiped down the linoleum counter it occurred to her that arguing about it might get her in trouble. If Scotty didn't come in the bar because of fighting with her, well then who else might avoid coming in either because they wanted to be with Scotty or they agreed with him and disagreed with her? She understood that her job was to make people happy, host a good time. The bar was their escape, not supposed to cause people headaches and stress.

But the injustice of it! It seemed hypocritical to pretend she agreed with people when she didn't.

The whole business frustrated her. Maybe she should quit working at the Pub sooner than she planned. It would be a stretch money-wise, but she could see if Judi and Sue needed help at the hotel. No locals came in there, so she wouldn't get in trouble running her mouth. Or Bud probably needed to hire someone to replace Joanne. Terrible thought. Besides, everyone local came in there.

As the end of her shift drew near, Mona became more and more uncomfortable. Should she fess up to Steve—or hope for things to blow over? Maybe nothing would come of it. She'd never fought with Scotty before, at least not since they were little kids. It might end up no big deal. She decided to lay low and keep her trap shut.

THIRTY-SIX

Saturday morning Maw and Peg woke up still unsure exactly how they'd pay their respects to Joanne. By now they both had heard explanations of why two obituaries, two funerals, and the firm line drawn in the turf between The Pole and June, Arlyce and Dottie. The fact that both funerals would take place around the same time meant choosing one camp over the other. No one could fake it, and that made Maw particularly uncomfortable. The three women represented good families in town, they were respectable and helpful citizens who might have meddled where they had no business, but Joanne had solicited their assistance. They'd gone out of their way for her. The newspaper account of Joanne's death revealed how she'd been housed in Otto's ice shanty and provided with bedding and food, and how June had discovered her when trying to bring her to the bus depot in Northfield. Plus, Joanne's daughters had given the women their blessing for having a memorial service for their mother, which counted for a lot.

The flip side meant ignoring The Pole, who Maw and Peg agreed was not a bad person, just somewhat troubled. He'd grown up in one of those huge Catholic families, his mom died when he was young and his father was a notorious drunk. Adam had raised himself, really, dropping out of school by eighth grade to work first as a farmhand, then on construction crews. Unlike his father, he didn't drink until he passed out in the bar or on the street. He was also capable of working, a feat his father never mastered, either. Sure, he had a violent streak, but most men did once they got done drinking a case of beer or a pint of whiskey—the fact that he took out his aggression mostly on his girlfriend didn't bother Maw, who believed Joanne was a free human being and could leave if she was inclined to do so. Besides, The Pole was a cheerful personality most of the time, and had done his fair share of good deeds around town. "Why," Maw pointed out while selecting a necktie from his dresser drawer, "he helps out on job sites when people are short-handed. He can drywall, shingle, pour concrete, frame and even handle electrical work. He looks out for the older people in town, kept Vera Schmidt's gutters cleaned out and windows washed until she died."

Peg nodded while working out the bunched and twisted leg of her pantyhose. "It's hard to blame him for Joanne's death when the police call it accidental."

It was a conundrum.

June had a steely look in her eye when Loyal came in from milking. His eggs and sausage links were on the table and she pointed to her wristwatch. "You've got a half hour to eat and get ready. We have to pick up Mom and Dad."

Loyal sat down obediently after washing his hands in the kitchen sink. He ate without talking and then retreated upstairs to take a shower. June cleared away his dishes while wondering what the day would bring. What if no one came to their memorial service for Joanne? How disappointing it would be to discover the town could forgive The Pole so easily and quickly. No, she told herself. Minimally her family, Arlyce's and Dottie's would attend. She felt certain the Coopers would come to church, as would other Lutheran families like the Longwells and Paulicks. Bud and the other employees from the supermarket probably had no love lost for The Pole. She decided that fifty people would be a decent turn out.

She wished she could sneak into St. Brigid's just to see how many people actually showed up there, but she'd have to rely on hearing about it through the town grapevine. Without asking, of course. It wouldn't do to gloat.

June checked her reflection in the mirror next to the front door. She fluffed out her hair around her ears and was glad to have an occasion to wear the pearl earrings Loyal had bought for her birthday a few years ago. They'd been an extravagant gift, she knew, and they weren't her taste at all. Still, it was wasteful to never wear them, so she did—to church and weddings and funerals. At least pearls went with everything, she supposed. Though a pair of twisted gold hoops would have looked better on her with her hair shorter.

Waiting for Loyal to finish getting ready, she restlessly puttered around the house, sorting mail, adjusting pillows on the couch, plucking dead leaves off a spider plant until she heard his feet on the stairs. She took a deep breath and squared her shoulders. It was time.

Arlyce knelt to tie Trapper's shoes while clenching her purse strap with her teeth. She stood, forgetting the open cabinet door above her from where she had grabbed a cup so Fisher could get a drink of water, and cracked her head hard against the bottom edge. A flash of stars burst across her eyes and she cut loose a string of curse words. The children stared at her with open eyes while she clutched at her skull. Her fingers felt no blood, but a good-sized lump had begun to form at the crown. "GODDAMN IT!" she screamed.

Steve rounded the corner into the room and froze before asking, "What happened?"

She pointed at the kids standing around her legs and screamed, "Would it kill you to give me a hand? My God, what are you doing?"

Steve looked down at his bare legs and feet and answered, "Nothing. Why?"

Gritting her teeth, Arlyce considered leaving the house alone. To hell with her lump of shit husband and getting four kids ready to parade in public. The only thing to consider was the numbers. They had to have a good showing for Joanne's service. She inhaled deeply and counted to ten in her head. "Can you *please* put on pants and finish getting ready? I have managed to get ready and dress and feed our children. You could at least pull yourself together."

"Okay, okay," Steve said. "You didn't say you needed help."

"I don't know, Steve. Four kids. Do the math."

"You don't have to be sarcastic." He disappeared down the hall and Arlyce heard the TV get switched off. Lazy asshole was probably lying in bed before he ran out by her. She turned to the kids, who somehow began unraveling while she was talking to her husband. Smoothing cowlicks with her licked palm and tucking in shirts, she hollered down the hall, "I want to leave in five minutes!"

Six of them would take up half a pew. There were twenty pews at St. Peter's. Plus the Butterfields, Traysons, the crew from Bud's Supermarket, the Coopers, Paulicks and Longwells. She calculated a half-full church. "Lord," she prayed out loud, "please fill that place and let Joanne see it full."

Dottie put her hands on her hips and took a deep breath before unloading on her firstborn child. "Scott Bartholomew Trayson, you get a tie on and get in that truck *right now.*"

Scotty pulled the covers over his head and groaned. "Leave me be, Ma."

"Don't make me say it again."

"So don't say it again."

Dottie yanked at the edge of a blanket, revealing Scotty's bare back and shoulders. "Why are you being so stubborn?"

"Why are you making such a big deal out of this?" Scotty sat up and glared at her. Her easygoing son never scowled. She stepped back in surprise. "I don't want to go. Anywhere. Leave me be."

"Mama?" Angie's voice came through the door. "Daddy says we should get a move on."

"Can you just tell me why you can't show respect to Joanne?" Dottie asked. "You knew her better than I did."

"I can't choose between you guys and The Pole. It isn't right. If I go to one funeral everyone at the other one will say I'm wrong. If I go to the other funeral, I'm wrong. I can't take a side, you know that. I work with him." Scotty pulled his pillow over his face and his muffled voice continued, "I wish I could go fishing."

"Shame on you! How can you live with yourself?" Dottie whisper-shouted. She turned on her heel and stomped out of his bedroom and down the hall. "I'm coming," she bellowed to the rest of her family. June and Arlyce would be pissed. They expected her to bring Scotty. At least he wasn't going to The Pole's funeral. That she knew of, anyway. Dottie kept an eye on the house while Gene backed out of the driveway. If that kid of hers snuck out behind her back to go to the Catholic church …

Dale and Dob shook The Pole's hand and expressed their sympathy in low voices. Organ music echoed through the church, against the stained glass windows and vaulted ceiling, across the altar and into the sacristy. "She was always friendly," Dale said. "I'm going to miss her behind the cash register at Bud's. Always ran the fastest lane, too."

The Pole nodded and brushed his calloused hands against his red eyes. Dob looked over his shoulder at Sal and Judi waiting in line behind them. "Well, like I said, the wives couldn't get away today, but they're sorry, too."

"Thank you." The Pole lowered his eyes and Dale nudged his brother with his elbow.

"Right then. Let us know if you need anything."

They retreated down the aisle, noting a few elderly couples waiting in the pews for the service to begin. They sat in one of the back pews and Dob sighed heavily, straining the buttons on his dress shirt. "Think we're doing the right thing?"

"It's a fair split," Dale said. "The wives are at the Lutheran church, we're here. We work with Adam, we can't side against him."

"I know." Dob stared ahead at the front of the church where the priest was speaking to The Pole and straightening his vestments. "It just feels wrong somehow."

Sue and Judi sat in the empty pew ahead of the Dohill brothers and Judi turned around. "It's so sad."

"I'm surprised you two are here," Dale said.

Sue shrugged. "We're midway through getting that deck built." Her expression was resigned and Judi reached over to hold her mother's hand.

It made sense to Dob. No one needing The Pole's help would go to the other funeral. That explained the old people sitting in the pews. The organ music stopped and the priest walked The Pole to the front pew. Dob discretely unbuttoned the top of his collar and waited for the mass to start.

June fought the urge to twist around in her seat and count heads.

Peripherally she could see the first few rows were pretty full, but were people still coming in? The pianist played the final chords of *May Sheep Gently Graze* and reached up to shuffle her music. Under the pretense of whispering in Mona's ear, June turned and looked at the back of the church. Two-thirds full. The female Dohills were a nice surprise, they must have split funeral duty with their husbands, she thought. She sat straighter when the pastor cleared his throat and thanked everyone for coming.

"It is with heavy hearts that we gather together to remember our sister, Joanne Graff. She was a friend to all she met. Who can forget her kindness to others, her smile greeting us at Bud's, her gentle spirit ..." As the pastor droned on, June relaxed. It didn't matter what was going on down the road at St. Brigid's. A hundred people had decided to come *here.*

When it was time for her to speak, June didn't feel afraid or nervous as she expected she might. A cool calm settled over her and she surveyed the room for a long moment before reading off the pages she'd written out last night. Mona gave her a small smile and nodded encouragement.

"Joanne's darkest moments weren't when she slid beneath the ice last week." The reaction in the room was palpable. Bodies leaned forward, the buzz of people gathered together ceased. She had their full attention.

"No, her darkest moments came before her lungs filled with water, before her heart stopped beating. Every time the person she should have been able to trust the most betrayed her, Joanne suffered. Every time she expected love and received a black eye, a broken arm, a bruise or a lump, that was her darkest moment."

Everyone's gaze stuck on June while she continued. "We ignored that darkness. Domestic abuse is an ugly thing. It makes us uncomfortable to look at it too closely, to notice it. But Joanne needed somebody to see it. She needed someone with fresh eyes and a healthy perspective to tell her it wasn't okay, and that she could do better."

June pointed to Arlyce, who sat in the front row bouncing Victoria on her leg. "My friend Arlyce is known for being direct." Scattered chuckles rippled through the room. June paused before continuing. "She didn't leave Joanne alone. She called her out for lying about falling down stairs or tripping on the ice. She told Joanne she could help her.

"We tried to help Joanne. We failed." June looked toward the rafters and blinked fast to keep the tears back. She sniffed and continued. "That doesn't have to be the end of the story. What you and I can do to make it up to her—to *apologize* for pretending that getting beat up was okay or too embarrassing to talk about—is to speak up, starting today. Right now, every time you see someone treated wrong, say something. Offer to help, offer to get help, tell them they don't have to stay where they are. Tell them they're not alone, they don't deserve to be hit or kicked or shoved around."

June pointed to herself. "*I* was chicken. I was too afraid to say anything to Joanne because I didn't think it was my business. I thought it was impolite. Boy, that was dumb." She shook her head. "I had nothing to lose. But ultimately Joanne lost her life."

June put her hands on both sides of the lectern for support. "We can honor Joanne's memory by not letting this happen again. Speak up. Offer help. I guarantee that if we do that, somewhere up there, Joanne will be smiling and forgive us."

The pastor stepped forward, and with his arm around June's shoulder, led a closing prayer. The church emptied out, everyone resuming regular life. June hugged Dottie, then Arlyce, and watched her herd her children down the sidewalk. Mona kissed her mother's cheek, whispering how proud she felt of her, and left with Jake by her side. Steve unlocked the Pub and turned on the lights. Bud returned to the supermarket and flipped the sign back to "Open." Dottie and Gene drove back to the farm where Dottie was grateful to see Scotty's truck still parked in the driveway.

June walked beside Loyal and Frank, Loyal pushed Nancy's chair and Nancy reached across to grab June's hand. "Shit."

June squeezed her mother's hand and gave her a tight smile. "Shit."

THIRTY-SEVEN

CARRIE AND TROY VANDERLEE shared the same dream: a quiet country home where they could raise their family with good Midwestern values and enjoy a safe, close community. Carrie's dream stemmed from a childhood spent watching and reenacting scenes from *Little House on the Prairie* and *The Waltons*. She fantasized about bringing homemade cakes to the community picnics, watching her children compete to capture a greased pig and seeing all her neighbors at church on Sunday. Troy's impulse came from a simpler place: he didn't like other people very much, so a few acres between him and his closest neighbor plus six-foot-high fencing struck him as the ideal set-up.

They'd run across an advertisement for Trayson's Crossings in one of several real estate catalogs they regularly skimmed while looking for their dream house. The development company explained that the lots had just been platted and they could be one of the first people to move in. After discussing the logistics of the forty-minute drive to their jobs in Northport, where Troy worked as an accountant and Carrie practiced nursing, they agreed that Northport did not offer the close, secluded community they yearned for—but Bassville! They knew a small town with only two churches and a river wending through would offer the quaint country lifestyle of their L.L. Bean-infused dreams.

Carrie buckled their daughters into the back seat of their station wagon and Troy double-checked that he'd locked the front door of their tri-level home in Northport. Their new house, they'd agreed, would be a classic Cape Cod. The girls, aged three and five, were contented with coloring books in the back seat and Carrie turned to her husband. "I really hope this works out. We need to build before Rebecca starts school."

Troy agreed, smiling fondly at his firstborn as he checked the rear view mirror and backed out of their driveway. His watch read 9:02. They planned to drive to the subdivision and explore the lots, then eat lunch at one of the local establishments and get a real feel for Bassville, maybe even meet some of their future friends and neighbors.

Two hours later the Vanderlees sat in the parking lot behind the Bassville Pub. Carrie worried about how they'd get the mud cleaned off the station wagon. Why on earth hadn't the town paved the main road? Her daughters had become restless and hungry, but several places, including the Bassville Pub and the grocery store on the corner had posted "Closed" signs. The one on the grocery store explained that the employees were attending a funeral. On one hand, it was really sweet that the whole town shut down to honor someone who'd died. On the other, it was pretty inconvenient to arrive in a ghost town without any open shops or restaurants.

Troy appreciated the majestic power of the flooded river rushing past the docks. He noticed how the water had risen to the edge of the parking lot and he wondered exactly how much higher it would get. He also contemplated the veracity of the realtor's claim of privacy in Trayson's Crossings. The map on the development's billboard showed more lots than he'd imagined, and while the realtor assured him that they could buy more than one lot to insure their privacy and of course not all of the lots would sell, why, it would be *years* before the development would be completely built up. He tapped his fingers on the steering wheel in time with the rhythmic kicking on the back of his seat.

Troy was about to suggest they drive towards home and find a place for lunch on the way when two cars pulled into the parking lot and people began walking towards the Pub's entrance. Lights were turned on inside the building and Troy looked at his wife. "Looks like they're opening."

"Finally!" Carrie exclaimed. She got out and helped unbuckle her daughters in the back seat. "Are you hungry, girls? Let's go eat hamburgers."

The four Vanderlees walked into the Pub and Rebecca began to cough from the smoke. "Oh dear," Carrie murmured. "I hope they have a nonsmoking section." She escorted the girls to one of the tables by the windows overlooking the river.

Troy approached the bar where a large man wearing a tight polo shirt was talking to a cluster of customers. He studied the men carefully. They looked rough and hard-working. His thin accountant's hands became embarrassing to him and he shoved them in his jacket pockets. "Hi, I was wondering if we could get some menus?"

The bartender pulled a stack of menus out of a rack by the cash register and handed them across the bar. "You need a beer or anything?"

"We'll probably just order sodas with our lunch."

The bartender nodded. "Let me know when you're ready to order."

The front door of the bar opened and in walked a line of people. Troy guessed they'd been at the funeral together since they seemed dressed up. The atmosphere became louder as one man with receding red hair and Coke-bottle glasses put money in the pool table and the balls tumbled out. "I'll rack 'em," he told one of the men he'd come in with, a barrel-chested man who looked a lot like another guy already seated at the bar. Troy returned to the table with the menus.

"Do they have a children's menu?" Carrie asked, flipping over the laminated booklet. "And did you ask if they have crayons for the girls?"

"I don't think it's that kind of restaurant," Troy said. "This is a bar, after all."

Rebecca continued to cough. "This is bad for her allergies, Troy," Carrie said.

"What do you want me to do?" Troy asked.

Carrie rolled her eyes and then leaned forward. "Baby, just try and relax. When we get home I'll put you in a steamy bath and we'll clear you up."

Rebecca nodded and began rotating in slow circles on her bar stool.

"Troy, make sure she doesn't fall off of that."

"She's fine."

More people entered the bar from the back door, and the vision Carrie had created of a small family-centered community began to dissipate. One tall, thin woman wearing dangling earrings took a drag off her cigarette before slinging a baby in a car seat atop the other pool table. Three boys wearing galoshes and dress pants started playing a game of tag around the other customers after helping themselves to glasses of soda behind the bar.

It became clear after several minutes that they'd have to order at the bar if they wanted any service, so Troy retraced his steps.

"You ready to order?" the bartender asked. "Sorry, I forgot about you sitting back there. Kind of got busy."

"No problem," Troy told him. "Can we get three burger baskets, two Cokes, a root beer and a milk?"

"Sure." The bartender scrawled something on a pad. "Fries with all of them?"

"Yes, please." Troy glanced back at Carrie who drew small frantic circles with her right hand, urging him to keep going. "And is there someplace else to sit? My daughter has allergies to cigarette smoke."

"Dining room's nonsmoking, kind of. Just go past the dart machines. Light switch is on your left."

"Thanks." Troy handed him the menus.

Troy returned to the table and helped Carrie guide the girls into the dining room where they sorted themselves around a table with a great view of the river. "Now this is more like it!" Carrie exclaimed.

They'd just pulled out the literature about the lots at Trayson's Crossings when a frail-looking old man pushing a plump old woman in a wheelchair came into the dining room. Carrie smiled at them, thinking how wonderful to expose her children to different ages and abilities. Bassville was a diverse community. "Hi!" she said.

"Hi!" the man replied. The woman nodded, her face creased with pleasure. She pointed at the girls. "Shit!"

Carrie's face fell. "Pardon me?"

The couple stood beside the table. "We usually sit here," the man said.

A sturdy-looking middle aged woman entered the dining room at this point and grasped the man's elbow. "Dad, we're going to sit at this table." She smiled briefly and nodded at the Vanderlees before moving a chair aside and guiding the wheelchair up to the table next to where they sat.

Carrie widened her eyes at Troy. He shrugged and continued

helping the girls build a tower with packets of jam and coffee creamers.

"Shit!" the woman in the wheelchair crowed.

"I'll say," the man agreed. "That river's going to flood a lot this year."

Flood? Troy thought. He leaned forward. "Excuse me, are you from here?"

The younger woman turned around to face him. "Yes. I'm June Butterfield, my parents," she gestured at the older couple, "used to own the Log Cabin. The bar up the street," she explained. "My husband and I have a dairy farm a few miles up the road."

"What were you saying about the river flooding?" Troy asked.

"Shit!" the old woman exclaimed. Rebecca giggled and Carrie shushed her.

"Every spring," June said with a shrug. "Ice melts, rain falls, the river floods. Happens every year. This year will be worse than usual, though."

The skinny woman with the baby walked in, exhaling a cloud of cigarette smoke. "I'm sorry to bother you, June, but can you help with Victoria while I get these lunch orders started?"

June took the baby girl into her arms and bounced her on her lap. "You okay out there?"

"Yeah." The woman glanced over her shoulder and then back at June. "We should've called Mona. It'll be all right."

The woman walked through the doorway leading to the kitchen and Carrie watched her stub out her cigarette in an ashtray on the counter before disappearing into a walk-in cooler. "Is it legal to smoke in a kitchen like that?" she whispered to Troy.

"Mommy, what's 'shit' mean?" Rebecca asked.

"Oh! Sweetie," Carrie lowered her voice. "Don't say that word."

"She said it." Rebecca pointed at the woman in the wheelchair.

"Thit!" squealed Elizabeth and Carrie held her finger over the toddler's mouth.

"No. Naughty."

The red-headed man from the pool table walked in and set down three sodas on the Vanderlees' table. "I forgot which one Steve said was the root beer, but I'm sure you'll figure it out."

"Do you have straws?" Carrie asked.

"Dunno." He turned to the other table. "Heya, Frank. Nancy. Can you believe they actually got me to work here now?"

"Shit!" Nancy replied. She beamed at him.

"What?" Frank leaned forward and cupped his ear. "I thought you worked at the mill."

"He's teasing, Dad." June put her hand on her dad's shoulder and looked up at the man. "Can you tell Loyal we're sitting back here when he turns up?"

"Sure thing."

"It seems like everyone knows each other here. Such a small town." Carrie made this comment loudly, addressing June.

"That's true." June spread her knees apart and gently eased the baby down to the floor where she could stand with support. "What brings you folks through town? It's not tourist season."

Troy laughed. "We were looking at a lot out at Trayson's Crossings."

The woman's expression became guarded. "Oh. I see."

"We'd love to raise our family in a small town. So much safer. Family values. Less anonymity than in the city," Carrie said. "Have you always lived here?"

"My whole life. Except for when I went to college," June said.

"Didn't you order her a milk?" Carrie asked Troy. "And Rebecca needs a smaller glass. She's going to spill this."

Troy stood. "I'll go ask."

Carrie gave the other table an apologetic nod. "You know how it is with little kids."

"Shit!" Nancy said agreeably.

Carrie cocked her head. "Do you mind?" She pointed at the girls.

"She can't help it, she had a stroke," June said in a weary voice.

"Oh. I'm sorry." Carrie felt chastened. Well, maybe an old lady saying 'shit' was kind of colorful, she guessed.

Troy had returned with a smaller glass in one hand when June stood up and started for the door. Clint Eastwood's clone stopped her with both hands on her shoulders. "Sweetie, don't."

"No. No way." She pushed him off and rushed into the bar area. The Vanderlees froze when the yelling and screaming started. The older couple at the table next to them leaned towards the door to listen while Carrie pulled her daughters onto her lap.

A crash and the sound of metal scraping reached their ears and Troy reached for his wallet. "Maybe I should pay for our drinks and we can grab McDonald's on the way home."

Carrie nodded, a shell-shocked glaze forming in her eyes. She stared at the door where a mass of bodies appeared to surge back and forth. Did she just see someone punch the guy who'd brought their drinks?

"It's your fault she's dead!"

"You have no right to do that!"

"I loved her! I loved her!"

Troy gathered his children, boosting one on each hip and said to his wife, "Stay close. We'll make a run for it."

The skinny woman with the dangly earrings walked into the dining room at that moment, carrying a tray with their food. "Cheeseburgers and fries!" she announced with a perky smile. "Hot off the grill!"

"Look," Troy said, "I don't think we should stay. I'm sorry." He felt bad, their food had been prepared and he understood that it cost money, but he couldn't sit with his children and eat while a brawl broke out twenty feet from their table.

"Oh, that?" The woman distributed the plastic baskets with burgers and fries while laughing. "That won't come to anything. Joe's here. He's just letting them blow off some steam."

"Joe?" Troy asked.

"Town cop," she explained. "He'll keep things under control."

Troy watched a burly, bearded man in a three-piece suit clench his fists and stare down the Clint Eastwood-clone. They circled each other and then the bearded man threw out an upper cut so fast, the other man flew backwards into the crush of people standing behind him. The bearded man bellowed, "Come on! Who's got the nuts? It's my right! I have my rights!"

The waitress pulled a bottle of ketchup out of her apron pocket. "They're fighting because The Pole killed his girlfriend and the funeral was today. June and I were hiding her in Otto's ice shanty, she drowned in the river. We, well, June, me and Dottie, got permission from Joanne's daughter to hold her funeral, but The Pole went ahead and had his own. He's just pissed." She shrugged, as if the entire situation were of no more consequence than needing an oil change or missing a dentist appointment.

"My God," Carrie breathed. She looked at Troy. "I'm sorry. There's nothing wrong with the suburbs. I don't want to move."

The woman tilted her head. "You want to move here? Dottie and her husband have all kinds of land for sale. Maybe you've heard of Trayson's Crossings? That's what they're calling it. Their last name."

Troy passed his younger daughter to his wife and used his free hand to dig out his wallet again. "We can't stay. This isn't safe." He pulled out a twenty and held it out to the woman. "Will this cover the burgers?"

"You want me to put them in a to-go box?" she asked.

A glass shattered in the bar and a deep voice was saying, "Calm down! Enough!"

"No." He bent his head low and led his family out of the dining room, around the corner and out the back door of the Bassville Pub. He snuck a peek to see that the big bearded man was crying now, his huge shoulders heaving with sobs while two other men guided him to sit on a bar stool.

Outside, in the parking lot, the Vanderlees buckled their daughters into the back seat and Troy gunned the engine. He and Carrie didn't speak until they reached the highway and passed the billboard announcing "White Bass Capital of the Western Hemisphere!"

"I never saw anything like that on *The Waltons*," Carrie observed wryly.

"You think it's something in the water supply? That had to be the weirdest collection of people I've ever met in my life."

Giggling, Carrie folded up the map the realtor had given them and dropped it on the floor mat. "That old lady, saying 'shit,' and that goofy-looking man bringing in our drinks."

"I mean," Troy chuckled, "if you're in the middle of a bar fight by noon, well, that's something special."

"What do you say we finish the basement and make a play room for the girls? And maybe redo the back patio with a bigger deck."

"I say whatever we do to our house is worth the money. We couldn't afford the therapy if we moved our kids to Bassville!"

THIRTY-EIGHT

Mona hunched her shoulders against the cold air and shivered. Her fingers fumbled with the key while she bounced on her toes. Finally she got the door unlocked and walked inside the Pub. She switched on the lights and made her way to the bar to unlock the front door. Her footsteps echoed through the empty bar. It had been over a week since Joanne's funeral and the bar fight that followed. Plywood still covered one broken window overlooking the river.

Mona turned on the OPEN sign and glanced over at Jake's little blue cottage on the other side of the Wissipaw. Ice chunks bashed and slugged against each other in the open water. Last night's town council meeting had ended in a unanimous decision to leave the culvert alone, so his place was safe. Gene had argued that other opportunities for development made more sense. People should build where the water couldn't reach it; allowing the river to disrupt properties that had sat on high ground for decades just for the sake of some wildlife didn't make sense. No one disagreed and after a short debate he called for the vote.

As Mona made her way to turn on the light above the pool table she caught sight of The Pole's truck, still parked in front of Grumpy's, though now a slip of blue paper fluttered where it was pinned beneath a windshield wiper. Nobody had seen him since the day of the funeral.

"Hey, lady. You got time to lean, you got time to clean!"

Mona turned toward Spade who had snuck in through the kitchen entrance. He pulled up a spot at the bar and dumped a pocketful of quarters in front of him. Busily he began sorting them into piles.

"You rob a Laundromat?" Mona asked.

"Nope. I robbed some HoChunk Indians," Spade said with a grin. He expertly flipped a coin into the air and caught it. "Slots."

"Congratulations." She moved behind the bar. "I have to get the coffee started. What'll you have?"

"Pepsi." He pushed three quarters across to her. "What were you looking at?"

"The Pole's truck. It's still parked across the street."

"Wasn't that something?" Spade asked. "I've known your dad a long time and I've never seen him punch a guy. That was incredible."

"It was something else," Mona agreed. She hadn't seen it happen, only heard about it over and over as Bassville wove the events of Joanne's funeral into another layer of the town's legends. "He still hasn't come back."

"Would you?" Spade asked. "I mean, whatever you believe—he killed her or he didn't—how does a guy walk around town with everyone second-guessing him?"

The door blew open, letting in a burst of cold air and Scotty and Beau. "Hey, beautiful." Beau leered at her.

"Hey, handsome," Mona flipped back at him. She measured coffee grounds from the Folgers canister into the filter. "Coffee'll be a few minutes."

242

"You taking breakfast orders?" Scotty asked.

"Sure. Arlyce isn't here yet, but I can start the grill. You guys are getting an early start on your day."

Scotty adjusted his baseball cap. "Yeah."

"I'm a working stiff today," Beau announced. "Stiff—heh. Get it?"

"Beau's helping me finish that deck over at the hotel. They want it ready before the walleye run starts and the weather looks like it'll hold for the next week so I hired him." Scotty nudged Beau with his elbow. "Think about that for a second, you're working for me! You're my crew!"

"Don't get cocky, pal. I can quit and don't you forget it."

Spade leaned into the conversation, his eyes wide behind his Coke bottle glasses. "Where do you think The Pole went?"

Scotty shrugged. "Dunno. But I gave Sue and Judi my word and I don't want to let them down. Guess I'm on my own now, at least for this job."

"What will you do next?" Mona wanted to know.

"Maybe work for the Dohills. Maybe keep working for myself. I've learned plenty, so it's not like I can't hire myself out for smaller jobs."

"Good for you," Mona said.

"Besides, I don't think The Pole can swing a hammer too well with a stab wound."

"That was *crazy*," Beau said. "I still can't get over that. I mean, I thought your dad was a goner when The Pole lunged at him. Not that I blame the guy—Loyal cracked him a good one. But when Dob grabbed him around the neck and pulled out that knife to settle him down…"

Scotty's arms flung out in a wide gesture as he completed the story Mona had heard over and over for a solid week. "He just went NUTS. Bar stools flying, Arlyce and Steve's kids hiding under the pool table and Dob takes one wild swipe."

"I just wanted to threaten him," a deep voice finished. They turned and looked at Dob who was walking in from the kitchen. "He moved so damn fast. Next thing I know my knife is stuck in his side like I'm carving up a deer or something."

"Hey, Dob," Mona said. The description of The Pole getting stabbed with a Bowie knife still made her a little queasy.

"What do you kids know today?" Dob asked. He took a seat beside Scotty. "I'll have coffee, Mona."

"You ever get that knife back?" Spade asked Dob.

"Son of a bitch ran off with it." Dob scowled and he slapped the bar with his meaty fist. "That's what I get for trying to help a friend. I'm out a good hunting knife and a decent carpenter for side jobs to boot."

"Who knows what would've happened if you hadn't stepped in though," Spade said. "I've never seen a guy go so crazy in my life."

"Wonder where he is," Scotty mused.

"Wonder if he'll ever come back," Mona said. *But if his truck's still sitting there over a week later, chances are probably not.* For the first few days she'd expected to see him skulk down the street, maybe see him walk into Grumpy's. She couldn't imagine where he'd run off to on foot. But if her dad punched The Pole like everyone said, well, it would take guts to show his face around town again. As hard as she tried, she couldn't imagine the sight of her father delivering a right hook to anyone. A shame she'd missed seeing it. She grabbed an order pad from the shelf below the cash register. "Okay, who wants what?"

An hour later the breakfast crowd began to settle up their bills. Mona was tapping the totals on the register's keys and making change when Jake walked in, his arms full of a bouquet of roses.

"Look at Mr. Romance." Beau smirked.

"What's the occasion?" Dob asked. "Not a whole year yet, is it?"

Snuffy applauded from his corner perch where he had tucked into a cheese and sausage omelet. "Frank! Nancy!" he barked. "Look at this kid!"

Jake's ears were pink, from cold or embarrassment Mona couldn't tell, but he didn't break his stride. He nodded at Spade and cleared his throat. "Mona."

Spade slipped behind him and dropped a quarter in the jukebox.

Mona's gaze shifted from side to side until she looked back up at Jake. "Jake."

The jukebox's mechanical whir filled her ears and Alabama started playing. *The Closer You Get*. Mona's fingers curled into fists and she took a deep breath. Her stomach twisted and she knew exactly what was about to happen.

Jake held out his hand to her and she came around the edge of the bar, conscious of everyone staring. There she stood in jeans and a long-sleeved polo shirt and *this* would be her moment, she thought. Jake's brown work boots gleamed with polish, their shine matching his eyes. He crouched onto one knee while holding her hand. "Mona, I love you. I can't see spending my life with anyone else by my side. Will you," he paused to press the bouquet of flowers into her free hand and reach into his shirt pocket to pull out a small box. "Will you marry me?"

Applause filled Mona's ears and she grinned down at Jake, feeling stupid and overjoyed at the same time.

"I asked your dad and I polished my boots. You can't ask a girl to marry you while you're wearing dirty boots. I'm on my way to Beyer's. They've offered me a hell of a contract. We can get married this summer before we move to Atlanta." He snapped open the dark blue velvet ring box to reveal a diamond solitaire setting. "Make me the happiest man, Mona."

Her joy plunged into despair and she blinked back tears. Damn him for doing this in front of everyone. She felt all of the pressure to say yes, she *should* say yes, everyone expected her to. Even she expected to—except—

Atlanta. She stared into Jake's blue eyes. He was a good man. He'd be good to her and she could almost, *almost* imagine their life together. She raised her eyes towards the slow churning Wissipaw River outside the bar's windows. Down that river was her parents' farm, her greenhouse, her family and friends. Her town council spot. Her mind raced through memories of Jenny calling her chickenshit, her dad helping her break up the acres he'd taken out of corn for her to grow vegetables, Jake's first tentative kiss against her lips while they stood on her front porch.

It would be so easy to say yes.

Shouldn't she be blurting it out by now?

The words caught in her throat, dry and brittle.

If she said no he'd leave and maybe never come back.

If she said no they'd be done. She never heard of anyone sticking together after saying no to a marriage proposal.

If she said yes ... did heartbreak actually feel like pain? Her heart burned in her chest. Her cheeks grew hot.

She knew the right answer sat lodged in her hesitation.

Frank had wheeled Nancy into the bar from the dining room and her grandma's voice echoed in her ears. "Shit."

She shook her head and burst into crying. "I'm so sorry, Jake. I can't. No."

Slowly Jake rose to his feet. He took one, then two stunned steps backwards. The shock on his expression mirrored her own.

"I'm so sorry," she whispered. Her hands clutched around the slim stems of the roses.

"I thought this was what you wanted, Mona." Jake held his hand out towards her for a moment, then pulled it back. "Goodbye then."

He shook his head and left the bar walking hunched over like an old man. The door slammed behind him.

Mona stood alone in the middle of the jukebox and pool table and barstools while her customers awkwardly pulled on their gloves and left their money beside their empty plates and cups. They tried to leave as quickly and quietly as possible. Snuffy helped Frank steer Nancy down the sidewalk. Beau and Scotty followed them. Spade clapped Mona once on her shoulder before walking out. Dob grunted some condolence she couldn't decipher before leaving, too.

Her stomach felt like someone had punched it. Her head ached. Mona walked back behind the bar and leaned her forehead against the cool metal door of the beer cooler, hot tears dripping down her face while she gulped back her sobbing. *It's not supposed to end like this. Maybe I feel this awful because I gave the wrong answer.* Mona scrubbed at her tears with the heel of her hand. *But it's too late. I can't say no to a marriage proposal and still have him. Why can't love be enough? Why can't he be enough?* The sweet perfume of the roses filled her lungs.

THIRTY-NINE

On April first Maw didn't feel like fooling around while he checked the minnow tanks before perching on the stool behind the cash register. He pulled Boyd Douglas's business card from where he'd tucked it between a cup of pens and a stack of cassette tapes. Static filled the line between dial tones and Maw felt glad he hadn't gotten the busy signal again. He'd left several messages with Real Reels, the production company Boyd Douglas worked for.

The forecast called for clear skies and fifty degrees, so the walleye fishermen should be moving in soon, Maw figured. He'd had posters printed up and taken out ad space in three newspapers describing Maw's Bait and Tackle as "featured on the *Discovery* channel." He wanted to be able to tell his customers and fans *when* they could see him featured, hence the long-distance charges he kept racking up with daily calls to Real Reels.

Finally a man's voice greeted him.

"This is Maw Cooper, from Maw's Bait and Tackle in Bassville, Wisconsin. I need to speak with Boyd Douglas about the documentary he filmed about me."

The man cleared his throat and paused before saying, "This is Boyd."

"Boyd! You're a tough guy to track down! Listen, I'm promoting the hell out of your movie, but I need to know your release date."

"Right. We're making edits and adding soundtrack right now."

"Okay, so when will it be on TV? On the *Discovery* channel?"

"Hold on."

Maw listened to muffled voices and impatiently twirled a spinnerbait in his left hand. Finally Boyd came back on the line. "It will air in October."

"And how's it looking? You need to come up and get any more footage of me or the shop? Maybe want to come during the white bass run so you can see the whole crazy business in full swing?"

"That's not a bad idea," Boyd said. "I might do that."

"You let me know and I'll take care of all the details on my end."

"Thank you, Maw. And I should probably tell you that my documentary about your bait shop won't be airing on the *Discovery* network."

Maw felt something in his guts drop. "Oh?"

"The work we produce for them features hard science and technical aspects of different professions. What you've got going in your bait shop is ... unique, but not scientific."

"What do you mean? I have a whole laboratory—you saw it!" Maw's voice rose with panic. He told *everyone* he'd be on cable TV.

"Maw, we're still going ahead with the project. Your story will have a different angle. I'm pitching a series about the psychology behind why people allow themselves to be tricked. I plan to include a Ripley's *Believe It Or Not* museum, a cult leader from Minnesota and a woman who works a psychic hotline number."

"But—that's not what we—we have a contract! You can't make me out as a scam artist!" Maw's throat choked while he sputtered out his protests.

"It's in the fine print, Maw. You signed contracts that gave me creative license with whatever film footage you provided. Don't worry, your name will be all over this project."

"I don't want to be promoted as a scam artist! I'm a bait shop owner!"

"A bait shop owner with a brilliant marketing strategy," Boyd agreed. "It's still great publicity."

"That's not our deal!"

"Actually, it is. Read your contract."

Maw slammed down the phone receiver and howled. Then he stormed back to his minnow lab to find the copies of the contract Boyd had left behind for him. He'd get a lawyer, he decided, and they'd find the loophole. He took a deep breath and looked at the aquarium with the blue-dyed water. And if he couldn't get out of the contract? The worst would be telling Peg—who would never let this rest. He dreaded telling her the truth. And he'd have to be upfront about what he believed: people want the charade.

Loyal and Gene's arrival was announced by the bells on the bait shop's door. Loyal thumbed through the stack of envelopes in his hands and shrugged at Gene while they surveyed the empty store. The neon "Open" sign was lit, the door was unlocked, the radio was playing. A minute later Maw came around the corner with a distracted expression on his face. "What's the good word, gentlemen? You're not fishing today," Maw said.

Loyal shook his head. "No, we're here to leave this zoning request from Pete Swenson. He wants to backfill the wetlands behind his place. You can read it over before the next meeting."

"Don't know why anyone'd disagree about keeping those culverts," Maw added while taking the envelope from Loyal. "You haven't even sold a lot in Trayson's Crossing, so it's not like there's competition. Don't know the point of adding land when what's for sale ain't selling. Still, taking them out would've made the fishermen happy."

"You know fishermen aren't going to buy a lot and build a house here, it's the people who live up the road in Northport that will. Those people don't care about fishing. They care about peace and quiet and safety," Loyal said.

"Not that the news lately promotes those qualities," Gene said bitterly and stuffed his fists in his jacket pockets. "Did you see the Channel 5 headline? 'Death on the Ice.' They ran that story for five straight days. It's terrible publicity. No one wants to move to a town associated with murder. How could anyone want to move here when that story is the only news about Bassville?"

Loyal thought about that couple in the bar last weekend, the ones with the two kids. They'd left when the fighting started. But maybe people didn't think about buying land and moving in the springtime. Heck, maybe there wasn't much of a market in the first place.

"So we need to distract people," Maw said to Gene.

"Or something," Gene agreed.

Maw squinted up at the ceiling and rubbed his hands together. "What we need is feel good news, a happy story that will make Bassville sound like a great place to live."

Loyal grunted.

"Of course, it would help our reputation if you didn't go around slugging people in bars, Rocky Balboa," Maw said to Loyal.

Loyal smoothed his chapped hand where the bruising still colored his cheek. "One time." He sighed. "It's not going to become a habit."

"I'm just teasing you," Maw told him. He leaned back with his elbows on the front counter. "Who knows? Maybe The Pole had it coming. You probably did the right thing. Anyway, he's gone now and I bet he's not coming back."

"Think he killed Joanne?" Gene asked.

Maw shrugged. "I don't know, but a guilty man doesn't run, right?"

Loyal tapped his finger on the manila envelope with the Swenson zoning request. "I'll leave this with you. We need to get moving, Gene."

"You're the marketing genius, Maw. Put your brain on selling lots, will you?"

"I'll come up with something, don't worry." Maw's brow furrowed while he thought. "A marketing campaign that will help the town and our local businesses. I'll put all of my energy and creative thinking into full gear."

FORTY

JUNE STRAIGHTENED HER BLOUSE and checked her hair in the bathroom mirror. She felt frumpy despite letting the ladies at the Best Little Hair House talk her into those frosted highlights to cover some of her grey. The cut was flattering, but now the soft lumpy bit under her chin was more obvious and when did her neck become so … textured? Maybe next week she'd take Mona shopping next week and treat herself to new clothes, too. Some updates would help her look good and feel good.

She reached for some concealer and dabbed it beneath her eyes. Since the funeral and the blow out with The Pole at the Pub, she'd kept a low profile. Her only public appearance had been to church and bringing her parents grocery shopping. The mocking voice of one woman still rang in her ears, "Joanne was a grown woman, she chose to live as she died. You have no business dragging Adam down, too." This had come from a woman in her thirties wearing skin-tight jeans and a low-cut Metallica T-shirt. She'd said this to June in the middle of the cereal aisle at Bud's Supermarket, and June had been rendered speechless by this verbal assault. She had no idea how or why the woman had any opinion at all, but her criticism stung. She'd expected to be hailed a hero for helping Joanne. Instead she'd heard that a line of people had offered The Pole their condolences before attending his funeral service for Joanne. She hadn't heard any names of those people, of course, but she could guess, based on who wasn't in attendance at the Lutheran service during the same time.

It seemed to her that defending Joanne had been morally right on every level. A man who beat up his girlfriend deserved to be shunned. It was the community's responsibility to punish lawbreakers, and killing someone certainly qualified as breaking the law. Yet despite her convictions, it seemed like a lot of people disagreed. Not Arlyce or Dottie, of course, but it destroyed her faith in people when her neighbors and friends were willing to accept and even condone The Pole's treatment of Joanne. It was monstrous. And depressing.

Still. She had to focus on Loyal and Dob. And Steve. They'd stood up to him and like the coward he was, he'd tucked his tail and ran. No one had seen him since and she'd heard from Dottie that the sheriff's department had towed his truck from where it sat parked in front of Grumpy's for a week after the funeral. Joe had told Dottie it still sat in the impound lot a month later, so everyone felt pretty sure he wasn't coming back.

June descended the stairs and poured herself a cup of coffee. She had to leave in fifteen minutes.

Was she too old-fashioned in her views about women? The woman at the grocery store looked pretty liberated with her nipples poking through the thin fabric of her T-shirt and her audacious attack on her. She never shared opinions so freely in public, yet the opinion expressed was one that discounted Joanne's helplessness. Who was the bigger advocate for women's rights? Her—a timid, mousy farmer's wife whose primary job was keeping house? Or the loud, sexy, confident woman in the grocery store?

She drank her coffee and hoped that she wasn't wasting her time. She'd failed in her attempts to help Joanne, but maybe she'd learn how to become more effective.

Loyal met her at the truck as she was buckling into the driver's seat. She rolled down the window and waited to hear his suggestion on which route to take through Northport or assure him she'd checked the gas gauge. He leaned against the door and squinted at the sky. "Good luck. I hope it turns out to be what you want."

"Thank you."

"I haven't told you this, but I'm proud of you, June."

June reached over and lay her hand on his. "And I'm thankful for you."

Loyal poked his head through the window and kissed her cheek. "Love you."

She was lucky, she thought while she steered the truck in the direction of the women's shelter in Northport where she had an appointment to learn about volunteering. She had the best man in the world on her side.

EPILOGUE

WALKING INTO THE TWO-STORY brick building, June fought back the urge to run to the safety of the truck. What if the people working there laughed at her? She had no real skill set to offer, she hadn't held a job since she was in her early twenties. She was out of touch, really. Her reflection in the glass doors demonstrated this fact, her slacks were a bit too short and old-ladyish, her pumps looked orthopedic compared to the heels worn by two women she passed on the street. Even her handbag looked dated.

She recalled the memory of Joanne's limp body dragged out of the water and lifted her chin. At a minimum she could answer phones, right? And she had her first clear sense of purpose since the kids were little. *On a mission from God*, she thought, like the Blues Brothers.

Inside the lobby, a wood-paneled room filled with cast-off couches and end tables bearing worn-out magazines, June approached the receptionist seated at a low metal desk.

"Good morning," the woman chirped. She wore huge hoop earrings and her dark hair in a loose bun. She looked exotic with almond-shaped eyes and a bulky-knit turtleneck sweater. "How can I help you?"

"Well," June cleared her throat. "I'd like to volunteer here."

"Wonderful!" The woman opened a file cabinet drawer and pulled out a folder. "What area did you think you'd like to help with? We have all kinds of opportunities ..."

An hour later June was returning to the parking lot with a folder full of reading material and an appointment for her orientation next week. She told the receptionist she'd be capable to volunteer as a runner and court watcher. The runner part was grunt work, filling in with paperwork and organizing and laundry as needed, really not much different from what she did at home for Loyal and the kids. The court watcher involved attending domestic violence court cases and reporting on the outcome. She thought that sounded interesting and useful.

June drove home elated. She could hardly wait to tell Loyal and her friends that starting next week she'd be *busy* three days a week, doing something that really mattered.

Acknowledgements

The evolution of a small town and its characters drove the stories in this novel. Real events inspired parts of this fish tale, but other parts came straight from my imagination. I remain mighty grateful to the storytellers who shared their personalities and adventures with me during my bartending years at the Bridge Bar in Fremont.

I feel grateful for the encouragement from readers of *Across the River*. Your questions about what happens next prodded me along. I know what it's like to wait for a sequel, I was a child when *Star Wars* came out and had to wait almost a decade between each installment. My friend Sharon Lillge threatened to get me drunk and force me to divulge what happens next to Jake and Mona after reading *Across the River*, she didn't want to wait around for me to write this book. So, thanks for being patient and thanks for wanting *more Bassville*.

Thanks to Becky Brown, for her keen eye as a copy editor.

A shout-out to Mitch Miskoviak for yet another brilliant cover design.

Love and admiration to the Screw Iowa Writers Workshop for their close edits, clever suggestions and holding me accountable in my writing. Marni Graff, Lauren Small, Mariana Damon, Nina Romano, you have blessed me beyond measure. This wouldn't have happened without you in my corner.

Beth Cole designed this book, the most behind-the-scenes job but something every reader appreciates.

About the Author

Melissa Westemeier lives with her husband and three sons in northeastern Wisconsin where she teaches high school English, writes, reads and messes around in her garden.

The author, age 6, serving up drinks with a smile behind her grandparents' basement bar.